GREEN GOSPEL

L.C. FIORE

Livingston Press
The University of West Alabama

Typesetting and page layout: Joe Taylor
Cover design and layout: Jennifer Brown
Cover photo: "King Giant," Haines Photo Co., Copyright 1915,
Library of Congress, Prints and Photos Division, J203757

Proofreading: Connie James, Joe Taylor,
Jamaree Collins, Valesha Fancher, Miakka Taylor

For my parents, Lyle and Ro

Livingston Press is part of The University of West Alabama,
and thereby has non-profit status.
Donations are tax-deductible:
brothers and sisters, we need 'em.

first edition

6 5 4 3 2 1

July 15, 2011

GREEN GOSPEL

To Bruce,

Recycle this book!

Florida
2002

ONE

The truck has stopped. She feels the truck has stopped although she has not yet opened her eyes. Sleeping or half-sleeping for a thousand miles, her body surrendered to the darkness and to the noise and to the deadening vibrations of the road. Now the jostling of the truck bed and the drumming of the wooden slats built up along the side of the bed are still. She is sitting upright, leaning against the planks with her knees drawn and her head resting on her arms. She opens her eyes; it is dark inside the back of the truck and a slightly less-dark light falls through the slits in the siding, between the bowed heads of other bodies sitting motionless across the bed. Ten or twelve men also do not lift their heads when they hear the sound of the chain pulling free of the tailgate lock. There is a pattering on the aluminum roof and when the tailgate opens she feels the insistent bite of rain.

She is closest to the gate on the driver's side. The smell of the unwashed men is cut by the fragrances of humidity and pine. The outside air blows through the back of the truck bed and cools the sweat along her arms. She has leaned against these men for balance, and for something else, courage maybe, for days, and now they lean forward as one body to taste the outside air. When the tailgate swings open, the man she remembers as Yahir is standing there motioning for her to step down.

Salte, he says. Get moving.

These are not her people. This is not what her grandparents

endured, nor her parents. And this is why they did not speak to her, why they did not even look at her when she hoisted herself onto the truck somewhere south of Tucson, only the one man who did not look at her but made room for her along the side, enough space for her pale arms thin as bone gleaming in the shadows of the truck, eastbound on Interstate 10. The smell was unbearable, the smell and the sounds of the cooped-up men, a steady murmur of hacking coughs and stuffed-up nostrils and some drooling man sucking the spit back into his mouth, over and over again. Isolated also by her softness; the hands of these men are callused, their faces hard as burned wood from laboring beneath the sun. The companionship of a blonde gringo — that's why Yahir accepted her as freight. She'd been brought along as entertainment. She had also said that she could pay.

She shoulders her backpack and slides across the floor to the open air. The rain gusts up from the road. The marsh and the wilderness and the palm fronds swaying are silver in the moonlight through the rain; the tops of trees snap and buck in the wind and the lushness is colored cobalt and steel in the night. Yahir's hands on her waist help her to the ground. She gathers her hair from her face and feels the rain on her lips and spits it out and she sees nothing down the road in either direction. Their journey began in the desert and will continue through the swamp and end somewhere in an orchard, somewhere, but here is where the ride ends for her, this flat, two-lane roadway without a single sign or mile marker, the unswerving roadway stretching through sheets of rain in either direction.

You've got to be kidding me, she says.

The money, Yahir says. Rapido.

She shrugs her backpack to the ground, a hiker's pack, green nylon, carbon frame — all of which strike her as absurd, squatting there on the rain-swept route, unclipping one pouch and threading her hands through the pockets, digging deeper, and finding nothing. Inside the truck, bodies stir. She unzips the hood. She pats down the side pockets, unclipping the *side compression straps*, yanking the *tool loops*, rummaging through the mesh dividers and finding no money. She feels the rainwater on the back of her neck and running down between her shoulder blades and she feels the wet seeping through the spaces between her toes.

Nos tenemos que ir. Dáme el dinero.

She empties her bag onto the ground: the knit ski-cap, a water bottle, a half-eaten bar of peanut brittle. The sum total of her possessions spread around her as she kneels on the flooding roadway watching freshwater from the sky dissolve the candy into sugary granules. She wants the water to rise up high enough that it drags her into the marsh; she is thinking of birds that tilt back their heads in a storm and drown.

¡Yahir, nos tenemos que ir a la chingada! says a voice from the truck cab.

All her life traveling alone and never this. She had listened to the road and she had fallen asleep and she had been careless and she had been robbed. Her money was in the lumbar pack and now the lumbar pack was in her hands and her money was somewhere in the truck. Folded damply in a pants pocket. Secured by the elastic band of someone's underwear. The worker who'd made room for her in Tucson; his perhaps. Or had they split it while she slept, or half-slept deeper than she thought, probing her person and then the *removable floating hood with internal mesh zip pocket*, finding her meager stash of money. At the bottom of the backpack, her fingers touch the sewing kit.

The money's not here, she says. It's gone.

Where could it go? Yahir shouts so the men in the truck can hear. Did it take a vacation? Did it decide how to spend itself and leave you here on the road, all by your lonesome?

The sewing kit is a square plastic box and she feels the lid and turns the box until her fingers find the latch. The lid opens and she can see the contents of the sewing kit with her fingers. She finds the shape of the scissors collapsed. She shifts the scissors into the cavity of her palm. Yahir laughs and inside the truck are shapeless sounds and a shifting of weight and someone stretching their legs out along the corrugated edges of the floor.

He says, If you can't pay money you'll pay some other way. We brought you out here at considerable risk to ourselves and to these men.

Tell me where to find you, she says. I'll pay you as soon as I settle somewhere.

Her arm is still deep inside the pack. She crouches near the license plate of the truck. The license plate says Oregon and behind the numbers a pine tree rises against mountains. Her eyes sting. She can feel the grime of her fugitive days rise to the surface of her skin like oil on the road after a light rain. The other man calls for him and Yahir turns and walks halfway to the front of the truck, stepping out into the middle of the road. She takes her hand from the pack and works the collapsed scissors from their lock and she opens the scissors and palms the thin, dull blades. She stands, feeling spasms in her calves, her legs still unwinding from the long road. Behind her is wild marsh and in either direction is endless two-lane highway and across the road are rain and fronds and soft ground and nowhere to run.

Muchacha don't have money, Yahir says.

She can't see him, but she hears the truck door open and shut. Then the driver appears, the shirtless white man she remembers from Tucson. His pierced nipple: junk metal welded to the swollen areola. He grabs her by the neck. He forces her against the tailgate. It happens so quickly she can't resist. He leans his weight against her until she is bending back across the bed. She struggles to find footing, to escape the vice around her neck, the incredible weight of him pinning her there.

No money, he snarls. His breath is rancid. How about jewelry? How about rare coins? Bars of gold?

Ask her for pot, Yahir says. Someone in the truck agrees.

It's all there, she says, but the shirtless man presses with greater force until her feet leave the ground. She is suspended against the tailgate and she feels her circulation pinched below her spine even as she's hung like a donkey-tail, kicking.

She says, It's everything I have. Please.

Her feet are on the ground again and the hand lets go of her neck. She sputters, trying to expel the rain or the feeling of suffocation or the fear that is more real to her now than anything she has ever felt — the rain or the hard edge of the tailgate in her back. Then he is pressing himself against her again and his fingers are running up beneath her shirt, the fast and powerful pinch of his fingers on her breasts.

What if you, then? he says. His mouth is on her ear and she can feel the quick, wet strokes of his tongue. What if we all take turns?

She feels his zipper against her stomach, her shirt pulled up halfway revealing her rib cage and her stomach to the blind sky. With one hand she resists him, but his body is slick with rain or sweat or his skin is wet like hers from oil rising. The zipper scrapes across her stomach; the zipper slices skin. Her legs and his perform a complicated dance, a classic struggle. He buries his face in her neck and his hands grope the waistband of her pants, fumbling with the buttons.

There are two parts of herself — one struggling against the man and one watching the men behind her shift and slide and prowl along the back of the truck bed. She is acutely aware of the crowded darkness behind her, the shapeless bodies noticing now, sitting up, moving closer, sliding across the floor—tapping one another and then withdrawing and then taking one another by the arm. They whisper back and forth, their eyes shifting to each other and then across the space behind her until their breath is one breath hot and shameless on the back of her neck, the untapped energy of twelve prisoners of the road.

She still palms the scissors. Yahir stands in the middle of the road, looking one direction, then the other. The button on her pants comes undone and she feels her pants collapse partway down her hips. There are hands on her shoulders, not the hands of her assailant but hands that are dark from soil and sun—first one hand, then two, scarred and callused hands that reach out from the darkness of the truck, from the wretched odor of unwashed man, from the redolence of fear. And this is what she shares with them, these men with whom she has traveled these many miles. They are similarly afraid. And the hands are gentle. They do not grope but run their fingers down the back of her neck, along the ends of her hair. These hands fear poverty and severance and these hands fear never seeing their families again; these hands fear the law. They fear death. She herself fears all of these things.

Hands grip her shoulders, and the grip of these hands collected is impatient, accelerating. She knows that if she lets this happen, she will die. She raises her right hand and other hands reach for it and take her by the wrist. She follows with her left, turning the scissors in her palm. She brings her fist down in a sweeping arc, fully extending and then cutting steeply. She plunges the blades into her assailant, behind his ear where his skull lolls upon his head. He screams, or she feels the scream in his musculature; she shoves the blades in as far as they will go, not thinking *Kill* but wanting it to be enough.

Her face is spattered by something warm, spit or blood, and then she tastes it on her tongue and it is blood. He spins from her, clutching the side of his head, blood spraying out from between his fingers and the handle of the scissors jutting out from between his fingers curled around his neck. She is spun to the ground. She crawls for the side of the road, wrestling her pants over her hips, trying to fasten them, trying to crawl away and also to fasten the buttons with her slick and trembling fingers.

When she reaches the side of the road she is sure that she will die here. She buries her head in her arms; she gives herself over to it. What fight she had drains out of her and runs with the water and the oil in the road. They will take her back into the truck and take from her whatever they want. They will leave her dead in the swamp where alligators will feast on her ruined remains.

El policia, Yahir shouts. Déjela.

The tailgate slams. She opens her eyes. Yahir helps the white man into the passenger's side of the truck and then Yahir is gone and the truck is pulling away, its taillights like two predatory eyes conceding into the rain-streaked bleakness of the road. It is some time before she is aware that the only sound in all the acreage is the sound of her own weeping.

Another car is suddenly close. She smells its tires. She lifts her head and across the road is naked pine forest illuminated, washed in the spotlight that has suddenly come on. The spotlight is mounted to the top of the patrol car and the patrol car squawks, once. The trunks of the pines are charred black to the highest reach of some long ago wildfire. There is no groundcover, nothing to shelter what, she wonders, foxes and gulls, frogs or fugitives like herself.

Her arms shake and her legs and body feel twisted like wreckage. She cannot trust the steadiness of any one part of herself. She crawls on her hands and knees. She collects her possessions from the side of the road and shovels them into her pack. *Double-ripstop nylon*. Nothing is dry. *Bottom compression straps*. She packs the ski-cap and leaves the peanut brittle, feeling guilty for the plastic wrapper and then packing it too. *Top loader*. Hearing a voice call out, You there, lie still.

She releases her pack and lies flat on her stomach, pressing her face to the asphalt. She tastes rainwater and oil and salt from the road. She is at the end. There is one police car and two men standing near it. Her ordeal is almost finished. She is lying in a puddle and the puddle tastes like the sea. She thinks this place has a particular smell that is wholly, fully what it is and she has never smelled it anywhere else. Certainly not at home, three thousand miles ago; many weeks now fleeing three thousand miles to avoid arrest, only to be left for dead on a Florida highway and handcuffed anyway.

The police are in no hurry and they let her lie there. She can hear their voices but can't hear what they're saying. The air is different here; thick and there is a citrus smell. Three years and thousands of miles and through it all, the Crestone 50 Women's Backpacking Pack. Thistle green. The straps not black, but *asphalt gray*.

She hears a low sound to her left, just off the road. A burbling sound — a bullfrog. The first call echoed by another. She sees something she thinks must be a hallucination, exhaustion playing tricks with her eyes. Frogs on the road, not one or two, but a scourge. She might be dreaming — she must be. The whole thing a pestilent bad dream.

One of the men is coming toward her. His body blocks the light. She lies there, not looking up. She should try to charm these men as she charmed the coyote but she is thinking already of waking up tomorrow to find herself in some new, dry place. Travel is progress, and so progress is all her life has been: half-considered flights that leave her hoping, as she does now that the police will not recognize her.

JOHN WHITNEY and his deputy, Cyrus Capron, were taking one last pass along state road 70, checking for flooding, when they saw the pickup truck and two men engaged in some sort of dispute. The men saw the siren lights and then there was a third man and the two men fled in the truck. The third they left crumpled on the side of the road. Only it turned out not to be a man at all, but a young woman. The woman was filthy but calm and when they found her she was stuffing her valuables back into her bag.

She crawled out of some dredge pond surely, Cyrus said.

Tourist maybe, Whitney said. Both officers sat in the car, considering.

Maybe she was on a date.

You know well as I, that truck was spics.

Whitney turned on the spotlight and got out of the car. He told the girl to lie down and she complied. He wanted to go after the truck, but instead they were going to help this girl who was probably in some kind of trouble, who was probably high or stoned or pregnant besides, who would kick and scream and hurl obscenities because that's what they all did, Florida's lower class, the white trash they liked to keep hidden in the south-central part of the state.

She's come a long way. Cyrus is out of the car now, pawing through the girl's pack. He holds up a brochure, river tours on the Rio Grande. He says, She's clean.

Whitney moves for his radio but decides to give it time, get her story. The girl's green pack is the kind of pack he's seen college kids carry.

He spits into the road. She must be on some kind of vacation.

It ain't tourist season, Cyrus says.

The sheriff pats her down and the girl says nothing and he doesn't find anything so he doesn't put her in handcuffs. Her body is straight and small and her flip-flops are cracked along the soles. No kind of walking shoe, these. The girl is white but she is much more cared for than the type of women he usually has to deal with on nights like this, with the fucking rain and a million fucking frogs out on the highway mating. He deals with people all the time. Even with bruises on her face and her hair matted down and lying there in a puddle breathing oil, he can take one look at her and know she's not trash. So the question becomes, what's a white girl doing with a truckload of Mexicans on a shit-ass night like this?

You got ID? He pulls at her elbow, gently, and helps her sit up.

I don't have anything, she tells him.

He can barely hear her voice above the rain. She blows air out of her mouth, clearing water from it. She's drowned, this girl, soaked to the bone. Her entire body shudders and he thinks maybe drugs, but he turns her arms over and finds no tracks. He reaches out; the deputy hands him the girl's backpack and then he helps the girl to her feet. He opens the back door and the girl climbs in. He thinks the size of her is deceptive. She's older than she looks. He slides the pack behind her into the car.

Cyrus has the partition open when he gets into the car again. Both of them are soaking wet and their ponchos spray water over everything, each time they move. The whole car smells like shit, like worms and wet dog. He turns around to look at her, flipping on the overhead. She recoils from the light and shields her eyes. Her shirt was white once, the pink star across her chest now faded. Her tits are small. Her hands show the deep grime he's seen before on drifters they drag in off the street, having gone weeks between showers. This suggests she is a runaway; the hiker's pack and the clothes she wears confirm it.

Thanks for bringing me in out of the rain, she says.

It's a funny thing for her to say. He shifts the car into drive and guides the car into the road.

Along the highway tonight is a great amphibious crossing. The state route cuts through mating ponds and so the frogs make the hard journey across the road to where the females are, weighing the risk of passing cars against their drive for snatch. A journey wrought with peril. The frogs move in tenuous clusters, advancing incrementally across the road. The still-living pass others mashed by car tires without so much as a second glance. They make their way three leaps forward, one sideways, one back. Whitney sees this every year and every year he can't believe the number of frogs that make the crossing—too many to avoid. The crossing takes up miles of the byway. There's no point trying to steer around them. He blows through. There are more than he can count, as far as he can see. His high beams cut the rain and the low fog moving now across the passage. Frogs straddle the lanes in dark clusters along the pavement, cowering beneath the fog and the steam rising up from the wilderness and leaning out across the road. Stupid frogs. Whitney checks his rearview mirror and thinks, Stupid girl.

Cyrus asks where she lives.

The overhead light is still on. The girl looks out the window with an expression he thinks is rootless, as if the answer might reveal itself to her from behind the viaduct or the ferns or the saw grass along the shoulder. He thinks she's already decided not to tell the truth. Freed of that, she can tell them anything, choose her favorite story and make it her own.

Tallahassee, she says. Spring break.

Alone?

I'm meeting friends later.

Who were those men you were with?

I wasn't with them.

Whitney thinks it's blood on her hands, slopped across her arm and along the bottom of her shirtsleeve. Nothing else dries like that. One of them made a play for her, maybe.

Cyrus says, You can't be walking around these parts alone. Especially at night.

Mexicans, Whitney says. Grove workers.

Pretty girl like you, we'd never hear from again.

There's no way to avoid running over the frogs and when he does the tires jump a little, like rolling over rocks or debris in the road. He accelerates, but driving faster means running straight over the frogs, no avoiding. They shouldn't be out in this; he needs to mark this date on the calendar for next year. These frogs and now they're bringing some kind of hassle back with them, this girl who says she's from the capitol.

You remember Richard Ladner? Cyrus says to both of them.

Sure, the sheriff says. I remember old Dick.

Man loved his boots.

Loved his boots, yes.

Avid fisherman, was what he was. Owned a small place down on Hillsborough. In his house, he had all kinds of skin up on the wall, snakes and alligators. Made his own boots.

Just stuff he happened to kill.

That's right. Just stuff he happened to kill.

Cyrus shuts off the overhead light, as if he'd meant to do it a while back. The passengers are all moonlight and swamp shadow. He says, The thing about walking in these parts is, you don't know what's waiting for you in the dark. We've got poisonous things down here, things with teeth. Not like those fancy streets you have in Tallahassee.

Fancy streets, Whitney says.

Take our friend. He was out walking his dogs one evening — a pack of dogs, now, big dogs. People said he fought them but I never saw truth to that.

Never any truth to that. He rescued them mainly, from the

track.

Well, I can't say they was racing dogs but anyway, there was a lot of them. He walked them every night down this road. One evening, alligator come out of the swamp and tore his leg off all the way up through his torso.

The girl doesn't gasp, doesn't flinch.

I mean, that leg was gone. Nothing to tie a prosthetic to. Nothing left.

Couldn't even call him Stumpy, Whitney says.

No you couldn't. You couldn't even call him that.

The sheriff is watching the girl in the mirror and he is hoping for a smile from her, just so he knows she's okay, but it's like she carries a burden that won't let her eyes light. She rests her elbow on the door and her fingers barely touch her lips, alternately in mindless patterns, a quiet rhythm. She is watching the naked pines roll past like she is expecting to see her nightmares come billowing up out of the ditch.

My favorite part of that story, Whitney says. The dogs dragged him all the way home. Have you heard that?

I hadn't, Capron says, although of course he has: He was probably the one who told him.

Dragged him a mile and a half to the hospital. Would have bled to death, otherwise. Dogs rescued their owner, in that case.

There's a lot about that story that don't make sense.

There is.

The sojourn of the frogs has been reenacted each spring of his entire life and for a million years before that, tadpoles budding limbs astride the lengthening days until voyaging across the east-west highway they've heard so much about from older frogs that've gone and then returned. Driving through it now, he and the deputy and this lost girl witness the tadpoles' only rite: a caravan for pussy. There are frogs mashed against the roadway like exploded oranges, some of the frogs still breathing but flattened and immobile, waiting for a second tire of mercy. Stupid frogs; stupid girl.

Cyrus turns around halfway in his seat. I never knew Arcadia was a spring break destination.

The great outdoors, she says. You understand.

Can't imagine there's much for college kids to do.

Camping, she returns. Plus, there's good people down this way.

That's because everyone down here is old.

The deputy puts his hand through the partition. I'm Cyrus. This is Sheriff Whitney.

Edie, she takes his partner's hand. Edie Richards.

He reaches his own hand through the partition and when she takes his hand he can barely feel it, her touch. Only the coldness of her touch. The absence.

Cyrus does the pussycat act. He nods and says, Don't mind the driver. He's a big pussycat deep down.

He hates the pussycat line. Cyrus thinks it's funny, but he doesn't see the humor—he's owned some mean tomcats in his life and the pussycat line cuts his authority somewhat. Outside, the rain has turned from sheets to mist. He runs over one frog, then several in succession. They jostle the car, like uneven road.

Edie leans forward and her eyes are two dark caverns. These frogs are really creeping me out.

THE FIRST THING Cyrus noticed, coming upon the girl, was that Edie was the same age his daughter would be this November. Despite the frog-strangler outside, despite the sheriff's suspicions, pulling up to the crumpled form in the road and seeing that it was a young female he had the strange thought, though it'd been nine years since his daughter was taken from him, nine years and still the first thing he thought seeing Edie was that his own daughter had risen from her watery grave to haunt the highway between Arcadia and Sarasota like a ghostly hitchhiker from some mournful backwoods song.

This is why he asked the sheriff to let the Mexicans go: He needed to stop for the girl. He couldn't get over the thought that it might be his own daughter lying there in the road, trapped in some sort of limbo, besetting roadside strangers with a plea for mercy in her spectral manner. He wanted to be sure it was not his own daughter drowning there. Because sometimes he still expects to see her, or wouldn't be surprised if he did — her death still not as real to him these many years as her life had been.

He knows there is a type of prayer that repeats the name of Christ endlessly. The name of his own daughter was Fay, and that is the word whispered unceasingly on his lips.

It was not his daughter, writhing in the exhaust fumes of the wetback truck, but this girl Edie who now sits in the squad car needing some sort of help. The pink star on her chest has collapsed in the folds of her T-shirt and everything hangs off of her ragged and damp. He considers for a moment the probable reaction of his wife, Katharine Anne. Then he stops considering and decides. He will offer this girl, who may or may not be from Tallahassee, and who is or is not planning to camp along the uninhabited marshes of state road 70, who is or is not meeting friends later — to this fallen girl he will offer his daughter's bed, his shower, his daughter's clothes if she likes, until she figures out where to next.

The car accelerates; its tires shiver through trenches of standing water. A dull roar sounds through the steamed-up windows, the moisture outside merging with the hot breath inside as the tires and the road become a single, fluid trajectory behind fogged glass, hurtling through the mist and the sound of nothing but water and road and a thin melody from the turned-down radio. Cyrus looks at the girl again and sees that her eyes are closed, her head bobbing with the gentle cadence of the road.

We're taking her in? he asks the sheriff.

I suppose. Get her something to eat. Figure out where to send her back to.

Awful lot of work for a Sunday night. Technically speaking, we should have been off an hour ago.

Whitney cracks the window, a cigarette balanced between his fingers and the wheel. He waits for the car lighter and then puts the screw to the cigarette. Cyrus waves at the smoke and cracks his window too.

The sheriff says, I don't see what choice we have. We take her in and let the state deal with her.

She's no runaway.

Crazy, then. The state's problem, either way.

She don't belong to nobody, Cyrus says. He doesn't need to, probably, but he pretends to just be thinking it all through. He says, Or if she does, then it's no one she wants to go back to.

He feels the sheriff simmering from across the car. He has a hard time reading the older man. He thinks it's because the sheriff is built solid as a bilge pump, two black eyes behind a flattened nose which never tell much of anything. There is never a movement, a tick or gesture that would show his thoughts on a subject either way.

Look, the deputy says. She's no criminal. I ain't seen her on *America's Most Wanted*. We picked her up, but that don't mean we treat her like she broke the law.

You're thinking of taking her in.

Just for the night.

Run this by Kat?

I haven't. And I don't need to. I'm the head of our house, John. I don't need to check in with the wife just to take a leak.

And you don't need to convince me. Whitney adjusts the mirror. He studies the sleeping girl. Shit, I'll be happy to be rid of her. Cute little thing though.

Through the dark center of town and along a back road they pass one-story homes and in the front yards, cars propped up on cinder-blocks and in the driveways, ski-boats or waverunners on trailer slips, the tarps that cover them snapping in the wind and pulling against their ties. The lights are on inside his home, one light in the front window where Katharine Anne will be reading one of her women's magazines.

At the curb, Cyrus gets out of the car and opens the back door. The girl is barely awake now or she is still asleep and can no longer differentiate between the two—waking and sleeping being one and the same.

He touches her arm. We're here, then.

He helps her out of the car and gathers her pack behind her. Whitney rolls down the window.

Be careful with her, he says. You need anything, you call. I'll be up.

Will do, Chief. Cyrus salutes, gently mocking the older man's tendency to treat him like a rookie although he's been on the force more than sixteen years. When the car pulls away the siren squawks once, both as a parting sound and, Cyrus decides, a sound to wake the neighbors. To remind them they sleep soundly beneath the watchful eye of Arcadia's sheriff.

Edie pauses at the foot of the path leading to the door. He waits for her. He says, Sheriff wanted to throw you in the slammer, but I talked him out of it.

She lifts her chin. It would be a smile, he thinks, in better weather. He says, I didn't see the point in putting you up in a motel, only to find you out on the road again tomorrow night.

Nice of you, she says.

She walks as if pulled by a string, led instead of driven. Her eyes and lips are a little too wide for her face, her thin nose. He watches her nose wrinkle as they cross the yard, at the smell rising up from the grass. Sulfur, the heavy reek of eggs.

Katharine Anne waits for them behind the screen door. What's this?

This is Edie, Cyrus says. She needs a place to stay.

I don't have nothing to make for dinner.

Go on and show her the second bedroom.

Edie slips past his wife and through the door whispering thank-you. She slinks, Cyrus decides, like a dog that knows she's done something wrong.

He follows both women into the kitchen, avoiding the hard glance his wife lays over him. He slinks a little bit too. He sets the pack on a chair and leans against the counter. He waits until his wife has led the girl down the hall and he hears them in the back bedroom, opening closet doors in the same room where his daughter slept, not much changed in there probably these last nine years. The dresses and the skirts and the denim jacket she wore in winter all still neatly hung and arranged by color. The wood hangers, the expectant smell of cherry wood.

In the bathroom he removes his belt, his holster and his radio. He hangs these on the back of the door. He washes his face in the sink and when he looks in the mirror again his wife is there, the skin around her eyes sunk and red, her lips pursed white. The colors are reversed, he thinks—once she had pale skin and lips like the flowers on a buckeye tree.

But nine years changes a person's color. Their only child had stood on the brink of adulthood. They turned their attention for one moment and she was taken from them. Kidnapped from the front steps of a museum, driven three miles in a car that was then broadsided by a municipal truck—a truck to pour concrete and make things last forever. Concrete to build skyscrapers, to retain water in swimming pools, to lay miles of sidewalk for people's feet, skipping over cracks. Silos and barn floors and concrete broken down to its parts — gravel and water and sand. Fifty miles from the coast and they see plenty of sand and plenty of water. Every day. Sand gets into their sheets at night and into the floor mats in the car. Constantly reminded of her, or of the way she died. Gravel lots; gravel in the aquariums of family friends; gravel as part of the liquid stone that has somehow come to replace whatever it was they'd once called marriage.

He tells his wife, John and I found her walking alone on 70. Pouring rain, this girl. Half-drowned.

There's a number to call, isn't there? she asks. The question is rhetorical — she knows there is.

She's older than she looks.

She could be anyone. She could rob us blind. Murder us in our sleep.

She weighs about fifty pounds.

He squeezes past his wife and goes into the kitchen. He can feel her following him; her eyes burn up the hairs on the back of his neck. He opens the refrigerator, brings out a beer. When the bottle is open he flips the cap toward the garbage. The cap rattles and slides along the floor and he doesn't bother to retrieve it.

She's meeting up with her pals in a few days, he says. She's tired. And hungry. She's all alone. Them's reasons enough.

Katharine Anne works the bow strings on her dress, deftly ironing out minute imperfections. Her hair is pulled back, a severity to her look.

This is your work, she says. You don't bring it home.

You'd rather I left her out there.

Just tell me when we got into the business of being saints.

It's only a night or two.

It's not our mission, Cyrus. We've wept our tears for other people's misery. I can't cry anymore. Not for anyone but me.

KATHARINE ANNE is rummaging in the freezer for something leftover when Edie enters the kitchen. The girl moves to the corner and tries to press herself against the built-ins, as if to slip between them and the wall, as if she carries some serpentine quality that allows her to thread slithering between close places. The built-ins are stacked with fine china and silver and ceramic bowls, purchased and inherited both. Edie's hair is dry and the bangs are tucked behind her ears and long pieces of hair hang uncollected at the back of her head. She wears fresh clothes, a sleeveless green shirt and low-slung jeans. The girl is small but the skin around her arms is loose, untried by labor. She rubs her bare feet against the brown-specked tile and the movement is cautious, timid, like someone younger. The clothes she wears were Fay's — nothing Kat remembers. She doesn't know what drawer she found them in. She thinks the sight of this stranger wearing her daughter's clothes — her daughter's wardrobe suddenly brought to life — should make her sad. But she feels only wonder at the details she has already forgotten and the carelessness with which she said, Go on and find something that fits.

Kat clatters the pots and pans and slides a skillet onto the stove. She turns the burner to high and then takes a Tupperware container and knocks it against the counter. She digs at the frozen food with a spoon and forces ice-chipped chunks of beans into the pan until she notices the girl still standing there.

You may as well sit, she tells her.

Edie moves to a chair, sitting straightly there with a practiced posture. Kat chops at the morsels beginning to steam in the skillet. The flat sound of the spoon and the pan rattling against the iron grill startles the girl, enough so her hands come off the table before she gathers them in again. Kat turns the food over; bits of meat separate from the tomato and onion and the smell of cumin drifts toward the ceiling fan.

Were you able to reach those friends of yours? Kat asks.

She stirs the pan, letting it sizzle. The girl does not answer, this young creature with unmarked skin, unblemished but for the silver ring in her bottom lip, the deliberate defacing of an otherwise strangely angelic face. Not pretty in the sense of movie stars, but trim: her nails show remnants of flaked-off white polish. The haircut, she can see now, cost money; Kat stands in her own kitchen with her hair pulled back to keep it out of the sweat of her face and neck, her own skin tanned and hard.

I wasn't exactly forthcoming about my situation, Edie says.

Kat tries to place the accent. She says, I thought you were a little old for spring break.

I'm not so old.

Kat bangs the spoon against the pan, clearing it of sauce. Trouble, then.

Trouble at home, yes.

Knocked up. A boy who doesn't want you anymore.

It'd be better if that was true. Edie smiles for the first time. I don't know what I was thinking, trying to cross the state on foot.

I'd say you weren't thinking at all. Kat tilts her head. Reach up in that cabinet and bring down some of those chips.

Edie opens the cabinet and digs through packages of economy-sized egg noodles and forty-ounce cans of tomatoes until she finds the bag of corn chips folded in half and held with a rubber band. She sets the bag on the table and helps set out three bowls and three spoons.

I know this isn't normal, Edie says. The women are paused, each holding onto one side of a serving bowl. She says, I'd never take advantage of someone's kindness. I don't usually find myself—I would very much appreciate a place to stay.

Kat says, Is your trouble with the law?

No.

My husband's a cop.

I know.

Kat lets go of the bowl and Edie places it in the center of the table. She dumps the corn chips and empties the bag.

Edie says, It's just trouble. The troubling kind.

Kat hears the shower shut off down the hall. She hears her husband come out of the bathroom and shut the bedroom door. She doles out chili to three place settings and sprinkles cheddar cheese across the tops.

She pushes a tub of sour cream toward the girl. Dig in.

The girl must be starving. Kat saw the way she licked the salt from her fingertips. But the girl has manners. She takes a modest portion of the cream. A handful of chips she arranges along the edge of the bowl. Using one as a sort of shovel, she works bits of bean and onion into her mouth, also pushing each morsel of beef to the side, submerging chips in the broth and then slurping at it. Avoiding the meat, eating around it.

Katharine Anne thinks if she were truly a Christian she would offer the girl something else. It isn't a matter of having enough to share. But she knows now all she needs to about this stranger. There might be truth to her story after all, that she comes from upstate. The girl eats with a certain prissiness, not to soil her fingers. She pats her mouth with her napkin. Despite the way she looked when Cyrus dragged her up to the front porch, like some catfish he'd caught in the Myakka, she knows now her family is moneyed. Her daddy a senator. Or president of the Rotary Club. Her lip-piercing bought with her parents' funds but strictly as a way to rebel against her upbringing. A way to act out, as their own daughter had with the streaks of purple and red in her hair. Of course, their daughter had pretty much grown out of that right before she passed, while this girl—for her, salvation is a phone call away. Her daddy like all the other daddies she knows who rear similar children and bail them out of trouble; Cyrus talks about it all the time. He'll come upon a one-car wreck, a teenager having wrapped her Volkswagen around a tree, to find the driver wandering the median, calling somebody on the phone. Not the authorities—Daddy was always the first call. A month later he'll see the same girl back on the road again in some meaner, more expensive machine. And if, as she suspects, it is the same with this girl Edie, what cares could she possibly have? Why, Kat wonders, does she not just make that call, as she has for each of her twenty-some-odd years?

EACH WORD that comes out of her mouth is a lie, Katharine Anne says. She is standing at her dresser, placing her earrings in a white box; there are seashells glued to the lid.

It's nice isn't it? Cyrus asks. Having someone else in the house again.

He lies on his back, spread out across the bed. The ceiling fan wobbles and faintly thrums and he reminds himself to tighten that tomorrow.

She's young, Kat says.

We weren't so truthful when we were her age.

When we were her age we were already married.

And we hadn't told a soul. Not even your parents. We were living in a trailer in Zolfo Springs. I was selling fresh meat, door to door. Trying to make you a rich woman.

She tucks the jewelry box into her sock drawer. I'm shutting the door tonight.

You know how hot it gets.

She goes to the bedroom door and closes it. She is wearing a T-shirt and blue shorts. She returns to the dresser and takes the jewelry box out again. She removes each balled-up roll, puts the box in the bottom drawer and covers it again with the socks. Then, grunting not from effort but to make him feel ashamed, she drags the rocking chair from its place in the corner and jimmies the top of the chair beneath the doorknob. When she climbs into bed, the mattress leans with her weight. He makes room for her and waits until she turns out the light.

She says, If we get up tomorrow and everything's still here, I'll reconsider.

He folds his arms behind his head. He is far from sleep. He listens to the whirl of the ceiling fan. He says, We'll want breakfast tomorrow. Me and the girl. The both of us.

TWO

Mae Carson is too young to feel this old — rundown and worn out. Working nights at Desoto County Memorial Hospital is something she chose and having chose this makes her happy, or provides the satisfaction others seem to enjoy from their own professions. But there are things she did not choose and that she did not choose them makes them different. There are the two sons she has raised largely on her own. There is the man she gave her entire being to, only to have him turn his back on her before the boys were halfway grown. These things she did not choose and she is stunned by the way in which they have unleashed themselves upon her life. She is haggard and threadbare and she struggles to keep her eyes open listening to what the sheriff has come to her house to say.

John Whitney sits at her kitchen table, drinking coffee that she prepared, Maxwell House Vanilla, with sugar mixed into the grounds to bring out the flavor. It is Saturday, her one day off a week. He has been to her house now every weekend for a year. He says the coffee is what keeps him coming back, but she is coming to suspect it has less to do with the flavor of the grounds and more to do with her boys.

I hope you don't mind my being here, he says. Maybe you still consider these official visits.

I don't think of you like that, she says.

Her kitchen table wobbles, owing to the slope of the floor. The table was her grandmother's and the table has sat in the same place for thirty years beneath the haze of cigarette smoke that is at least that old. She stamps hers out in the ashtray where, like a bloom, the filters overflow the dish. The ashtray says *Jackson Hole, Wyoming* and she owns others that say *Maui, Maui* or *I HEART New York*, although she hasn't been to any of these places—only once has she traveled outside of Florida. She has collected enough so that friends of hers, and family, bring back ashtrays from the faraway places they visit. She owns an ashtray from the Cape of Good Hope, in South Africa. She had to look it up on a map.

You might think about getting some help out here, he says.

I can't afford no maid.

Someone to baby-sit then, even once a week.

Sweet tea suns on the countertop; the lemon slices float belly-up like tourists in a hot spring. The sheriff has delivered a bag of clothes, hand-me-downs that people donated or that he found set out on the street. He barely mentioned the clothes when he came in; he put the garbage bag aside and said it was for the boys. She did not dote over the clothes right away but left them for later when she can go through the offerings in private and not be shamed.

That the sheriff is seated at her kitchen table alarms her, even though she knows John and knows he means well. Still, each time she sees his car in the driveway she can't help but worry. It's been like this since her husband left. The sheriff says his visits have nothing to do with child welfare or social services; if he weren't here he'd be at the Holy Donut where they don't put sugar in their coffee grounds, not like she does. Despite this assurance, she can't relax—he's brusque and he always seems to be saying one thing while looking out for another. Her husband had trouble with the law and what happened was, it finally caught up to him. For the last time a year ago.

It's getting to be flu season. He taps a cigarette out of his pack. The boys will need shots.

He might say more but he gums up when both of her boys come into the kitchen. Troy, the oldest, still has baby fat on his arms and legs but shows signs of being handsome, looking more like his father every day. Evan, the youngest, is a squirming live wire — she can't believe his strength sometimes. Both of them are clean, even if their T-shirts are ragged around the collars. She's glad at least there's that: she hasn't dressed her children in filth.

Mind your manners, she tells them.

Good morning, Sheriff, Troy says. Evan moves nearer to his brother. They stand there blinking a little because they were watching TV with the light off, even though she's told them not to.

I've brought you both something, Whitney says. He reaches into his pocket and when he shows his hand again he's holding two silver dollars. The boys take a few steps toward him, walking stiff-legged and remembering their posture, keeping their hands at their sides and not reaching, just as she's taught them. So well-behaved, her boys.

What do we say? she asks.

Evan makes a kind of sound. She thinks at first it might be a word, constructed language, but he makes the sound again and it is more of a whine coming from the back of his throat. Nothing more than that. He tugs on his brother's shirtsleeve.

He wants to play outside, Troy says.

Take him then, she says.

He's afraid of the wasps.

He's afraid, or you're afraid?

Nobody likes the wasps, Mama.

The boys turn from the kitchen but she calls them back. What do we say to our guest?

Thank you, Sheriff Whitney, Troy says.

Evan performs a sort of half-bow alongside his brother. Then they disappear again and the front door slams.

Evan still isn't talking, the sheriff says.

She stands up from her chair, working out a kink in her back, between her shoulders. Last night she had to move a patient twice by herself because the other nurse didn't show up for her shift.

Whitney says, I got a call from Todd Peters. You remember him. Cleaned himself up good, by the way. Holding down a steady job.

Praise the Lord.

Neighbor's kid hammered nails into the tires on his Bronco. Todd had yelled at the kid earlier for something, trampling his begonias maybe. Thing is, I'd have a hard time hammering nails into a tire, much less this six-year-old boy.

Boy must have been angry.

Goes to show, kids act out in strange ways.

Mae picks up the ashtray with her cigarette still burning. She dumps the butts in the garbage can below the sink, saving her cigarette at the last moment. She slips it into her mouth and sets the ashtray back on the table.

She says, The boys will want lunch when they come in. Will you be staying?

Depends what's on the menu.

It's better to keep moving, she thinks—she has all of this nervous energy. She wishes he'd say what's on his mind. She opens the cabinet above her head and sets out the jar of peanut butter and the jar of marshmallow fluff.

He shakes his head. Far be it from me to turn down, what is that, Fluffernutter, but I think I'll be moving on.

Don't be scared of the Fluff.

That stuff don't take too well to my insides.

It's just marshmallows.

Even so.

She lays out eight pieces of bread and spreads four with peanut butter. She says, It's not his being quiet that worries me. I know that's just his way of acting out or maybe trying to deal with his daddy being gone.

You've talked to the boys about it, then.

There's not much to say. She scrapes at the last bit of marshmallow and spreads it evenly across the other slices. She says, When a pet dies, I can handle that. But what do I tell my boys now? Sorry your father is a raging drunk. A good-for-nothing. You may see him again, or you may not, but either way it's probably best if you forgot him.

Plenty of people turn out fine, raised by one parent. My mother raised me from the time I was twelve years old.

I know she did.

She had help though. Family. That sort of thing.

We got no family in these parts.

She offers to refill his coffee but he declines. She wonders if she should tell him. She wants to, although she's afraid of how it might sound. It may end up like a strike against her. Then she thinks she should have made her boys stay indoors, with the wasps outside. She should have had the wasps exterminated. She decides she'll make a show of serving fruit along with the sandwiches so he sees at least they're eating healthy. Then she reminds herself to have faith in people—Sheriff Whitney has seen her family through its worst times. He wouldn't abandon them now.

She says, The hardest part is, since my husband left, Evan's been having nightmares.

Go on.

Not nightmares exactly. But he's been waking up scared. They're like night terrors, what he has. I'm up all hours, praying over him, and he still wakes up sometimes like the world's ending.

I never had night terrors, he says. But kids have bad dreams, don't they?

It's more than that, more than what he said, but there's no use making a big deal of it. She lets the conversation drop and wraps a sandwich in a Ziploc bag. When Whitney stands up from the table she gives it to him.

You're so kind, she says. Coming over here each week.

You're doing real good now. He adjusts his wide-brimmed hat and glances at his reflection in the microwave oven. Things keep on, you won't need to worry about my coming out here anymore. Of course, I may still drop by—I can't get coffee this good anywhere else in town.

Now, stop.

He pockets the sandwich. She walks him to the door, hurrying a little, maybe too much. She feels a certain amount of relief with him leaving; already she's replaying everything she said in her mind. She doesn't know if the cops can take her children away— she thinks they must be able to if they think there's reason.

He says, I did get a call from the school counselor yesterday.

Mae can't stop the words when they come—her heart bursts. There ain't no trace of harm on those boys. Not one trace.

It's the little things, Mae. They need to be at school on time and they need baths regular. They need to do their schoolwork. I'm trying to help you as much as I can, but you have to do your part. Do what's expected. Those boys show up to school again with so much as a hair out of place, it won't be me out here next time.

Please, she says.

The sheriff steps into the sunshine. Think about getting yourself a little help out here. Even just somebody to watch the boys and make sure they're getting all the things they need.

You find time for yourself and keep sticking to that job of yours, things'll turn out.

She asks, Why is it you care so much about us, Sheriff?

The sun is at his back and she's blinded by it so that she only sees the shadow of him standing in the yard. The truth is, he says, I feel somewhat responsible for you having ever fallen in love with that joker in the first place. I should have left him out there on the street that night, instead of dragging him inside for you to fall head over heels for.

He nods goodbye and walks to where his car is parked beneath the shade. She stands on her front porch, watching the sheriff turn his patrol car up the gravel drive.

Head over heels, the sheriff had said. Head over heels and here she is almost a widow, or as good as widowed anyway and not yet forty. Paychecks spent before they arrive and still she works six days a week at the hospital, working nights for the extra pay. The sheriff squawks the siren once and he is gone and that's the end result of her hard work, the fruit of her labor—hand-me-downs collected for her boys to wear. Other people's trash. Because they think she can't clothe her own sons—and maybe she can't after all. Inside the house she sees the garbage bag lying there and she prays her boys can rise above it. Head over heels, the sheriff said. All she remembers now are facts.

It was on the night shift, ten years ago. There were race riots on television. A black man had been beaten by the police in Los Angeles the year before, and all of it had been captured on film. The news channels played the clips again, all day and night. The LAPD had pulled the man over on the highway and the man was black and the man resisted and then the man was beaten by a dozen officers who appeared to continue striking blows even when the man was on the ground. It all played out on television and the nation watched the riots that followed the verdict handed down upon the officers: shop windows shattered, smoke in the streets, black bodies running through neighborhoods that looked war-torn like Beirut and not Los Angeles, California, in the United States of America. All of this was playing on the televisions so you couldn't get away from it—it was all anybody talked about at work. They picked up the conversation where they'd left off the summer before. Debating whether or not the cops were right or wrong. Whether it took that much force to bring down a perp who was high on PCP—they debated the medical evidence of it all. This is what they were watching, she and another nurse, when they looked up from the television and saw John Whitney dragging the filthiest sort of trash into their unit. She remembers disengaging from the screen—her attention caught more by the smell than anything else—and seeing the new admit and being thankful at least that he was white. She felt the national tension, maybe, and was relieved that the man was Caucasian and not some other race so that she would not have to talk about the events of the day or try to understand them—she would be able to feel vengeful and she would be able to do her job and then she would be able to go home and forget it all.

The man was bleeding from a head wound and it was like the events on the West Coast had somehow traversed three thousand miles to land themselves in her hospital bed. Brutality as a national pandemic until she saw the man was drunk and that he wore a flannel shirt with the sleeves torn off, the kind the real backwoods boys wear. His sneakers were untied and the laces dragged and got caught up in his step—he could hardly walk. The sheriff carried him into the clinic, cursing because the stranger had shat himself and the stench that came in with him was worse than sewage, a smell that burned her nose. Drifter wasn't even the right word for him—he was something that had crawled up out of the ground.

We'll book him in the morning, Whitney said. Get this loser

cleaned up first.

Whitney dropped him on the bed and they strapped him down, even though the fight had long since flowed out of him: Above his eye was dug out to the bone. His license said Vester Carson, twenty-eight, of North Carolina.

No one knew the stranger. The other nurse said, Man with these good looks is dangerous. Especially when he's got the taste.

They cut the clothes off his body and wiped him down as best they could and she remembers the irritation they found on his skin although they had mistook it for some kind of rash. She cleaned the wound and the doctor came in and stitched up the eye and when it was only she and the drunk again, she could not dismiss from her mind the slight swell of his belly and the hair that ran in a straight line from his navel down — her favorite part of a man. That was the thing about Vester Carson's good looks: they could cut through all of that mess and make everything else seem incidental.

Even when the morning shift arrived, Mae stayed with the new admit. She said she had a special interest in this one. She changed the dressing every few hours and watched the flutterings his eyeballs made behind their lids. She wondered what such a man dreamt about.

Word spread that the stranger had sat by himself near the waitress stand, drinking Jack on the rocks and not saying much of anything until he got up off the stool and lost his balance and when he fell he cracked his head wide open, a wound that left a trail of blood the length of the bar, down the slope of the floor. He asked for another round and the bartender refused. Then he became belligerent. In the end, nobody laid a hand on him; he was just falling-down drunk.

Is he in big trouble? she asked the sheriff.

We're not in the business of rehabilitating drunks, he said. Let me know once he's sober.

She knew women who collected men like her own father had collected busted-out radios to one day fix. She was never one of those. Men were as foreign to her as Africa. But Vester Carson made her bold. He made her want to try the things she'd always wanted to do, or say the things she'd held inside. If only, she thinks now, she'd paid attention to the warnings that clattered about him like tin cans tied to strings, she might have been warded off for good. But he was handsome and wore a tattoo on his arm of a Bengal tiger and when he was sober he could talk a nun out of her chastity belt. Not that she needed any convincing.

Are you my Molly Pitcher? he asked once he was awake.

She went to his bedside. Do you know where you are?

It's not the Ritz, but it's not bad.

She held a glass of water to his lips and he sipped from it. She said, You need to get that drinking under control.

His eyes shone like stars in a pond. It's not the drinking that's the problem. It's the alcohol.

Already she had made up her mind. She pulled back a corner of the sheet and ran her hand along his foot. She let her hand slide over his bridge and she touched his ankle; he had nice skin then and only a few raised bumps across his shoulders. It might have been heat rash; it might have been acne. She hardly noticed. He said he was a veteran of the Gulf War and she told him he was brave. Then she touched him and made him come right there in the bed and she had never done that for a man before. She had learned early on that heavy girls disappear just like ugly girls—immediately and forever. For her, weight had always been a problem. But this man stroked her with words and he made her laugh like no one else and she could do the wash on his abdomen it was so tight and lean. When the sheriff came back later that night he found her in the same position as when he'd left.

Thought you were gonna call me when he woke up, he said.

He just come awake.

I'm dying for a smoke, Vester said.

Whitney booked him and he spent a few nights at Desoto County. In her off-hours she sat in a chair outside his cell and they studied the unfamiliar shapes of one another. He was drying out and it was a hard road. His hair was tight black curls and every coil held demons. He expelled cigarette smoke and watched her through its shifting; he offered one to her and she accepted. He lit the matchbook with one hand and put the flame to her cigarette. She had never smoked a cigarette before and the menthol was both scathing and somehow satisfying. She liked the cloud that hovered in her lungs although she wasn't sure why; she liked the burn. He said he wanted to see her touch herself and so she did — she made herself go right there on the folding chair in the middle of the row of jail cells with a young Todd Peters in the cell across the way, probably watching her too and making himself go as she did. But Vester just sat there watching. When she finished she found herself sunken in the chair with her legs open and she was surprised how easily she'd given herself over to it. He drew on his cigarette and said he could listen to the sounds she made for the rest of his life and die happy.

He was being held on bail that he couldn't pay. He said he'd have the money once his pension came. He wanted her to cash the check for him but instead she paid the bail in full. Her grandmother had passed a year or so before, leaving her the house on Origen Road. She knew Whitney and the rest of them and she made special arrangements so when Vester walked out a free man he wore not the torn-up clothes he'd been brought in wearing but a white linen suit that one of the cops had found for him, who knows where, in the stuff that people just leave behind. The suit was a little too big around the shoulders but he looked dapper. They drove to her house. She prepared a big lunch but he threw her down on the bed and said he had no use for food unless it was the taste of her. They didn't have use for clothes either, as days went by and she called into work sick and then she was sick for a week, both of them rendered immobile with a paralyzing hunger for one another.

Weeks passed. There were no thoughts during those heady days. No plans. Just living — how she'd always wanted to live. They drove to Tennessee to celebrate two months of cohabitation, the longest either had committed to anything except, he said, his tour of duty and even that wasn't entirely up to him — and they were married in a helicopter flying over the Cumberland Valley. They bought a videotape of the ceremony but the cameraman forgot to connect a certain cord and so they had the images but not the words either of them said, just several silent minutes of sprawling Tennessee mountains, their lips mouthing devotions that someone had taken the trouble to write and that they both seemed to say with great feeling. Vester drew a military check and benefits from the base in Miami and he worked around the house and fixed her busted outlets and cleaned the gutters and painted her kitchen and the house took on a life of its own, a new birth, and so, she felt, did they. They stayed up all hours transitioning the house from that of her grandmother with her dark wood paneling to something that was theirs — somehow lighter. They spent the weekends with the phone off the hook and the door locked and she let the mail sit unopened.

In-between their honeymooning they watched television, clips of the riots in Los Angeles and of Rodney King, being subdued by police.

Right there, Vester would say.

Where? I don't see it.

Right there. He moved for something on his waist.

Meanwhile the batons continued to fall — five or six uniformed officers delivered the blows with the black man lying heavy as stone on the ground. It had been a routine traffic stop, the newspapers said. And then flames consumed south-central Los Angeles. The worse the rioting became and the more the newspapers screamed the more ravenous she and Vester became for one another. She felt the national tension and she felt its release as she and her new husband consumed one another, watching the flames on the television screen reflected in her bedroom window, all the images reversed. Rodney King moving not his right arm this time, but his left.

Why won't he just lie still? she asked.

Drugs don't let you be still, he said.

On the television screen, King lies on his stomach and there are seven or eight policemen standing there and it is like the eye of a storm, a moment where everyone catches their breath and a car passes and all is quiet. Mae hopes the clip will be different this time, running not two-minutes and forty-nine seconds but something shorter—not even worth airing. King turns over and the blows rain down and how can a man who has been kicked and beaten find the strength to get up again? He must be deaf. He must be high or stoned. There are ten police officers standing around and some people in plainclothes just happening by and then there are too many men for her to count, the beaten man on his knees now being handcuffed in the light from the cruisers.

You can't hear what's being said, Vester told her. You don't know what the cops are hearing. We see this video but it's not the whole story. We need the sound to know for sure.

All she had were images—images from the City of Angels broadcast into her home for the past year and a half; images of Vester sober for half that long; images of her shape changing in the full-length mirror because suddenly she was bearing a child. But she missed the sound—she needed the sound to know for sure, something other than the watery, unfocused images that played themselves out on her television screen.

She hadn't known he kept his bottles hidden. He chewed mints and wore his Old Spice heavy. Expectations would have been different, had she known. He began going out in the evenings and crawling into bed with her as dawn broke, dragging liters of liquor and the grime and the sand of the streets and the reek of the Cuban whores while she pretended to sleep through it all.

It began with her pregnancy when all of her energy was focused on the coming child. She had no energy to spare. She hoped each new morning would find a changed man in her bed, domesticated like a puppy brought home from the pound. Foolish thoughts, she knows now looking back.

Troy was born. And then she was pregnant again, almost right away, although she couldn't figure out how. Remembering now and feeling surprise that she ever allowed him to take her—she must have understood even then that she was second or third in just that night alone.

Home with the infant, the noise and the disruption of routine, Vester's absences extended. One night turned into two agonizing weeks. Kat Capron came to the house twice a day to help with the infant. She brought diapers and baby formula and warm compresses for her feet—all stuff people donated at the church. Mae didn't know that, then. She wasn't conscious enough to grasp the magnitude of the generosity being shown her—how deep the well ran. The Caprons had only just lost their daughter; she knows that now. Kat's daughter was not two months in the grave and she was sitting on Mae's couch and Mae was lamenting the details of her own pathetic story and poor Kat had just lost her daughter, her only daughter, and was subjected to Mae's miserable weeping.

The phone calls started, Vester phoning from a strip joint up I-75, *All Nude, All Day*, asking her to bring the boy so he could see him and when she refused, his voice quieter but more intense like the tip of a slow knife, making threats that described in detail the way he would approach her house and watch the lights go off as he lay waiting in the bushes—he still had his key, didn't she realize?—and he would murder her and murder the unborn child and steal back his son. She believed him. She did not question. She fled to the Caprons'. She stayed there several weeks. Eventually, he started calling there, too.

She remembers huddling in the corner of the kitchen watching Cyrus talk to Vester on the phone, talking him down, lying for her, telling him he didn't know where she was. Rejecting his threats. Laughing at the threats as if he couldn't touch them—and she realizes now he couldn't. The Caprons lost everything when they lost their daughter. There was nothing left to fear. Not from him. Not from anyone.

It was almost winter, after she'd put Troy to bed. They were still living with the Caprons. She heard Vester's voice calling out from the yard. She went to the window and saw him standing on the curb in a coat and tie with his hair gelled and combed straight back. In his arm was a bouquet of yellow roses, her favorite, and behind him a white 1979 Camaro with only the most unnoticeable rust stains around the tire wells.

It's for you, baby, he said. Let's take it for a spin.

She didn't ask where he'd gotten the car, or the suit. The child leapt inside of her and she ran right back to him and by the end of that night they were living together again. But now she paid all of the bills, his checks already spoken for by an illegitimate child he had with a woman in Virginia. It's easy for her to look back now and see how easily he manipulated her, how he asked almost every day who else would love a fat woman but him? All the time reminding her of her size, saying, Nobody would love you better. She wanted what was best for her son and for the baby and she made herself believe that what was best for them was a normal home, with a mother and father, no matter what else came.

Her water broke. Evan was born at 4:34 A.M. the next morning. And if the first child had driven Vester away, the second seemed to anchor him there. He gathered the infant in his arms and spoke about what kind of life they'd live together. Years passed. Short bursts of his drinking followed by months of sobriety and repentance and church-going and clear-headed charm and wit and all the qualities she saw in him that first night in the hospital bed. A pleasant dream with dark underpinnings, something in the periphery of her vision during those years, not what she couldn't hear but what she couldn't see—the police officers who began off-camera but drew closer as the event unfolded, witnesses and then participants drawn to the violence despite every reasonable thought.

She remained vigilant. If their marriage was a dream she slept with one eye open, reminding herself to enjoy the moments even as they were happening. It's terrible to be that self-aware, she thinks, that prescient. Evan was three years old when she taught him to recite his home address and phone number. Troy had already learned his, barely five himself. Then one night, a little over a year ago, she went to work, leaving the boys in the care of their father. They'd been left with him before. He was capable when he wanted to be. But two o'clock in the morning, Whitney came into the triage leading Troy by the hand and carrying Evan on his shoulder. He'd wrapped his jacket around the youngest boy and the boy slept.

What've they done? she asked.

Whitney set the boys down on two empty chairs and took off his hat and ran a hand over the buzz-cut closeness of his scalp. He said, They turned the lights on at the Bar-Knuckle. The boys were sitting in the corner, quiet as mice. Bartender asked where they lived and they said their father told them to wait there.

Mae knelt on the floor and touched her sons with the back of her hand as if they might be running fevers.

Whitney said, Owing to the fact I know you and Vester, and I know your circumstances, we'll let it go. I don't have to tell you, a judge won't approve of bringing a toddler to a bar. You'd lose them right quick if it ever goes to court.

Troy is eight years old now, Evan six. She is a single mother keeping together a three-bedroom house way out in the country. She lives her life in scrubs. She tucks the boys into bed and goes to work at the ER and comes home the next morning to make them breakfast and sleep a few hours while they watch television, until she is up again to make lunch or run errands or take them to the church to play with friends. She lives her life in pajamas. Pink scrubs and blue scrubs and red scrubs with green wreathes when it is Christmastime. Needing time of her own to settle adult things and all the other aspects of her life but feeling guilty if she ever pawns off her boys in order to do so.

Not that there aren't plenty of volunteers. It seems the entire congregation of Christ by the Sea has offered to watch her boys at one time or another. They love her boys and for that she is grateful. She has lost count of how many times a person has said to her, Whenever I think there aren't enough hours in the day, I just think on Mae Carson, how you work yourself to exhaustion and raise those boys and still find time to give back to the church. There are always other kids at the church for the boys to play with, at all hours, and there are often free meals.

In the lobby of the church hangs a white cross trimmed with silver. The cross is four feet tall, its crossbars thinly modern. It hangs at an angle between the ceiling and the wall, suspended in flight. Floodlights illuminate the cross and at night she stands in the parking lot and through the glass doors sees the cross hanging in the foyer. Witnessing this, she catches something on the air, a dewy taste on her tongue. It is fleeting. Like a dream she can't quite remember. How the whole night opens out for her at such moments, crushed beneath the vastness of Creation. How when she and Vester had only just started living together they drove to Tennessee in her run-down Datsun. How they were married in a helicopter and then drove to a motel nestled in the foothills. How they couldn't keep their hands off one another, clothes only a barrier between their need and the fulfillment of that need. How on their last evening in the valley he made her wear a blindfold and drove her many miles up a mountain. She felt the incline of the car and knew they drove steeply up. The car flattened out and she put down the window and breathed in the damp air, musty and slightly chilled, with a note of the pine forest that spread for thousands of acres. When the car stopped, he opened her door and led her along blacktop and then to grass. When he removed the blindfold, she saw she stood on the edge of a cliff. Below her was mountainside and at the bottom of the mountain was farmland and beyond that a ridge of mountains. Behind the mountains, the sunset. She does not know enough colors to describe the sunset that day. She could see a farmhouse on the valley floor, and the road they had driven up. Vester touched her arm and said, Turn around.

She turned and found herself at the base of an enormous cross. The cross was three stories high, maybe four. Its beams were thick as train cars. The cross shone with brilliant white radiance, lit by four spotlights. Around the cross were a wrought-iron fence and plaques on the brickwork which honored veterans.

What is this place? she asked.

I don't know, he said. A guy at the Waffle House said we needed to see it.

She walked the perimeter of the cross. There was no one else around. She found it impossible to imagine its undertaking—the clearing away of the trees and the paving of the road (the way they came just two-lane road stretching forever into the forest) and then the building of the cross—the faith behind the project. That was the power of symbols—they needed no words, no other sound.

Vester stood on the edge of the precipice and hollered into the valley. She sometimes imagined a white-bearded man with a pack on his back, pots and pans and a tambourine clattering from the pack, and inside the pack exotic medicines and island remedies, a rhesus monkey trailing behind. Vester was like that—a snake oil show. Each day brought a new tall tale that made her laugh and love him even more than she had the day before. He'd stop to pick up a smooth, rounded stone and say it was an arrowhead and then he'd tell the story of the Indian brave who lost it, how the brave shot the arrow, his last arrow, in a valiant effort to save the woman he loved—the squaw. The story would go on and on, him just making it up the whole time, and he would be worlds away then, gone from her. But sometimes she could follow him into those imagined worlds or see as clearly as he did the end result of his current scheme and for those moments she loved him best of all.

Him standing on the edge of the cliff shouting her name into the valley—that's what the metal cross in the foyer of Christ by the Sea reminds her of. It should evoke humility, she thinks, or reverence. But instead it reminds her of the one man she's ever loved. She loved Vester Carson. After all of it, she loved him. And when Christ was asked how many times to forgive thine enemies he said not one hundred times but one hundred times one hundred. Maybe, after all these years, she wasn't there yet.

THREE

Bankruptcy. He likes to turn the word over in his mouth, to chew it like cud. He imagines the word paraded across a stage by twelve Las Vegas showgirls, their bare tits bouncing. A series of ruptured things: his marriage, his faith, a burst money sack bleeding out—bankruptcy.

From his office window Pastor Reginald Dancer can see the road and across the sloping front lawn of the church the sign that rises from the sawgrass and milkweeds. The church itself: concrete and stucco, gleaming white, with vertical panes of tinted glass pushing the pallid foundation toward Heaven. When the church was built, it was the only structure for three miles in either direction. Now parishioners come from ten times that far away to pass beneath the sign and through the glass doors of the church, to pass beneath the cross suspended mid-flight above the atrium.

It is his greatest source of pride, this sign. Not because it is beautiful, although it is, and not because it is by far the largest in Desoto County. The magnificence of the gesture exists for him in the permanence of his name carved into the rock, cast so as never to be interchanged with another. He is the pastor of this church and has been since its inception; his office affords him a view of the sign and he watches it change over the course of a day, the different ways in which light falls across it. The gray light in morning, the fiery-orange at sundown.

The first mark that bore his name he drew himself with a Sharpie on a sheet of printer paper, back when typing paper had perforated edges that needed to be folded and then removed, sixteen years ago. He taped this sign to the door of the Almond Room at the Holiday Inn as an afterthought, because the entire congregation—all five—was already seated in a small circle of folding chairs. That Sunday, he preached the first chapter of Jeremiah—*Today I appoint you over nations and over kingdoms, to pluck up and to pull down, to destroy and to overthrow, to build and to plant.* The flowers of the almond tree, he told the fellowship, bloomed earlier than most. This impatient blossoming was the fulfillment of God's promise and the predication of His strict, forthcoming judgment.

There had been five that first week and the next week there had been seven and after two months they'd outgrown the Almond Room. They found a third floor meeting room in town where the whiteboard outside the door bore removable black letters that the security guard changed, depending. They shared this room with, among others, a class that taught English to Cuban and Haitian refugees. This group met prior to theirs and when time came for Sunday service, many of the students stayed. In this way he met John Whitney, who was attending the class with his mother. He was only just talking about running for sheriff then. Their numbers diversified and swelled and the space grew cramped, but they remained thankful for the continued evidence of God's work in their lives.

Their current incarnation on Roan Street is the true monument to God's covenant. And when Noah's family stepped down from the Ark and their feet touched dry land for the first time in months, God filled the sky with a rainbow, an emblem of His eternal pledge. He made a promise to the town of Arcadia as well, in the form of the sign, in the austere tranquility of the limestone by day and the way in which at night the cool fuscia lamps, tucked into the rocks below the water, cause the stone and the water beneath it to flow like wine.

When they purchased the land and decided to build the church, none of them anticipated so much growth so quickly. It may have hurt them, he thinks looking back. Within six months of occupying the newly-constructed church (there was still drywall in places and holes in the ceiling that revealed the guts and innards of electrical wire and steel coils) he was naming deacons and hiring an assistant pastor and two secretaries and forming a Pastoral Committee to oversee leadership of the burgeoning flock.

Offerings poured in. The church became a must-stop for evangelists on the senior circuit—Christ by the Sea had caught the tail-end of that boom. All the major names in America's fundamentalist movement preached at Reginald Dancer's pulpit in the late eighties and early nineties: evangelists, musicians and touring companies; weight lifters for Jesus, Christian rap artists, Christian punk bands. There were healing services where the church filled to overflowing—the faithful stood in classrooms watching miracles occur on twelve-inch monitors. On nights like these he felt the entire town, the county, the entire state of Florida was packed inside his church, driving in from Sarasota or Fort Pierce to hear God's word through the Sony deluxe sound system. Just to purchase a cassette tape of the Reverend Reginald Dancer's sermons. Just to feel the charge, the power of multitudes in worship. Their numbers reached three thousand members.

The Building Committee said, Buy the sign. He spared no expense. It is hard for him to believe now, looking back, but the cost of the sign was nothing compared to what they spent to bring Moses Persimmon or Matt Dobson or Ben Leland in on a Wednesday night, or what it cost to make the church handicap accessible, or what it cost to pay salaries, his included. But the sign had been a rallying point for the church, something tangible for the givers of tithes to see each Sunday when they came to service, to reassure them their offerings were accomplishing the great and glorious will of God. Now each day the sign seems more and more like a monument to sinful pride. His personal tower of Babel, something the church or himself alone is being punished for.

He watches the sign and beyond the sign the road and the cars passing on it. No one slows to read it, not anymore. Christ by the Sea has become an institution — more than that, it has become part of the memory of the town. A car with out-of-state plates might slow to let its passengers absorb the gleaming church and beyond the church a field of mirrors, or so it must seem, before being carried past. Unknowingly streaming past what was once the epicenter of the Evangelical movement in America; not knowing the strange tower rising out of the mirrored field beyond was meant to start a new movement, a synergy between the gospel and a groundbreaking ministry of conservation.

He can still hear his father-in-law's voice: Solar cells, my boy, solar energy. Six words had spurred the downfall of a nation — his nation. The nation of Christ by the Sea. The good doctor, Lawrence Gauche, was the father of Nadine Gauche to whom the pastor had been married. The doctor approached Christ by the Sea with an investment plan, an opportunity for growth. The church owned five hundred acres of Florida marshland. The doctor owned several hundred thousand shares in a company called SunStorm, LLC, and he was making a killing in Arizona developing technology to cheaply and efficiently harness solar energy and then selling the solar power to the utility companies at a very profitable rate. The plan was simple enough; the church could do the same. Christ by the Sea agreed to sell a hundred acres. The church would receive a percentage of the profits, and as an added incentive, Dr. Gauche pledged six million of his own dollars to be donated to the church at a million per year. He flew his own crew in from Tempe and gave the church the rights to a hundred thousand shares of SunStorm, LLC. Once the company went public the shares would be worth a great deal—but for now they are worth even less than the heavy card stock they are printed on, less than the cost of the LaserJet toner.

Each day he sees the same view from his office window: the slope of the lawn and the sign and beyond the sign the road with cars passing on it. Farther down the road, if he stretches his neck to see, which he sometimes does because a part of him loves misery, or so he's come to believe, he can see to where the new development is going up, casting a longer and longer shadow across his church. Construction cranes loom in the distance like giraffes grazing from the clouds; the ever-present sound of jackhammers and the grinding of engines of heavy machines. This ongoing development is the third act in his tragedy, the third portion of his woebegone trifecta. There is the church he is bound to lose. There are solar panels that sit unused like fine china on a hundred pristine acres. And now this development, overseen by his ex-wife, where the buzz saws and the bulldozers and the spinning cylinders of cement are an extension of her consciousness, the way she grated on him in marriage and now torments him in bachelorhood and will no doubt haunt him in the Great Beyond. Nadine Gauche, the former Mrs. Reverend Reginald Dancer.

And wasn't it for prideful reasons he agreed to meet with her a year ago? After she—no, not her, but her assistant—called to schedule an appointment. As if they hadn't shared a bathroom for twenty years, hadn't washed their face in the same sink beside the other one brushing their teeth? As if she didn't know he'd let his own secretary go for budgetary reasons with the feeling, because she was elderly, of tossing his own grandmother out into the street?

And then she was sitting in the swivel-back chair across his desk, her legs crossed, her posture perfectly emitting the sense of being wrapped-up tight. A coiled spring, like a toy racing car he might have wound up and let fly down the tiled hallways of his youth.

Her hair was pulled back; the coat-sweater she wore clasped her throat. Hard and coiled was his ex-wife, the bit of bare flesh on her kneecap uninviting as the tap of her callused heel against the sole of her sensible flats. If he'd harbored any last thought of one day finding his way home again, slipping his head and shoulders beneath her knee-length skirt, the insistent clicking of her heel squelched it for good.

He gave it over to God. He could let it go. But her bare legs drove him mad. She knew this, of course—her bare knees a negotiating tactic, pure evil, heartbreakingly simple.

How've you been? he gulped.

Picture perfect. She allowed a crisp nod that punctuated this summation to the affirmative. I know how busy you are this time of year—believe me, I know—so I'll be short. I represent Tyler Development. It's a subsidiary my father owned. We know that Christ by the Sea is having some trouble making ends meet. And we think we can help you alleviate some of those financial concerns.

He wanted to scream. Concerns? She caused these concerns.

But she said, Tyler is willing to make an offer—to put in a bid for roughly three hundred acres of the land currently held by Christ by the Sea.

What kind of bid?

A very good one. Eight thousand an acre.

That was hard for him to believe. He took a moment to let the number slosh around inside his brain. Only several years before they'd purchased all five hundred acres for two per—a four-hundred percent increase in value.

He asked, What are you planning to build?

That's not really your concern.

If you're planning on preserving it as a natural habitat, I'm much more inclined to listen. As opposed to say, building a NASCAR track.

No NASCAR track. She smiled and allowed a small laugh, a brief moment to glance down and straighten the papers on her lap. It was like seeing someone he knew — but hadn't seen in quite some time — pass fleetingly on a crowded train. There was a time that just one look from him could make her feel nervous like that.

She said, For the time being we'd keep it undeveloped. We see it as an investment, more than anything. But in the future it would be reasonable to expect a gated community. Single-family homes. A golf course, eighteen holes woven through the community.

Where are these people coming from? The people to live in these homes?

You should see it over in Sarasota, she said. She flipped her pen front to end, end to front. You can't get anywhere in less than fifteen minutes. This time of year is the worst. And more and more people are living there full-time. It's not a resort town anymore. There are real businesses, real banks. When the rest of the world needs to get away, they come to Sarasota. So what do the good people of Sarasota do, or the good citizens of Venice Beach? They'll live in Arcadia and commute into the city just like they do up north.

Interesting theory.

It's the future, Reg. It's staring right at you and you can't even see it.

She'd said the same thing four years ago when her father first approached him with the SunStorm, LLC proposal. Except she had batted her eyes then and made it clear that he should feel blessed, anointed. Her daddy was doing him a favor; her father could build anywhere. But it made sense to use the church's land, and the church could benefit. She could run the operation like another one of her pet projects. Which she quickly grew bored with. As she would with this plan to develop suburbs for the suburbs. Still, she had not batted her eyes when she suggested this development—there was nothing else sketched upon her face but cold business and sordid cash.

It will have to go before Church Council, he said. But I'm telling you now, up front, that it will take twelve an acre, at least, to make it happen.

That land is nothing but…bog. Home to the swamp creature.

That land is the future, Nadine. You said so yourself.

She sighed. She shook her head. It was like she pitied him. She said, We'll meet you halfway. Tell the council we'll make it an even ten. Three hundred acres, three million dollars. Math so simple, even you can understand it. And we'll make the mortgage very favorable to the church. Our apologies, of course, for not being able to pay it outright.

And if we get a better offer from someone else?

Are there any other offers, period?

There were no other offers, of course. The Church Council approved the sale. It was impossible not to, faced with their obscene amount of debt. Tyler Development secured a mortgage on the land. This fixed amount of monthly income relieved the church of some of its financial pressure. But even now, a year later, they continue to scrape by, weighed down by their overhead, cut off at the knees by their declining membership, and saddled with an investment deal gone sour.

Bankruptcy. The word shipwrecked on a rocky shore, suffocated by the seaweed and the barnacles.

In his more paranoid moments, he muses bitterly that this was her plan all along. Her old man didn't plan to die of course, two years into his commitment—he probably didn't want to die at all. But it proved to be only a minor setback in Nadine's vision for the future. In fact, it provided her a true weapon, when before she'd had none. With her father dead, her interest in solar energy waning for quite some time, her interest in marriage waning for quite some time before that, it was a simple thing to contest the estate and tie up the four million dollars Dr. Gauche still owed Christ by the Sea. This was all it took to bring construction on the solar panels grinding to a halt—enough to turn those hundred acres from a guaranteed cash cow into a white elephant. An elephant that feasted more or less straight out of the offering plate.

His father-in-law was barely in the grave when Nadine left him. She moved to a one-bedroom condominium in Punta Gordo, as if she were just waiting for the good doctor to die before making their separation official. She took nothing—she hardly took any clothes. Once she was rich she wanted nothing to do with their humble origins, the chest of drawers they'd bought from the flea market, sanded and stained and held onto all those years, the first piece of furniture they purchased as a married couple. And even with the contestation of the will, even with SunStorm, LLC dead in the water, she had other things—newer, richer things—to keep her busy.

History was littered with pastors befallen by personal tragedy or crushed beneath the awesome responsibility of serving as God's conduit on Earth. Such men, when they fell, were always discovered stinking drunk in a nudie club outside Jacksonville or were rumored to be touring the heartland by motorcycle. These church leaders, once found, were rushed straightaway to a recovery home in some other parish for a pre-determined time, granted a leave of absence for a psychological sabbatical. Sometimes they emerged new men. Other times they quit the cloth altogether, liquidated their possessions, and flew to Tibet.

In the back of his mind he thought he always knew just how he too would go off the deep end if given the chance. But he lacked the imagination to bring his own bender into focus. He lacked the creativity to do it right. In the end, he couldn't orchestrate his own fall from grace, as even Lucifer had done so many years ago. And so he sat. And sat. And he waited. And he stared at the wall. And one day he no longer felt like sitting, and that was the end of it.

Now he was in the cash-flow business. Before he was in the business of saving souls, but now cash needed to flow — from the mortgage paid by Tyler Development into the pockets of the SunStorm, LLC investors and into the mortgage owed by his church on the hundred acres and the building it still owned. But no matter how many different ways he entered the numbers on his Casio, they always fell short.

Bankruptcy. He might thread the word with string and fly it on a beach somewhere with other, lighter kites that sail more easily on the swifter currents of air.

He wonders how a falling man knows when he's hit bottom. The light changes and across the yard he sees the sign differently. The darker night makes the sign appear less imposed upon the landscape. But everything is imposed at one time or another — the sign, the church. Arcadia imposed upon a swamp two hundred years ago. Florida nothing but will imposed upon the land. And now uninhabited brick mansions are imposed upon three hundred acres he once owned, and beyond the seal of his office window, behind the great sounds of new construction, beyond that industrial cacophony, is Nadine, the former Mrs. Reverend Reginald Dancer.

Daylight fades across the slope of the lawn outside. The lamps click on and tint the water and stone a rose-colored haze. He knows that even Lot had everything stripped from him — Nadine can take this too.

Mae Carson remembers her first visit to Christ by the Sea. She was running late that Sunday; when she drove up to the church the parking lot was nearly filled. The lawn was smooth and manicured as a putting green and the church stood solidly upon the slope with regal beauty. The sun flashed blindingly from the windshields in the parking lot and the sun caused the white concrete exterior of Christ by the Sea to glow with radiance, and it seemed to her, all of this light, as a sign. Struck blind, was how she felt, like Saul on the road to Damascus so many years ago.

She entered the church through the glass doors, cautiously as if not wanting to leave fingerprints. Despite the sunlight outside, the interior of the atrium felt cool as shade; she was welcomed by the sound of bubbling water and praise music piped over the sound system. The lobby was packed with church-goers, mostly white. They stood in groups of twos and threes around the stone fountain and the ferns and the aloe plants billowing from their clay jars. There was the sense of an evening out, despite the early-morning hour — there was a bag and coat check and when Mae glanced up toward the skylight she had the feeling of falling toward blue sky. She saw that most of the men wore slacks and golf shirts or pastel button-downs. She saw teenagers wearing shorts, even, and most women were not, as she was, in their Sunday best, but dressed simply in flowing skirts or loose slacks. The red ribbons on her shirt, her white pumps, the Fergie bow in her hair, proclaimed her social class more than if she'd come to the church in beach clothes.

There was a foldout table spread with bagels and donuts, cream cheese and butter, orange juice, coffee and milk. She shied away from the platters thinking surely it wasn't for her, not for any visitor who happened to drop by just because she was scared and pregnant with her first and never knew when her husband was coming home. In the auditorium she found no seats open on the floor. She climbed the stairs to the balcony where a soundman and two video cameras recorded the service.

Up until that morning she had thought of Church as organs and hymnals and severe confessions of faith. But here was a full band set up across the stage. There was a drum set and two electric guitars, an electric bass and keys; there was a three-piece brass section and three back-up singers, female, and a married couple she would later learn were the praise and worship leaders — full-salaried. The man and the woman held microphones and when the music began, Mae was washed again with the feeling of falling, a hollowness deep in her gut. The first song was not halfway through when the singers hollered praises and lifted their hands toward the sky and by the end of the song they were calling out strange words and imploring the audience to do the same — Praise Him! Give your praises to the Lord! — and there was a strange surge in the congregation, three thousand maybe, who all raised their hands and seemed to shake or bounce as they called back, Hallelujah, Jesus, Hallelujah. She was hypnotized, but also sure that she should run. She'd wandered into some kind of cult. Pentecostals: She was looking for snakes. But the singers shouted, Amen! and each time a single voice rose from the chorus she felt the cold burst again in her belly, not so much falling as the fear of falling, a palpable hum of emotion welling up inside of her, emotion that she did not have the strength to sort out. She felt dizzied by the music. Women waved colored flags at the foot of the stage, all of them engaged in choreography, waving and snapping back the yellow and red and olive-green banners. Mae kept rhythm by clapping her hands, as best she could. There was fervor on the floor below and she felt certain she could never keep up — three thousand people were heading in some mystical direction she did not think she would be able to go.

Then the music slowed as quickly as it had crested. The music slowed and the people swayed, many with their hands still lifted up. They closed their eyes and sang the slow songs without even glancing at the words. These songs were so unlike the hymns that she remembered, "Nearer My God to Thee" or "What a Friend I Have in Jesus." The lyrics to these new worship songs were printed in her bulletin and also they scrolled across television monitors hung from the corners of the hall. She concentrated on the monitors and sung the words and tried to look purposeful because she didn't want to seem rude, but she also didn't think that she could close her eyes and sway and lift her hands upturned toward Heaven.

When the music began trailing off, some of the congregation was led weeping out into the foyer. A young man took his place behind the glass pulpit. Everyone sat down and the music tapered and she did not think that this could be the pastor, the Reverend Reginald Dancer with his name on the stone wall outside. He wore a light blue shirt and Chino slacks. No collar. No tie. The top button of his shirt was open and the shirt hung straightly over his chest and arms and his skin was tinted orange from exercise and sun. Not one strand of hair was out of place, but swept up in the front and kept loose and a little long. His hands never strayed from the sides of the pulpit. She couldn't take her eyes off of him, even before he said a word.

But it was his voice that transfixed. She no longer remembers what the pastor preached that morning, but she remembers the sensation of listening to his voice for the first time. She'd once seen a kind of tribal man on television, with bones in his nose and ears, putting his mouth to the end of a long, carved tube and creating a sound that she somehow felt more than heard—it hummed inside of her instead of entering the usual way through the ears. Listening to Pastor Reg was like that; she remembers how surprised she was to look at her watch and see the sermon had run two hours.

Someone leaned over and said to her, The Spirit really moved this morning, praise Jesus.

Praise Jesus, she said back.

Coffee Hour followed. Katharine Anne Capron introduced herself and spoke with her for the duration, making her feel welcome and less like the only stranger at a big party. Fay Capron was there too, tugging at her mother's shirtsleeve. Mae remembers thinking how pretty the girl would one day be—how already she hunched over to hide her height but that in a few years the boys would notice the length of her legs, the fine turn of the bones in her wrists. Katharine Anne went back and forth between the two, her daughter who was whining for something, Mae can't remember what, and this visitor to Christ by the Sea who was stationary and skirted with polka dots so enormous they might have covered a piece of furniture if there hadn't been a head attached to them. When Fay had fluttered off, Katharine Anne launched into what sounded like an apology. Saying perhaps Mae had noticed something strange about the service or maybe she had overheard certain conversations and wasn't sure what to make of them. The need to acknowledge problems head on, to confront them, to nip them in the bud. To be upfront with people. She said it hadn't always been like that—the church was going through a rough patch but she saw no reason the church wouldn't get through it, in the end. She told Mae the story of Reginald Dancer building the church from a small meeting room in a hotel out by the interstate. How when they'd moved to a rental space, all he talked about was one day building their own. And when the time finally came, he wouldn't listen to reason or advice from any of the members who had been with him since the beginning. Instead, he built Christ by the Sea and spared no expense. She emphasized this—no expense. He purchased an enormous tract of land, five hundred acres of the wettest Florida soil. Nothing around for miles then, this being long before the wave of new construction that seemed to be sweeping the state. From the moment they broke ground, all he talked about was God's Master Plan. That's what he called it, Master Plan, like a scheme hatched by a madman in a prison tower. He would say that God's vision for their church was to be visible — he said this word a lot, visible, visibility – to be a shining light with national sway. A beacon — again, his word — in the Florida wilderness that would one day attract the multitudes to its doors. Thousands of members, believers and non-believers, gentiles and Jews.

Katharine Anne said her husband, Cyrus, who was one of the church elders, suggested such reasoning might have worked for Walt Disney but that didn't mean their church would find the wild so hospitable or the people so willing to drive in from the coasts.

Until the church was finally built and people really did drive in from hundreds of miles away to hear Pastor Reginald Dancer sermonize. To hear the band and to feel part of the energy of God. To see the healing services, which they quickly became known for. The church exploded and the elders like Cyrus took it upon themselves to solidify the hierarchy of governing, because they could see a need for it, as the church grew from something small and special into an institution, a self-sustaining body.

Offerings poured in and the congregation outgrew the two services on Sundays, and soon there was something going on at the church every night of the week. But the elders sensed trouble. It appeared that if God was talking about His Master Plan, He was talking only to Pastor Reg. Cyrus pointed to the numbers and urged the pastor and the lay ministers to be vigilant about the spiritual health of the church, even as it seemed like every day the pastor was only concerned with garnishing global press and landing spots on cable networks and hearing his own voice on radio shows and muscling politicians and most of all concerned with attracting new members—obsessed with growth. Most of all ignoring the troubles at home.

Katharine Anne told her, The pastor's wife is just a little thing. She grew up in Massachusetts, something of an actress, or at least she could sing and dance well enough. She came down to Florida for college because all she ever wanted was to be a character at Disney World. Don't misunderstand me—this was her Dream. And once she'd achieved that, which she did no problem, being of the right age, diminutive size, and pretty, the only thing left to do was start a family. But the domestic life never took.

Mae thinks it would be hard to be the pastor, but harder still to be the pastor's wife. On the one hand, nothing but a trophy, her spiritual obligations vague at best and marginalized in Scripture. Nadine could manage just fine when Christ by the Sea was a Bible study meeting in the Holiday Inn or even after they moved to the upper room. It wasn't full-time then and she could put on her Disney face once a week to play the role of Pastor's Wife. But when the church moved into its permanent space and when its membership began to grow, the women looked to her for leadership. Nadine attacked it the only way she knew how, as a sorority president might, with a rah-rah attitude that was high-energy but ultimately content-free. She could not untangle herself from the prissiness of theme park mascoting, all cheeky smiles and peppy show. Where she might have shown tact, she tightened herself around each fundraising effort, each ladies' luncheon, until every event became a chore. Church is many things but it is not work, and it began to feel like work for the other women. The way Nadine understood it, the rest of them were ungrateful for her hard labor. She lashed out at volunteers. And whether it was this perceived lack of gratitude or whether she began to come to grips with the fact that she was not suited for ministry, she began a downward spiral that ended with the Dancers' divorce.

Mae thinks some women go and get married and take responsibility for their homes. Others get married and start to behave like children. There's just no telling.

Nadine's father passed away and then Nadine moved to Punta Gordo. By this time, the church had long ceased drawing the A-list evangelists. All focus was on the solar farm going up next door. By the time of the divorce, the congregation was whittled down to a third of what it had been, but even those numbers were enough to fill the auditorium each Sunday. The divorce of the Reverend and Mrs. Reginald Dancer made statewide news. And the pastor was unhinged.

With the SunStorm LLC project abandoned, the pastor abandoned the green gospel the church had been founded on. Changing horses midstream was not enough of a metaphor — he changed entire waterways. He began to prepare his church for the Rapture. Beginning with a condemnation of Hollywood, what he called a purveyor of secular movies lacking moral center. This denouncement culminated in a Wednesday night service where parishioners burned their video libraries in a fire pit out back of the church. Not just smut, but Disney movies and spaghetti westerns and musicals. In the ensuing months, he began to preach on the origins of the Church as he sought, he said, to prepare his ministry for the coming of the Kingdom of God.

He begged for a return to aesthetic virtue. He pleaded for modesty. Women should wear only long dresses. Women should keep their hair tied up. Be true revolutionaries, he told the congregation, and serve your God.

Church members were directed to dissect each aspect of modern life. From music to television to the observance of Halloween, they sought the spiritual center of it all. For Mae, it meant filtering the cartoons her boys watched. Taken to its logical conclusion, this filtering left her boys with nothing but educational programming.

She began to have her own doubts about her family's future at Christ by the Sea. She turned to prayer, and waited to be led.

Now the pastor spends nearly every waking hour at the church. He is the kind of man who, faced with the potential for failure, steadies himself and works harder, stays later. Mae judges from the amount of time he spends within the whitewashed walls of Christ by the Sea, the potential for failure looms large.

She asked him once why he spent so much time alone, stowed away in his office surrounded by memories and Bibles.

Why is it you spend all of your free time at the church, he asked her, instead of taking your boys out on the river or to visit friends?

This is what the Lord saw fit to bless me with, she said.

So you understand, the pastor said.

But Mae knew this was not the reason. The pastor had reached the point in his life where the unknown held more power than the known. Suddenly, or perhaps not so suddenly, his life had been reduced to metaphor. He could hide despite the glass doors of the church; he could slip between the cracks of the plaster fountain, or seat himself on its bench and run his finger across the water's surface and if someone happened by he could speak with them and offer the generalities and encouraging words he had collected during sixteen years of pastoral counseling — all without the threat of real human interaction. He would not be tainted by the suffering of others. His heart would not be touched.

She allowed him this, and did not judge him for it. She knew a man could suffer only so much anguish before deciding he'd finally had enough.

DOWN THE HALL she can hear the voices of the children's choir singing together not in harmony but close enough to hold a melody. The upright piano clanks beneath their voices and there is one central key that seems to drag. She is surprised that already they are practicing for the pageant but then she knows little of musical preparation. Perhaps it simply takes that long to gel.

Past the rehearsal room and through the foyer she finds the pastor's office lit. His door is cracked and she pushes it open, tapping her knuckles against the wood. He stands with his back to her, hunched over a pullout drawer in an exhibit of thin drawers running floor to ceiling. This rosewood bookcase spans the length of his office wall. Its shelves are stacked with bibles and the *Anchor Bible* series of introductions to the gospels and the letters of Paul. Thin paperbacks too, with titles like *To Trust Again* and *Even Angels Pray*. Behind a glass window are mementos from his football days, a program from his Senior Night, a ribbon anointing him top scholar-athlete, and a football scrawled with signatures she can't quite read. Near the door hang his diploma and framed handwritten notes from, she presumes, dignitaries and the like — she doesn't know enough about politics to recognize the names but she sees the seal on the heads of these letters and thinks they look official. Dancer has his magnifying glass pressed to the drawer. She is almost close enough to view its contents when he feels her presence and slides the drawer closed.

His voice betrays neither surprise nor annoyance. Mae Carson, your devotion is unparalleled.

It's due to my working nights, she says. Can't sleep like a normal person anymore, even on my few days off.

That makes two of us. He crosses to his desk and pushes the magnifying glass across thickly-bound files.

He will provide, Pastor.

She touches his shoulder and she is careful to keep the touch light and friendly, platonic. Her hand is safe there, balanced on the strongest part of a man. She thinks if they were lovers she might slide her arm around his waist and push her lips to his, to offer reassurance. To let him know that she still believes in him and in the church. She lets her hand trace the outline of his arm and she squeezes him gently at the elbow. She wants to change the subject, to get his mind on something else.

She says, What do you keep in those drawers?

Just things that I collect.

The knob of one drawer is cool to the touch. She says, Like postage stamps?

She knows that he is watching her and watching her hand, and her hand on the knob is a game of chicken — she wouldn't dare, or would she? Then he moves for her and takes her by the wrist. The pressure of his forefinger and thumb she feels all the way down to her groin.

I appreciate your prayers, he says.

He leads her from the bookcase to the window. There is a bench seat there and they take it. The window is open and they can hear a bullfrog somewhere off in the drainage pond or in the wrecked land behind the church, abutting the new development. Otherwise the world outside is dark and impenetrable. She is glad for the open window, for the breeze.

He touches her knee and then withdraws his hand. She tries to judge the offering but cannot. He asks how things are at home.

Status quo, she says.

No word from Vester?

Not since April, when they caught him trespassing in our pond.

And you? Managing?

Mae shakes her head. Some days are better than others. Some days I go to work just fine. Some days I can't seem to drag myself out of bed — and that's when things start going downhill.

She and the pastor are both looking out to different parts of the darkness. Nothing is said for quite some time. She has come to recognize these silences as natural with him. It is during these silences he listens for the Spirit. It is him letting the Spirit move between him and whomever he is with. He believes this sort of quiet is vital for this purpose, following the guidance of the Holy Ghost. She squirms as the minutes drag on and he studies her without saying anything more. It's that he doesn't quite look at her, but somewhere just off, as if she carries something on her shoulder that would tell him all he needs to say.

The sheriff was over to my house just this morning, she says.

I haven't talked to John in a long time.

He's the same as ever. Lonely old man, living by himself.

He's not that old, is he?

Probably not. Still, I don't like to think of him eating his suppers alone. He's good to us. He was telling me about the other night, he picked a girl up off the side of the highway.

A girl, you mean, a streetwalker?

I don't think so. She pretends to adjust her seat but ends up inching closer to the pastor, close enough to smell the heaviness of his breath. She says, Young girl. Maybe twenty years old. John thought she was a runaway. She's staying out at the Caprons'.

The pastor says nothing. She asks, Do you think it's queer of them to take in a complete stranger?

Dancer smiles and then stands. She hears the bullfrog, lowing. The lonely bullfrog like her own loneliness broadcast to the drainage ditch and to the road.

He says, I think the Caprons, Cyrus in particular, are still looking for meaning, even after all this time.

She's heard his voice sound like this before, as if channeling something warm and dark and deep. He is standing very still, hands folded. He watches her, although she is only sitting on his window seat like she does each night she visits him.

He says, I see a real challenge for you. Vester may be back

one day. You'll have to set aside your pride, when he returns. His rightful place is at the head of your household.

I struggle with pride, Pastor.

Each of us does.

John dropped off a bag of clothes for the boys today and I couldn't hardly look at them I was so ashamed.

God is still finding ways to work through you, through all of us.

She knows that in her heart of hearts she never wants to see her husband again. She doesn't see how forgiveness could really be in God's plan, not after the way Vester treated them for so long.

She says, I haven't heard from him. I don't know if he's in jail, or if he's dead, or if he's living some entire life with some other woman in some other state…and I'm tired, Pastor. I'm so tired I can barely walk.

He goes to her. He sits and pats her hand and the gesture breaks her heart. He puts one arm around her and lets her weep into his shirt collar. The shirt he wears is the thinnest cotton; her tears turn the fabric a deep shade of red.

FOUR

Hexagonal clusters of solar panels tilt on their aluminum frames and shiver cool as sentinels in the sun. Like baby's tears fanning outward across the wetland, four quadrants converge on a solar tower which rises out of the coverage of tinted mirrors and absorbs the reflection of a thousand heliostats shining up at it from the ground. Like a black beetle, still and shimmering, the solar farm covers a hundred acres.

Pastor Reginald Dancer and Cyrus Capron drive toward the center of the infield. They pass close enough to see the blue mirrors inside the solar panels, the dish arrays programmed to track the path of the sun across the sky. But there is no movement now, and no sound save for the squad car's tires kicking up sand and dust along the road.

Otherworldly, isn't it? Dancer says.

Eerie as hell, Cyrus says.

The deputy's clipboard rests on the bench seat between them. Clipped to it are several pages of safety measures and a security checklist outlining standards that the solar farm, even dark, must meet. When they drove into the farm, the pastor made a big show of getting out of the squad car and unlocking the gate, waving Cyrus through and then locking the gate behind them. He performed this task with all the grim-faced determinism of established routine, although he'd only just bought the lock and chain at the Wal-Mart and affixed it to the gate the night before. The pastor believes that Cyrus is a pushover, a pancake who spent his afternoons as a gangly youth not playing with other kids but simply running, from one end of town to the other. Running in circles sometimes. They're not very churchlike, the pastor knows, these cold calculations, especially given the tragedies that have befallen Cyrus since. But if anyone in the Desoto County Sheriff's Department might be convinced to turn a blind eye, it's this deputy, and if there's one higher power Dancer still believes in, it's the power of persuasion. They've known one another a long time, after all.

They park at the foot of the solar tower. The tower is built like an oil derrick, with several stories of crosshatched iron supporting the viewing platform and the central receiver. On any given day, the heat that is generated and then converted or stored might drive turbines that, fully operational, could power the grid for all of south-central Florida. For now it is a tangled waste of metal and potential energy.

Fay did a science project on solar power. Cyrus stands at the open car door, shading his eyes to stare up through the I-beams. She bought one of those big, Styrofoam balls and spray-painted it yellow. We hung it from her bedroom ceiling, after.

Dancer shuts the car door. That was a fine project. One of the best that year.

The deputy hitches up his belt. He has no hips to speak of, so his gun and his radio hang low. He walks to the cage door at the bottom of the tower and jiggles the lock.

Got a key for this?

Dancer digs the keychain from his pants pocket. Rust flakes away when he keys the lock. The teeth resist and then pull open.

Watch your step, he says.

The stairs zigzag up the interior of the tower. The deputy begins the slow-footed ascent through the core of the thing, his footsteps heavy and hollow. The pastor removes his hat and when it's clear Cyrus won't change his mind he heads up the stairs behind him.

When the Caprons lost their daughter, it was like the heart had been ripped out of every person within a hundred miles — of everyone who knew her. Dancer thinks it does the girl a great disservice to remember her as more than what she was. She was the daughter of Cyrus and Kat Capron and she did win third place in the dance team competition in Fort Lauderdale and she did dance each Sunday with the Hallelujah Happy Feet and he remembers her always dancing with the youngest children at weddings and parties, making them feel part of the grownup world that she was only peripherally a part of herself. And although everyone who met Fay Capron loved her instantly and blindly (this is true) she had her faults. She bit her nails and flirted too much with older boys; rumors circulated of her rolling in the bushes at the high school during football games. But then it is a wonderful service of the human memory that filters out the bad and painful parts, if it remembers them at all, and polishes the reputations of the deceased.

Fay Capron was a teenage girl. She was more devoted than most daughters, more obedient, more helpful around the house. She had a quiet smile and was just growing into her long bones. She was active with the youth group; she was a good student. She made perfect origami cootie catchers. Fay Capron was thirteen years old.

The pastor remembers it as if he were there. Anyone who paid attention to the news during those few weeks remembers it this way, because the exact moment of abduction was caught on camera and played on the nightly news for weeks following. Because of this, he can't resist the urge to transpose himself upon the girl whenever he thinks of it — no one can. He's seen the footage so many times, he's watched it frame by frame, and sometimes the girl on the video is Fay Capron and sometimes it is another girl he imagines in her place and sometimes it is him, judging and then anticipating his own actions before performing them on the granular black and white television screen.

The Caprons were in Sarasota for the day, visiting the Ringling Museum. They spent the morning taking in the rose garden and the collectible big-top charm, the Howard Brothers circus model; the Rubens; the Van Dyck; the Poussin. Outside the museum's entrance Fay was left alone, her parents not having come out of the bathrooms yet, or the coat check, or they were making one quick phone call before hitting the road.

The security camera finds her standing below the cast-iron statue of Poseidon, god of the sea. Fay touches the tip of his spear, his trident. She circles the base of the statue; the camera follows her. It is footage destined to be taped over later, divested of meaning: a bored teenager waits for her parents. Her particular actions, touching the tip of the trident and then withdrawing from it as if she found the point too sharp, the way she circled the base of the monument trailing one hand along the stone as if she were only killing time are given weight only by what happened next.

A man approaches you. A man you don't know. The man is old like your father and he has a belly like your father although the rest of him is thin. A beer belly, you've heard it called. Something about the man makes you uncomfortable but you're thinking he's just like the other somewhat creepy men who say things to you sometimes, things you can't decipher and that you chalk up to the adult world, things adults whisper to young ladies in crowded elevators or dark movie theaters or in the light of day, just like this, while you wait for your parents to come out of the museum—does this man really think you are alone?

There's something strange about his face—pockmarked. He doesn't say anything, doesn't smile when he reaches out his hand

and you reach out yours and then he takes your wrist with a quick turn of his. His grip is tight, like the handcuffs your dad carries that he sometimes lets you mess around with, except your dad always has the key to get you out, when you've tired of playing. Your dad, who with your mom should be coming out of those museum doors any minute. You feel your stomach heave because you don't know this man and this is some new experience; the grip he has on you is starting to hurt. You can't shake it. He drags you out of the camera's frame. You lean back, trying to free your wrist — you don't want to go with him but it's useless. He's got you.

Strangers will watch the tape and wonder why you reached for his hand. They will wonder why you didn't shout for help or run away. Already you're asking yourself the same questions. Because you didn't reach for his hand — he grabbed you. He must have grabbed you. Who would have done something stupid like that? Reach for a stranger's hand. You've heard the warnings a million times. Your whole entire life. Don't talk to strangers. Don't ride in cars with strange men. Why now, after thirteen — almost fourteen years — would you forget? Why would you all of a sudden have gone and done something stupid like that? Someone offers their hand, someone not entirely trustworthy upon first glance, and you take it without thinking? But you did. You know this, deep down. He reached out his hand and you took it. Because you know boys, or you think you've dealt with all different kinds, but as you hurry your feet to keep up with this ugly man, to keep from falling down and being dragged, you know unequivocally that you have never dealt with this sort — all around him is danger. It's happening so quickly you can't consider what you should have done, only what you must do now. The thought to scream never crosses your mind.

These same questions will be asked by talking heads on the nightly news for months. You and this man will be branded together upon the public consciousness. This strange, deformed man whose name you will never learn will be linked to you for eternity. Your meeting played repeatedly for months following and then randomly for twenty-five years after that, on retrospectives or Learning Channel specials on child safety, broadcast in middle-school classrooms to pre-teens who couldn't care less. Your life as an example, finally, of what not to do. This man enters your life for fifteen minutes and yet has the most profound impact on it: your name forever uttered by mothers as a warning, like the Bogeyman or gypsies, as in, Remember little Fay Capron who strayed too far from home one day and never saw her mom and dad again.

This stranger wrenches your arm and the pain is real. You try not to worry about whether or not you wanted him to reach for you, a little bit. Out of rebellion or curiosity wondering what it might be like with an adult. But there's no use wrestling with this question: Did she, or didn't she? Don't beat yourself up over it. The question of Did she, or didn't she? She reached for him, or didn't she? She knew him, she recognized him, she wanted to go with him…or didn't she?

You don't even notice you've been kidnapped until he's dragging you through the parking lot. It's one of those perfect Florida days. March, early afternoon, and somehow there's not a single person outside, no one crossing the turnabout and no cars waiting at the bottom of the stairs. It must be a lull, you think, between the morning and the afternoon and you and this strange man cut through it like a surfboard, passing bronze statues of naked men and in the parking lot all the steaming cars with silver shades behind their windshields, minivans with blankets and remnants of fast-food breakfasts and many out-of-state plates but not as many as you would think. The air is thick with lemon. You know at last what this man plans to do precisely because there's no one here to see him do it.

But someone has seen him—a woman. She saw him grab you. That's how you know you didn't reach for him: The woman saw him grab you and yelled for help. Her screaming bloody murder trails you into the back seat of the car.

Dumb bitch, the man says, wrestling the seatbelt around your waist although you are not struggling. Stupid cunt.

He says the word your mother hates and that you are strictly forbidden to say. And yet the word seems at home in the back seat, where the smell of cigarettes has settled deep into the cloth. Fabric hangs in great swaths from the roof, pinned in place with silver tacks. The ceiling sags like dead skin. There is hardly room for your feet with all the clutter on the floor: crushed packs of cigarettes, crushed soda cans, crumpled pages of roadmaps and newspapers and cassette tapes. The garbage around your new tennis shoes offers its own cacophony, a restless shifting even when you haven't moved. In the front seat, the man pushes all of his weight against the gearshift and throws the car into reverse.

There is no mistaking it—you are being kidnapped. This really happens to people. You are surprised to discover it's not just something you've irrationally feared your entire life. It's not just something that's woken you up in the middle of the night, when you've dreamt of being kidnapped by men who speak a language you don't recognize. The men are always dark-skinned in your dreams, but now that it's really happened, now that you are really being kidnapped, the abduction is being carried out by a white American male, age forty to forty-five, of average height and balding. He's driving a white car with a brownish interior the color of red clay. The thing about your nightmares is you are never abducted outside an art museum in Sarasota of all places. And yet this is exactly the way it has gone down.

The light through the windshield is calcified the color of amber. The car shakes as it clears each speed bump—you are still in the museum parking lot, racing toward the exit. You steady yourself with both hands. The car seems to straighten out as it peels into the road; you are thrown back against the seat as the vehicle gains speed. You wonder when you'll start to cry.

Your field of vision is absorbed by the seats and the rearview mirror above them. In the mirror you can see the way his eye regards the road. The eye shudders as the car shudders; it flashes with the glare and it sharpens at the sound of sirens behind you. You don't even think the sirens are for you until the eye seems to panic. The gray pupil swims with venom.

This is the eye that liked what it saw. The sirens are very loud now but you don't dare raise your head to look—you think it's best to stay perfectly still and to be a good girl. Bruised and knobby knees, khaki shorts and the outline of a training bra beneath your *Panama Joe* T-shirt—the eye picked you out of the crowd. In the ancient art exhibit. In front of *Male Figure with Leopard Skin and Kilt.* Or back at the hotel, and trailed you here. The eye drives very fast and you drive this way for a very long time. You drive for so long you think you might run out of road. You think the eye knows all of your secrets.

There are secrets you haven't even told your best friend Lacey Petersen. Secrets that no one saw you do. Lies you told, or half-lies. Things you do when you're alone. The way you stare at yourself naked in your parents' full-length mirror when you're supposed to be taking a shower. The way you cross your legs—your newest trick.

The garbage beneath your feet rustles whenever there is a great shifting, each time the car turns. The light through the windshield flutters like 8mm film and you wonder what the eye has planned. The eye has come to punish you for your transgressions…which are like sins, you remember. You think of the church your parents go to and the women there and how disappointed they will be in the way that you've turned out. The eye looks from you to your legs in the mirror, to your crotch. And now you start to cry, not because you are afraid of this man or what he might do, but because you can't even think of something to pray or what you might offer Jesus as a bargaining chip—you plead with Him to get you out of this, this one time, and you'll never kiss another boy again.

You hear the sirens. You remember your dad is a policeman. You think he's probably with them now, in the front car, speeding to your rescue. This is what your father does for a living—he stops crimes from happening. He catches bad guys. This is what he's told you since you were old enough to understand that people have jobs. When other girls feared burglars or rapists you didn't, because you were safe in your home at night with your dad the cop. Even if his rules are a little strict. Even if he badgers you too much. Any moment, you think. Any moment your father, the deputy of the Desoto County Sheriff's Department, will open this car door and carry you home.

Officially, the 1987 Oldsmobile runs a red light. It is broadsided in the intersection by a municipal truck. The truck outweighs the Oldsmobile by a ton or more. The truck alters the car's forward motion and pushes it perpendicular from its intended course. The abrupt change in direction snaps the necks of both the passenger and the unwitting driver; the truck pushes the Oldsmobile sideways through the intersection nearly three hundred feet before finally being stopped by a low retaining wall and the inevitable drag of the earth against the car's rumpled fuselage as it comes apart across a hundred yards of road.

AT THE TOP of the solar tower, both men pause to catch their breath. From the platform looking down, the tower is like the needle of a record player threading the eyehole of a smooth, black disk.

Cyrus reaches for his sunglasses. Light converted to electricity. Am I right?

Dancer nods. The sun puts out heat. The solar panels reflect that heat. This receiver here, above our heads, captures the sunlight and converts it to energy.

The hottest spot in Desoto County, Cyrus laughs.

This is not your run-of-the-mill solar farm, the pastor says. Not some retired hippie somewhere erecting a semi-conductor in his backyard. This solar farm, our farm, would have revolutionized energy production. If we were operational, this solar farm would generate as much power as the Hoover Dam.

Cyrus whistles through his teeth but for Dancer the words mean nothing: what could have been and old regret. He feels briefly the old excitement coming back but doesn't let it overtake him — he doesn't like to think about how close they were to making real money with this thing.

He says, Most solar cells are built with a kind of alloy. Silicon is cheap but not very efficient. The best mirrors are made with a blend, like the best coffees or some might argue, the best wines. Instead of light and dark roasts, or a robust Bordeaux, you have aluminum and arsenic, gallium and nitrogen. These are more efficient, although they still waste energy. Before now, this was the best anyone could do.

The deputy is half listening. He leans over the rail, working something in his jowl. He lets loose a rope of white spit that soon pulls apart in the wind.

Our cells are different, says the pastor, ignoring the deputy and remembering instead the sales pitch he made to countless investors, all of whom turned him down. These solar panels are made from a single system of alloys incorporating indium. Indium, blended with nitrogen and gallium, can convert the entire spectrum of sunlight to usable energy. It's a major breakthrough. Expensive to build, but the conversion rate…. It would have been a boon for our church. It would have put Arcadia on the map. Because we know exactly how much sunlight will cost next year, and the year after that.

Cyrus draws a hand across his mouth; some spittle clings to his cheek. No one else is interested?

Not one single inquiry. No one else can handle the technology. Even if they could, Nadine has it all tied up in the courts.

I'm sorry to hear.

Dancer dismisses the sentiment with a wave of his hand. The thing that weighs the most on him is this: despite the particulars and despite the varying details, he and Nadine are no different from millions of other Americans who are divorced.

Walking the perimeter of the platform affords an unobstructed view in any direction. To the southwest they overlook the development going up behind the church, where brick mansions poke their heads out of the ground like termites. Both men take it in without comment, until Cyrus laughs, and then Dancer laughs too.

The pastor says, She couldn't have stuck it to me any better if she'd branded her initials into the sun.

Windfall Estates.

It's perfect for Nadine, he says. She can torture the earth; she can raise entire villages and then spend hours arguing over what color marble she wants installed in the kitchen.

She was never much cut out to be a pastor's wife.

He slaps Cyrus on the back once and they leave it there. Each day the Lord makes it clearer to him that his marriage was doomed and nothing but bullheadedness kept him involved with it for so long. Everyone saw it but him.

The Lord has great things in store for me, Dancer says. I believe the Lord wants me for His own.

I'm sure he has your full attention now, given our finances.

Dancer leans against the rail. The sun is up now and shining brightly over the deputy's shoulder. The pastor left his own sunglasses in the car.

He says, I hear you have a young woman living with you.

About three weeks, Capron nods. The sheriff and I, we picked her up out on 70, in a rainstorm. A real dam-buster.

Has she indicated to you at all where she might be from?

She says Tallahassee, but Katharine Anne thinks this may not be true.

She thinks the girl might be lying.

Katharine Anne, she sometimes has an intuition about things is all.

Spirit of the Lord, Dancer says, but he is thinking himself about men of the Bible who told half-truths for God's purpose. There are plain-old lies and then there are divine lies; he is thinking on instances of holy subterfuge.

Cyrus says, It's given Katharine Anne a little break. And I won't lie to you — it has been nice having a third around the house again. I've long believed ours is a family meant to stand on three legs.

Tri-pedal, Dancer says and then he lets the thought sail over the railing and into the sky. He is thinking of Joshua and his spies in Jericho, of the prostitute and the red sash hung from the upper-story window.

He says, You know Mae Carson, and her boys.

Katharine Anne helped her through her second pregnancy, with her husband gone.

They have it tough now, Dancer says. Him being gone. It's all she can do to maintain that house and get herself to work and try to give those boys something of an upbringing.

Cyrus removes his hat and works his fist inside, loosening the band. He sets the cap on his head again and pulls it snug.

I know what you're driving at, he says. We're not keeping her.

I'm not saying you are.

We've grown used to her though. We've grown attached in just a few short weeks.

It is a challenge, Dancer thinks, like coaxing a cherished toy from a small child, a safety blanket the child has outgrown. He shakes his head. What of later Christians who hid in catacombs, the apostles after the crucifixion? They kept the memory of Christ alive in much the same way, by anointing a stand-in for the friend they lost. Wasn't he himself, as pastor, part of that lineage? Peering over the rail at the array of solar mirrors below, he expects them to rustle like branches of dried leaves.

I could bring her by, Cyrus says. If the girl is interested. We'd have to talk to her, of course.

This young woman—

Edie.

If Edie is looking for somewhere more permanent, the Carson home might be a fit.

If she's interested.

Of course.

I know what you're thinking, Cyrus says. And it isn't true. There's no one can replace Fay. It's a burden I'll take with me to my grave.

Both men descend the staircase. Dancer secures the bottom door and leads the deputy across the infield, to what he refers to as the tin drum. But the generating station is hollow inside, empty. Cyrus only ducks his head in before moving on. They walk the perimeter. Cyrus reaches up and drops several of the ladders clinging to the outside edge. Each ladder rattles and clangs against the hollow structure, showering them with sand and dirt as the ladders slide.

I'm going to have to recommend we put a barbed-wire fence around this property, Cyrus says. And these ladders need to be secured.

Deputy—

I know as well as anyone the church has money problems. But we're going to have far worse trouble if some dumb, drunk high-school kid wanders in here and breaks his neck falling off the roof.

Give me time, at least.

Thirty days, but I'd recommend doing it tomorrow. That, or hire a night watchman.

Dancer raises both hands in surrender. He walks away, kicking at the dirt. He hears Cyrus rustling the pages on his clipboard. Now he'll have to talk to Nadine. Maybe she can use security as well, someone to look after both properties; they can split the cost. Make things more entangled than they already are.

Cyrus calls to him. Don't feel bad. I'd lay this on you whether you were my pastor or you were my worstest enemy. Besides, if you get this farm up and running, you'll be needing security just to escort the truckloads of money coming into this place. Am I right?

But Dancer does not hear him. He remembers another example of divine misrepresentation. There is the story of Esau and his brother, Jacob. How their mother Rebekah dressed Jacob, the youngest, in the skins of goats so that he could trick his father into granting him the paternal blessing—the whole of Isaac's fortune. And later, when Esau returned from the hunt, having done all of what his father asked, there were no blessings left for him save one: *By your sword you shall live, and you shall serve your brother; but when you break loose, you shall break his yoke from your neck.*

SATURDAY MORNING finds Mae Carson scattering compost across her flowerbeds, beneath the boxwoods and the stagger-bush and around the base of the mangrove tree. She carries armfuls from the compost mound: years of grass trimmings and top soil and fallen branches. She hears Troy struggling to start the push-mower in the backyard, the sound of the starter-cord being pulled and pulled again with no response. He's flooded the engine, but she lets him struggle. It does her boys no service to be helping them every time they meet a challenge. The sooner they learn to tend to themselves, the better.

She hears the sound of a car on the road and then sees the patrol car turning down her drive. Its tires kick out gravel and rocks and when it draws closer she can see Cyrus Capron behind the wheel and in the passenger's seat the girl they spoke about, some kind of drifter who's been staying with them. If it's not the sheriff dropping by with a garbage bag full of hand-me-downs — most of which were torn or moldy and that she threw away — it's his deputy trying to pawn off a charity case he's grown tired of. Already she has too many mouths to feed.

The deputy parks beneath the shade of the camphor laurel and the two of them sit in the car with the engine running for quite some time. Mae dumps the rest of what she carries near the rainspout. She calls out for her boys and then her boys appear from around the back of the house, sweating and filthy from the tool shed.

You been crawling around on the floor in there? she asks the eldest. She paws at him and wipes grease marks from his face.

I hate grass, he tells her.

You find me a good deal on Astroturf and we'll lay that down instead.

Why do we gotta cut it? It only grows back.

Mind yourselves, Mae tells them both. We've got visitors.

A car door opens and Cyrus walks around to hold the door open for the girl. Mae waits for them on the front steps already thinking the girl must be something like royalty, men holding doors open for her all the time. Cyrus pulls something out of the back seat and it's a large, green backpack like the kind to take camping. He carries it up the path, lagging behind the girl protectively. Already Mae wonders how much help this girl can be around the house. It doesn't look like she has the strength to lift her hand to write. Her bones are thin and her complexion is pale; she seems to float across the yard, leaving no footprints in the grass.

Good morning Deputy Capron, Troy says.

Mae wipes her hands on the front of her pants and welcomes the girl, Edie. She says, Have they not been feeding you over at Cyrus' place? You liable to blow away any time the wind picks up.

They feed me plenty, Edie says.

You got a quick metabolism then. It's a blessing. Don't take it for granted.

These are the boys, Cyrus says. Troy and Evan.

The wind picks up and showers pollen across the yard. The air is filled with pink and white blooms. Edie steps toward the boys and kneels before them, tucking her feet beneath her skirt in the manner befitting someone holy. She takes each of the boys' hands in turn and holds them for a moment, either studying them or feeling for their pulse. She kneels there smiling, showing no teeth.

You smell nice, Troy says.

She lifts her wrist to her nose, and then offers her wrist to the boy. She says, I smell almonds. And what else?

Vanilla, he says.

Of course, Edie says, smelling for herself once more. Vanilla cream.

Edie is thinking of staying with us for a little while, Mae says.

We have chickens, Troy says.

Edie clasps her hands in the cotton folds of her lap. I'd love to meet them.

Green Gospel 81

Don't be bothering her with those birds, Mae says.

I don't mind, the girl says, half-turning as if she only just remembered she was there.

The boys race off around the side of the house, Evan trailing his older brother by several yards. Mae takes the backpack from the deputy and the backpack is as light as her own hopes are empty. She invites them both inside.

Cyrus declines. But I'll be around a while, give you two time to get acquainted.

The wind lets up and across the walk the pollen lays down in thickly curling patterns. The approach looks different in light of this strange girl—the flowerbeds unplanned, the weeds rampant, the compost below the boxwoods sloppily laid.

I heard they picked you up on 70, she says.

The girl's face shows a certain repose. There's a clarity to her eyes that is striking. She says, I find hitchhiking to be a lost art.

I heard they picked you up in a rainstorm like something half-drowned.

I said it was a lost art. Not one I've mastered.

Entering her own house on the heels of this stranger causes Mae to see her home in a new way. But it is not the newness of something just-bought. It is the reluctance that accompanies each purchase, the guilt or the not wanting to use the thing for fear that over time it will blend in with the old or the not-so-new things she already owns. Inside, she notices the faint odor of cats, when she doesn't usually; she notices how unpleasant the smell of other people's cooking can be, even if the food turns out to be delicious. The carpeting in the entryway is stained with the mud and the mess of two half-grown boys; dark paneling runs the length of the hall, making the house seem smaller than it truly is—a cramped, shadowy space beneath piles of board games and broken lamps and forgotten toys, plain old junk, file boxes she took from church that are packed now with old lottery tickets, Florida Lotto or Play 4 or Mega Money—a year's salary in slips of paper now packed into boxes and stacked with other uselessness, to the ceiling in some corners. They pass by the archway of the living room where the blankets and pillows the boys set up as a fort the night before still consume the sleeper sofa and the La-Z-Boy: They named it Fort Carson. She leads the girl directly into the kitchen which she has, at least, recently swept. She offers a seat at her table.

She says, Feel free to smoke.

I'm not much of a smoker, Edie says. But you go ahead.

The girl's head is set upon a swivel. She seems to observe every detail as if she would write it down later. Mae feels shame at the chips along the countertop, the cracked linoleum on the floor, places along the ceiling where the sunburst paint leaked over from the wall. When the girl leans her elbows on the table, the table nearly flips. Mae rushes to stuff the folded piece of cardboard beneath the errant leg again, the cardboard having been kicked out. But she won't apologize. She won't—not for this. She does the best she can, and the girl will accept them or she will not. It makes no difference to her either way.

I can't stand it, the woman says. She produces sugar and cream and places it on the plastic tablecloth. All these people running around with their holier-than-thou attitudes, telling us we can't smoke here and we can't smoke there. Mark my words, this kitchen will be the last place on earth a consumer of Turkish and domestic blend tobacco can feel at home.

It doesn't bother me. The girl leans through a burst of smoke. It really doesn't.

Mae places coffee in front of the guest. People forget how to enjoy the finer things, because they're afraid of what can kill you. That's what we hear all the time from these so-called experts. Everything gives you cancer: microwaves, cell phones, bread.

Edie stirs cream and sugar into her mug, the sugar poured like sand from a shoe after a long walk on the beach. You have a lovely home.

Oh, she says, taken aback by the compliment.

The girl holds up the ashtray and shows her the picture of the Golden Gate Bridge. Have you been?

I'm not sure where that came from.

Do you actually raise chickens?

Mae dumps the coffee grounds into the trash. A neighbor gifted them to us. Next thing we knew, we had a family.

Rooster in the hen house.

Mae forces a laugh. I think they came that way, I'm not sure.

Edie leans her elbows on the table again and the table holds. She pushes the coffee mug back and forth between her fingers.

The girl says, We had all kinds of animals growing up. We had a llama.

What on earth did you do with a llama?

Mostly he just stood there, it's true.

People own all kinds of crazy pets sometimes.

Mae thinks there is something about the girl that seems to dismiss the need for pleasantries, for small talk. The conversation is straining, something stale in the air, stale generalities. Or like two dogs sniffing at one another, circling. Through the front window she can see Cyrus leaning against his car. She hears Edie sniffle and catches her wiping her nose with the back of her hand.

She pulls a long roll of paper towels and gives a handful to the girl. Are you sick?

Something in the air down here. The girl blows her nose. I didn't know I had allergies until I came to Florida.

Where are you from originally?

I didn't know I had allergies until I came farther south. I was born and raised here, in Tallahassee.

Mae seats herself next to the girl, very close. She holds out her hand and takes the used paper towels and balls them in her fist.

She says, You seem like a nice girl. I don't know your story, and I can't say I want to know. But if I find you've been taking advantage of that poor man out there, if you've been taking advantage of the Caprons' kindness, I will split you like a hog.

The girl doesn't flinch. I plan to repay the kindness shown me.

It happens quick: There is a window open above the sink and the screen she has not replaced since it blew out in the storm several months ago. She hears the flutter of wings against the sill and looks up in time to see the blur and fury of wings push through the space below the open window, rattling the glass in the window frame and upsetting a clay vase into which she often deposits shiny things, pennies or shells or stray earrings she finds after the services at church. The collectibles scatter one direction and in the other goes the bird — there is a bird now inside the house.

She thinks at first it is a pigeon or a dove — the creature hurls itself against the ceiling as if surprised to find itself suddenly enclosed, to find boundaries and solids where before there was only open air. But it is no pigeon, and no peaceful dove. The bird is black with a white undercarriage and a streak of red feathers in its crown — it beats its wings against the ceiling light before darting toward the floor. Mae drops her cigarette and looks for something to throw over this beast, a blanket or placemat. The bird tears toward the ceiling again, wings extended, and its wingtips scatter pages and the magnets that once held them to the freezer door. The room is filled with the sound of beating wings and the sound of pages snapping and the magnets and pennies and misplaced things clattering across the tile. When the bird rests atop the cupboard its face peers out from beneath an ashen hood.

An owl, Mae says.

It's no owl, says the girl.

Mae stops; the kitchen falls suddenly still as if the sound of the girl's voice alone has stilled the pages and the pennies rolling across the floor and the ghost bird now motionless atop the cabinetry, motionless but for its heaving breast. It peers at them with eyes like polished stones, stretching finally the length of its talons and scraping against the blonde faux-wood. Mae does not breathe. She is afraid to move, afraid to set the creature back into its terrified spin.

But the girl moves. Edie rises from her chair and the bird watches her lift the chair and carry it soundlessly to a place below the cabinets. The bird not moving but shuddering beneath its folded wings. Edie sets the chair and steps onto it and then onto the countertop. She reaches for the bird; her fingers stretch across infinite space. The ghost bird shuffles backward and presses itself against the wall; it spreads its wings and Mae is stunned by the great expanse, a yard wide at least, and the strength the wings contain, filling her kitchen wall with primal, pigmented patterns. Edie reaches for the bird and the bird takes flight, rushing into her waiting arms as if the girl had called it to her. The bird collapsed — no, went running — into her embrace.

Mae steadies the girl as she descends from the countertop to the chair. Edie presses the bird against her shoulder and holds it there, stroking the red-feathered streak that bursts like a handkerchief from a magician's sleeve. It's the way the sunlight falls through the curtain trim or the smell of the wild on this creature, the smell of dark places and night blood, that causes Mae to back away slightly when girl and beast finally touch ground.

It's the softest thing I've ever felt, says the girl.

Watch your earrings, says the woman.

Mae reaches for her cigarette, now burned to the filter. She sees the paper scattered across the floor like some great wind has passed through. She watches the girl slip down the hallway and she hears her own boys outside, closing the chicken coop. Even as she moves toward the front door she is thinking the girl can stay. That maybe before she never believed in signs, or she believed in them but failed to see them. Even as she opens the front door and waves the deputy away she sees clearly the girl must stay on—that signs exist only if she has the sense to recognize them.

FIVE

The window beside her bed is open. The darkness outside is like a stranger she shares a seat with on a crowded bus, between them a respectful but narrow distance. Numbers on the alarm clock expand or sharpen, alternately close and then far away. She is restless due to the time change. She is restless because of the heat.

She hears one of the boys calling for her from the far end of the house — Troy, she thinks, because the little one doesn't talk. The older boy calls to her by name. She lies in bed listening until he calls for her a second time and she is sure that he has called for her, Edie. Blundering down the hallway, she hears a second sound like a bird has gotten loose inside of the house — perhaps the ghost bird has returned and with it the piercing sound of something trapped inside a room, beating its wings against the windows and walls. She moves faster. Troy calls out for her again and the dark hallway is unfamiliar to her hands sifting through the shadows and rattling framed pictures and following the smooth emptiness of the living room arch. She hurries to the bedroom door. A revolving nightlight casts a blue haze across the ceiling and the walls and the haze is speckled by rotating, golden stars. Her hand reaches for a light switch but finds nothing. In the dim turning light she sees Troy sitting up in bed, his legs drawn to his chest. He points across the room to where his brother, Evan, is coiled along the floor, his eyes full as two black moons. The younger boy presses himself against the floor and makes the bird noise again: one shrieking note.

Two chains hang from the ceiling fan. She reaches for them and pulls both chains and when the light comes on Evan screams like he's been burned. He pitches himself beneath the desk and grips the legs of the chair with both hands; he wheels the chair back and forth and out from him again. He unleashes a sound like evil whipping through the trees and even as she moves for him she knows he does not see her—this sound meant for a terror only visible to him.

He's not awake, Troy says.

Evan laughs. It is not joy but arrogance behind the sound. The laughter is much too old. She reaches for him but he spins, ramming himself against the desk. He rips into a torrent of obscenities and when she's heard enough she reaches below the desk and finds the collar of his nightshirt, taking it with her fist. She plants her feet; she hauls him out from below the desk with him kicking at her and calling her a liar.

So he can speak after all. She shouts at him to wake. She grips his jaw and might pinch his tongue between her fingers, to make it stop.

His body goes limp. The laughter ends. She cradles him and in her arms he is heavier now. She drags him to the bed and lays him over it. The moment has passed and she is afraid to make any noise for fear of waking him again into that fearful, half-waking state.

It is quiet only for a moment. Laughter bubbles up again from the boy and his eyes come open and now the laughter sounds very pleased, the satisfied laughter of a victor. His body shudders; he is kicking at her with his feet and throwing off the bedclothes—tangling them both within the cotton folds. She untangles herself from the sheets and then boosts herself upon the boy to straddle him and take him by the shoulders. She says his name. She says his name again louder. A steady mantra of his birthright, each time louder. When he quits the struggle she feels his body slack and sink into the mattress.

His skin is clammy. She touches his forehead and then takes each of his small hands within her own and warms them. She climbs out of the bed and pulls the covers up over the shivering boy. She tucks the sheets around his body while the older brother watches her.

We should pray, Troy says.

Is that what your mom does?

Edie takes the older boy's hand and he reaches across the bed to touch his brother's foot below the covers. Evan's T-shirt is damp when she moves her hand across it. She searches for a suitable prayer — it's been a long time. They stand listening to the chains of the ceiling fan clacking, to the toilet running, to the rustle of a real bird somewhere tucked inside the eaves. A car passes on the road; a moth beats its wings against the spotlight near the door; there are dogs barking on the property neighboring theirs, or farther away. Then all is quiet, as if the air has gone suddenly out of the room. Evan lies on his stomach with his eyes closed and one hand thrown over his head, propped awkwardly against the headboard. She places his arm at his side. When his breath evens out she knows he has found sleep.

Back into bed you, she tells the older boy.

She pulls the ceiling fan chain and the room goes dark again and the gold stars resume their orbit from the ceiling to the walls to the floor. She stands in the doorway listening, and leaves the door cracked when she slips finally into the hall.

She is awake for good, despite not having slept. Her heart races. She goes onto the back porch and curls up along the wicker love seat. The cushion is damp. She hears chicks stirring in their nesting chips. Something flutters across the pond; a loon calls out and she hears no response. She hears then the sounds of countless non-responses. The night is full of them. Deafening cries of loneliness fall unanswered—the shifting of garbage can wheels in the gravel walk. In their wake, the noiseless echo it seems that she has heard throughout her life, a life of call and no response, where something shouted into a well does not come ringing back again but lies deathly still at the bottom.

She gathers her legs and wraps her arms around them. She runs her hands along her bare knees letting the back of her hand drift across her legs so the hair brushes against her knuckles. She remembers the long ordeal riding in the back of the grapefruit truck across the southern United States. She has not slept more than a few hours since. The air conditioner kicks on and startles her, drowning out all other sounds.

She rises and moves across the porch and through the screen door out into the yard. She wears running shorts and a Billabong T-shirt the Caprons let her keep, nothing she would have bought herself. She's never even surfed, but it seems to suit the new persona she's taken on, the role of live-in nanny. Earning room and board with a small stipend on top if there's anything left over at the end of the month—a new life of certain contradictions she's only just beginning to understand. For example, she's been in Florida for weeks now and hasn't seen a single palm tree.

There are other trees she can name. Ever since she was a child she's known laurel oak from black walnut, black tupelo from white cedar. Her father an amateur conservationist who taught her these things. He led day programs for school children on weekends, teaching them about the value of land.

From the front yard she can see no other houses, only woods and the pond and beyond these the road. Down the drive and across the road she sees a water tower bubbling up from behind the cover of shortleaf and slash pine. She considers the sleeping children; they'll sleep a while longer. She walks toward the water tower, her bare feet pinched by the gravel drive and then soothed by the pavement of the road. Across the road, on the forest floor, pine needles carpet the path and lead her to the base of the municipal structure. A slight breeze and then cooler air beneath the pines raises gooseflesh on her arms.

At the water tower, she grips the ladder and peers up through the crossbeams. The gangway will not be locked—they never are. There was a time she never thought of things as having limits. Locks meant for unlocking. Fences meant to be scaled. There was a time she ignored arbitrary designations of ownership. There was a time she could not resist the urge to climb whenever the mood struck. She loved the world better from up high, people made more sense; patterns became clear with a little distance. People warned her not to climb because she might fall, but she laughed at them and enjoyed the feeling of superiority that came having reached the summit, looking down at their worrying. Who will catch you? they always asked. She never needed someone to catch her, until she finally did.

She begins the ascent, feeling rust flake off beneath her hands and feet. She reaches the trapdoor and pushes against it and when it opens she pulls herself through. On the walkway, the tread feels thick as marbles on the soles of her feet. There is the smell of water that has stood too long. She sits below the railing and lets her feet dangle over the pine trees and the road and beyond that a trail of lights she does not recognize. She can see where Mae's home lies dark. She wonders at how far away California seems. She considers her enemies, who she once considered her friends—no doubt sleeping now on the far edge of the western continent. It is because of them she is here and it is because of them she cannot sleep and it seems like very little in return for what she's given, which is everything.

She sat like this for days once, on a platform four feet wide in God's Valley along the Oregon coast, to protest a lumber company's plans to clear-cut hundreds of acres of old growth timber. Twenty or so protestors erected platforms high in redwoods and spruces and hemlocks whose limbs were eighteen or twenty inches in diameter — ancient trees. The trees were ancient and the trees were old growth timber and the trees protected species of wildlife: the spotted owl, or her favorite, the marbled murrelet, which was something like the offspring of a penguin and a duck. Edie and her cohorts scaled these trees in climbing harnesses and dragged with them enough food and water to last a week. Crackers and nuts and fruit; Wonder bread and peanut brittle. Looking back, she thinks she must not have thought she'd be there very long at all. She must have considered it more like a picnic than something that might drag on without end.

When night fell they heard the trucks, and the flatbeds carried wide spotlights that flooded the canopy like daylight. Concert-sized speakers on the backs of these flatbeds shook the trees. First, gut-punching death metal, drums like machinegun fire, and then music that was like country music but not quite, a yodeling vocal line straining above accordions and kettle drums in a relentless two-step. She and the other tree-sitters called out to one another (they couldn't see each other but they knew each other's voices) and they made up lyrics to these queer songs and loudly made a game of it until morning came and exhaustion settled over them with the dew.

Deprivation of sleep she had expected. The music, she could handle. With morning came a change in the audio program: droning lectures on astronomy, fossils and the mating habits of dung beetles. All mostly fascinating to the ones for whom the lectures were intended to bore — this was the stuff they sometimes listened to on their own, high or stoned. They would not be coming down from their roosts any time soon, not for these lectures; it was more like a slow night in the dorm. When the protest reached the twenty-four hour mark the death metal came again. Now, the volume was adjusted sporadically; tracks were cut short or repeated several times. She amused herself by guessing at the limit of the government's CD collection, recognizing tracks by PanzerChrist and the Lunatic Gods, Faith No More and Napalm Death. Limited, at best. She tried to memorize each track so she could make a mix tape of these songs later. The afternoon grew short and the lights came on again and the music kept on and still no one slept but no one came down from the trees either.

She could stand on the platform and stretch her legs. But what she had imagined as a week spent basking in the ancient forest became steamy afternoons and insect bites inflamed on her wrists and on her neck. The smell of herself as the hours turned to days; the tranquility of the forest became body odor and black plumes of exhaust from the trucks below, the rumbling of their idle engines below every other sound. After forty hours she wrapped herself in a blanket to shield herself from the sun. The blanket itched and she felt her body overheating and she discarded the blanket before she drank too much water and still she shivered with pain each time the wind blew across her skin. For all her preparation, she had forgotten something as basic as sun block.

Just over three days and many of the tree-sitters began to come down. She peered over the ledge to watch policemen extract protestors from the lowest branches. Her friends were so weak they offered no resistance. The police dragged them into the back of a paddy wagon and she remembers being surprised at this— she thought paddy wagons had gone the way of gas lamps or cobblestone streets.

A boy perched not too far away managed to land a bottle of sun block on her platform and so she had that, at least. The bottle read, *Banana Boat: Helps Protect Skin From Premature Aging.* After she applied the cream to her skin, she tried to throw the bottle back to him, but he too had climbed down. She began to lose track of who had gone and who remained. Almost no one spoke now, all of them conserving strength. The adrenaline of the first few days had worn off and each minute stretched infinitely. She read the back of the sun block. The lotion was made by a pharmaceutical company in Delray Beach. *UVA & UVB Lotion, SBF 15* came recommended by the Skin Cancer Foundation.

She lay down and tried to stretch out. She read the back of the sun block and then she made mental lists: species of trees, species of animals, then genus, the books of the Bible, then in order, then backwards, then every holiday she could name in every country — the perfect mix tape. She planned Christmas gifts for everyone she knew for forty years hence. She rubbed lotion into her arms and legs and relished the *moisturizing formula with Aloe Vera and Vitamin E.*

Going on five days — one hundred and twenty hours — the press arrived. Reporters and cameramen and photographers gathered at the base of her redwood tree and called to her. Someone had a bullhorn. Looking back, she thinks she should have spoken to the press. She understands better the power of the media and the greater power of those who control it. But then she had seen the newsmen as being on the same side as the people she was trying to fight. When the media arrived she had already achieved a state of sleeping with her eyes open and it was all she could do to peer over the ledge and see the news channel vans and the antennas and the satellite disks and then roll back over again. Her skin crawled as if she had a fever coming on, or maybe her fever had come and then broken. She tasted blood on her lips and when she touched them with her tongue her lips felt like sandpaper. Her water ran low. She allowed herself a mouthful only every hour, then every two. The music pounded and she slept now despite it, a sleep fitful not with nightmares but with a pinwheel of faces from her past that spun in her dreams beneath the bright hiss and pop of sparklers, set to the music of that forest, "When I'm in Love I Yodel" and "Macabre Operetta." Her skin was hard as baked mud. Soon, she stopped sweating. She felt every swallow of water down every part of her. More and more of her friends came down from the trees and they were dragged into the backs of white vans and sped from the property.

After one week, the forest was silent. The trucks drove away, carrying their speakers with them. She tried to call out, but found no voice. She heard no one else in the trees and she knew then that she was alone.

Delirium. She lay still and then opened her eyes to find that hours had passed and that she had slept without meaning to. The canopy of leaves above her head breathed with many lungs; she listened to birdsong like code and tried to crack it. She counted its rhythmic patterns with small movements of her fingers against the wooden slats. She felt a fissure in her body, her soul just one long, oily strand rising from her navel to wrap itself in the branches above. Her soul as thick vine; her soul siphoned carbon dioxide from the tree and turned the tree black. Her vine glowed in the shadows of that forest like a phosphorescent worm.

The sound of chainsaws woke her on the morning of the tenth day. She rolled over and peered at the ground below and saw actual lumberjacks, like on the side of a syrup bottle, running their chainsaws through the branches of her tree. They cast the severed limbs aside and each discarded limb brought her closer to total isolation, a barren march up the wide, tall trunk of her redwood tree. When she closed her eyes she heard the sound of weeping, like a hymn sung before a battle already lost. She heard the soul of her tree rise fuming into the night above the harsh crack and splinter of broken timber, the rustling whoosh of tree limbs falling, and the tree limbs landed with a sound softer than that: the muffled cry of man's progress unimpeded. There were no branches left save for the ones that held her. Below, ladders were unhinged and leaned against the trunk. They were coming for her. They would be here soon. She was on her stomach looking down and then her fingers unfastened the harness and she thought to change platforms, to keep moving, and reached for the next platform, reaching out before her hands flew from her side and suddenly the heat of the sun and the heat of tears evaporated in the expanse of daylight as she fell through it.

She dropped like a wrench from a construction lift. Reports said she fell sixty feet to the forest floor. Her spleen ruptured; several ribs shattered; both ankles snapped. Her collarbone cracked like bathroom tile. Her liver, shrunken from dehydration, was left bruised and bleeding; one cracked rib stopped a centimeter short of puncturing her lung. The doctors said she would be lucky if she were ever able to run again.

A month in the hospital, a month in a rehabilitation center — she missed half of her junior year. She was, in fact, the last to come down.

SHE WAKES to the smell of something faintly sulfurous. It is morning. Cars pass on the road below. She is embarrassed to have fallen asleep — the woman, Mae, is probably already home. What will she think when she finds Edie gone, the two boys sleeping unwatched and unprotected? She hurries to the ladder and descends, scampering quickly down, or as quickly as her aching body will allow, moving but also nursing the treacherous flare-up of her old injuries.

Across the road and up the gravel drive, Mae's home leans across the pond, nestled in among the cover of hawthorns and palmettos. One with its surroundings, part of the natural habitat almost, like pennywort on the surface of the pond or the raspberry vines creeping up the side of the house. Edie's feet are wet; bits of rock and blades of grass are plastered between her toes. Mae's Buick is parked in the open garage and Edie again feels a flash of panic: She should not have been gone so long. She lets herself in through the porch screen door. The darkness is retained within the walls and in the living room she finds Mae collapsed in her La-Z-Boy, her legs protruding like quills from beneath a thin afghan. The woman is asleep. On the television is an infomercial for a kitchen appliance that is both blender and saucepan. Edie thinks to turn the television off but worries the change in volume might rouse the woman; she wants the day for her own. She pads into her bedroom and shuts the door. She slips from her nightclothes into a long, white skirt and sandals. In the bathroom, she washes her face and pulls back her hair. The mirror above the sink is crowded with magnets and stickers, passages of Scripture flourished with rabbits and birds. She holds the hair band in her teeth, as psalms and proverbs buzz about her reflection. Though her color has not fully returned, she looks better than she did when she arrived, more filled out and not so skeletal. She pinches a thin fold of skin along her waist, a new development. She needs to get out for a while, reading, *A cheerful heart is a good medicine, but a downcast spirit dries up the bones.* In her bedroom again she drags her backpack from the closet. She has not opened the backpack since that night on the side of the road, with the frogs and the burned-out pine forest around her, and the smell of the open pack speeds her swiftly to that place again while she removes her sewing kit and the knit ski-cap and the plastic wrappers and when she is sure the backpack is empty she stows these items in the backpack again and closes it.

In the kitchen, she writes a quick note and clips the note to the freezer door. The magnet is a ladybug and the note says she has gone out but will be home for dinner.

When she leaves the house there is daylight breaking and steam rising off the pond. Mae has said that she can use the Buick whenever she wants, but she saw a bicycle in the garage and she goes to it now. The bike is a cruiser, peach with a white stripe and high handlebars and white tire wells. Its tires are flat; she rummages through the mostly-junk; she finds a bicycle pump and fills the tires. Twisting the backpack over her shoulders, she pedals the bicycle down the drive and out into the road, changing gears until her legs push in languid strides. There is little traffic. She rides fearlessly around blind turns, gaining speed with little effort along the flat roads, the topography like a tabletop and different in every way from the endless hills and winding paths of the Pacific coast. She imagines her lungs opening wide. She pedals faster, feeling the inactivity of the last few weeks burn off her skin the way beads of water evaporate on Mae's cast-iron skillet.

Arcadia Welcomes You. There is an Albertsons grocery on the corner and she parks her bicycle outside, not having a lock but deciding to leave it anyway, knowing it will be there when she returns. She enters the store, pausing at the register to let her eyes adjust to the fluorescents and the feeling of time standing still, the feeling inside the store that it could be any time of day and any time of year — any grocery store in America. Rows of bath products and greeting cards, sweet-smelling candles and discounted Halloween costumes, costumes with fabric the consistency of foil; she makes her way to the back of the store and loads several cans of wet cat food into her basket, as much as she can afford. She finds bottled water. She paces the produce aisle, basket in hand, before choosing one green apple and one cinnamon-raisin granola bar. There is music being piped in and it flutters down the aisles, a duet between a man and a woman about what else but love. She feels something well up in her throat and she is caught off-guard by this response, nearly moved to tears by what, commercial music. It makes her sad to shop for groceries alone. It is not the being alone that makes her sad but the shopping for groceries in an unfamiliar place, where the aisles are arranged by some regional logic, indecipherable to outsiders, and the colors of the products are strange. A new place where she has ended up far from anyone she knows. It should not make her melancholy, this quick trip through the aisles, but it does—because the goods are more or less the same and yet the labels that are familiar—brands of soup, bags of pretzels and chips—are not enough to balance the dairy brands that are so different in each part of the country, the milk here not her familiar Dean's but something called Pet—not at all appealing, Pet milk. Despite the advertising money spent, the white-washing of regional character with something more Americana, it is their familiarity which causes a sense of loss—the familiarity of the brands driving home the unfamiliarity and heart-breaking loneliness of shopping at a strange grocery store alone. It would be better if she had someone with her. She needs to hear the sound of her own voice.

It is a relief to find the Indian girl behind the register; she greets the cashier like an old friend, her greeting bright and overly-cheery. She asks is there an internet café somewhere in town and the girl lets a small laugh-breath escape, shaking her head. The cashier clamps down her bills in the drawer and says there's nothing like that—the only place she knows with internet is the library.

In the parking lot again, she shrugs the backpack over her shoulders and pedals down Brevard Avenue; past the DeSoto Banking Corporation, the recorder office, the empty slate livestock market; Advance Auto Parts, Suburban propane, the offices of John Weltin, Land Surveyor. These give way to restaurants set back from the road: Nav-A-Gator Bar & Grill, Slim's Deep South BBQ, Clock Restaurant, Howie's Pizzeria, Brenda Lee's Downtown

Deli, the Tea Room, Boo Radley's, and the Bar-Knuckle. The sheer number of restaurants, per capita, must be one of the largest in the world. The sky is enormous, the land flat, the buildings low. The sun, though barely risen, rides on her handlebars. On every other corner stand green signs with white letters and arrows on the signs pointing to the most important destinations, the Arcadian landmarks: Whidden Park, the courthouse, the library. All catering to Florida's number-one industry: tourism. The road is now busy with traffic, but it would be a blessing, she thinks, to have this traffic in San Francisco. The sidewalks are nearly empty, only a few seniors getting a jumpstart on the day in order to be ready for bed after the early-bird special. No one pays her any attention. For the first time in months she feels truly anonymous, as if the openness of the roadway and of the town hides her rather than reveals. Whereas in the city she was hyper-conscious of both herself and her surroundings, vigilant of danger but also scrutinized by the urban-elite, here in Arcadia, taking a right on Hickory, following the reflective white arrows on the green-painted signs, she feels unadulterated, inconspicuous bliss.

The entrance to the library winds through a dim hallway lined with bulletin boards that announce upcoming events, the Shriners' dinner or the Golden Oldie Dance on Saturday — taste Chester's World Famous tapioca pudding. The first floor bustles, the line at the checkout counter seven deep. Mothers clog the aisles with strollers and older women cluster around the new releases. But the bustling is silent, a hundred hushed movements. The squeak of stroller wheels, the tapping of computer keys — Edie heads upstairs to the second floor where the balcony overlooks the lobby. One side of the mezzanine is stacked with media shelves, major national magazines and a week's worth of newspapers. She takes several of these to a table near a glass wall shaded by two dogwoods outside. Setting out her apple and her breakfast bar, she searches for her name nestled somewhere in the pages.

She checks the tables of contents. She reads national news summarized in three-sentence blurbs. She scans headlines and finds no mention. She turns to the newspapers, casting aside unlikely sections to pour through national and regional news, paying close attention to articles tucked near the back where wire stories are often inserted as filler or shrouded by advertisements. Again, she finds nothing. She allows herself to entertain the thought that she has shaken them or that she has truly managed to disappear. She gnaws her apple. An older man crosses the library and sits at a table close by. Back home, the library tables are crowded with homeless who come inside to enjoy the air conditioning. But here it is only her and the elderly gentleman who finds the crossword in the local paper and puts the tip of his pen to his tongue, something she hasn't seen anyone do except in movies. She thinks it's all so perfect, so quiet. The people of Arcadia have given up keeping track of the tragedies and battles the rest of the country may wage hourly; they've left the rest of the nation to it so that they themselves might enjoy the silent challenge of fitting words in vertical or horizontal squares, spurred by evasive clues.

She returns the magazines and the newspapers to their shelves. She drops her breakfast in the trash. She carries her backpack by its straps, the groceries heavy. She wanders the second floor until she finds four cubicles, each arranged with a computer older than any computer she remembers having used. She sits behind the terminal facing the stairs. Free internet access is hard for her to believe, but here it is. She's been shielded from the world for more than a month now, almost two. She connects to the internet and navigates a search engine, but three letters into her name she stops, remembering the trouble that has led up to this moment and how it may have all begun with something as innocuous as this, a few keystrokes broadcast over miles of fiber-optic cable. It hits her suddenly, her total isolation. She can't make calls. She can't check email. She cannot even type her name. Because it is traceable, all of it, to the IP of the library's computer, or to a phoneline in Arcadia, and any movement might suggest her location. For the moment, her location is all she has.

She tells herself it's only vanity. That is why she wanted to search her name. As long as no one knows her whereabouts, she is free.

But her freedom is relative; liberty only in opposition to its counter, jail. She slumps in the wooden chair suddenly surrounded by inaccessible items. She cannot even get a library card, and this thought makes her sadder than it maybe should. People must reinvent themselves all the time. But even something as simple as finding a job — impossible without a past. She has no history now, having left it all behind the moment she boarded an east-bound truck with a dozen migrant workers, the moment she was left on the side of the road to drown. She inhabits now a strange limbo, with no past, and nothing certain but for each present moment as it comes.

Outside again, she finds her bicycle parked where she left it, as she suspected it would be. Across the street is the post office and she considers, briefly, before going inside. She lingers in the lobby, near the PO boxes. On the wall are posted hundreds of missing person profiles. In the center of these, a glass frame displays the FBI's ten most-wanted. She is relieved not to see her own face here, and laughs trying to imagine her photograph beside the olive-skinned faces the Bureau is most desperate to apprehend. She sees how ridiculous and unfounded her fears must be. They have bigger fish to fry. Terrorists. Murderers. Rapists. And what is Edie Aberdeen of Ann Arbor, Michigan, in the face of criminals such as these?

As for missing persons — each missing person is not missing

to themselves. Every missing person knows just where they are, every second of the day.

She heads north on Hillsborough and turns into the parking lot of a seafood restaurant, the Blue Terrapin. Several restaurants share parking lots in a blacktop landing strip. Behind the Chinese Fortune she finds what she is looking for. She parks her bike and peers behind the dumpsters; she kicks at the cardboard boxes and the boxes with wooden slats. Kneeling, she removes the cat food from her plastic bag. The lids pop when the lids peel away and the smell of moist liver parts and crude protein are as unmistakable as any smell.

She sets the tins in a circle around her. Before long, the first cat appears, slinking out from underneath the dumpster and putting its nose against the food. She does not reach for the stray. Several cats emerge and eat together shoulder-to-shoulder, like prisoners, silently and bearing a sense of duty. The cats look healthy enough, underfed perhaps. She doesn't notice any lesions or wounds. And she doesn't reach for them, although she'd like to run her hand through their fur and whisper to them, so that they and maybe she might feel less alone. When the tins are empty, she gathers them inside her plastic bag and sets the bag inside the dumpster. She opens her backpack and empties its contents, all the totems and talismans of her past: the sewing kit, the plastic wrappers—but she catches the ski-cap before it falls. She cannot bring herself to throw it away, not yet, although if there is any piece of evidence that might incriminate her, it is this. She restores the ski-cap to her bag while the cats circle once, lingering briefly before scattering back to the places from where they came.

She has the thought to head back home, but instead follows Roan Street on its way out of town, past older homes and trailers that seem less cared for. She still feels a certain energy that needs to be expended, the dormancy of her last several weeks. She crosses an overpass above an inlet, and at the top of an incline the immense limestone signage welcomes her to Christ by the Sea.

She recognizes the name. She read a bulletin in the Caprons' home about a Labor Day picnic. She knows also that Mae is often here. Some connection through the church was how the Caprons found her this job. She pauses her bike at the bottom of the lawn and absorbs the gleaming, white monstrosity, resting plump and content atop the embankment. Already, she thinks, the architecture is outdated, its obvious homage to modernism and the complete disregard for its environment. Flaunting, even, its disregard. And if there is justice it lies in the fact that in twenty or thirty years the church will not feel modern at all but pleasantly outdated, like the keyboard guitar or clear cola.

She turns left, down a street running parallel with the church. She passes land that has been leveled and now supports what looks to be a solar farm, like the kind she saw everywhere out west. Its appearance feels anachronistic, to come upon these solar panels suddenly. The blue solar panels stand silent and she turns her head not to be blinded, seeing sunspots on the road. Beyond this, she sees the new development rising to the south, several roof-peaks now peering over the line of trees. She pedals hard, finds the entrance to the subdivision. She feels the nausea that began when she saw the church now blossom into full-blown rage.

The housing development is bordered by low boxwoods and azalea. The entrance is framed by two-tiered, brick walls. The entrance and the egress lanes are separated by a grass isle and on this island are an empty guardhouse and a brick sign that reads *Windfall Estates*. It is also on this island that she sees her first palm tree since arriving in Florida; she follows an avenue of struthious, Royal palms all the way in.

There are finished homes built facing a side street to her left but she pushes on, taking her second left past more finished homes and around a sweeping bend that filters into the side of the development abutting the church. Riding along these paved but unnamed streets she has the sensation that one wrong turn will lead her back again to the main road. It is impossible to be lost in this series of circles and arcs.

Toward the back of the subdivision, in its deepest recess, she finds a baseball diamond and a sandpit the size of two large swimming pools; imported beach that will one day host volleyball nets and community grills. Along the back road, the houses are still unfinished. Concrete pallets promise houses even larger than those she has seen. Concrete footprints and deep gouges in the earth and the ends of tubing in the earth and not one tree on any property, the lawns not yet seeded, nothing but acres of red mud and formidable piles of sand, sparse wind casting clumps of soil across driveways leading to houses not yet built.

The road caves in on itself and then abates. Seeing it a second time, it seems to her that a great wind has come and leveled each house leaving only cornerstones. There are footprints for houses not separated by twenty feet at their closest corners. Houses that face opposite streets but share backyards, identical sheds on opposite corners of their property lines. She counts only a few variants in design, maybe four, which the builders then expand with exterior trim and paint. Cathedrals, or keeps: The smallest models still with three garage doors and situated close enough that, stepping out onto his back deck, the owner of one house might peer directly into his neighbor's.

She heads toward the entrance again, but makes a left on the main road running along the western edge. To her right, the outskirts of the development are cleared but still wild. Tall, dry grass conceals wooden stakes that fly pink and blue ribbons. Marking zoning, or marking future foundations; marking perhaps, the footprint of the putting green. She makes a hard left and submerges again into the heart of the development, thinking the design resembles the state of Wyoming with three streets curving through its center. There is the occasional parked truck but she seems to be the only person moving through the streets—streets that will one day bear names like Sandpiper or Foggy Horn. The driveways will soon be scattered with crushed seashells brought in from the coast. Each tenant is already choosing particulars for their interior design: the tile, the countertop, the faucets, the bathroom trim, the light switches—to dim or not to dim—down to four possible styles of mailbox. Their lifestyle choices restricted by the development's constitution, by its governing board. What car to drive. What paint colors they are allowed to choose. Behind all this opulence she wonders about certain animals that must have been displaced, about runoff and clean water, about the environmental calamity of it all.

Parking her bicycle in front of a finished home—no occupants yet, but the skeleton there—she tries to see herself residing in mansions such as these. Mansions that might have been spit out of a Monopoly game board. Such a place, she thinks, will never recover from its checkered origin. While ducks roast in the kitchen and housekeepers are imported and dismissed like luxury items, the earth beneath them shrugs and sighs and slowly eats into their foundations. Storms will one day batter their weather-proof awnings and shake their wrought-iron gates to clog gutters and drains and overflow the sewers. So that in twenty or thirty years or in a hundred copious centuries from now nature will come again to claim its own.

Maybe, she thinks. Or maybe not. This might be something she tells herself to calm her anger. To medicate her sense of injustice, her rage. There is no one to defend the earth, like a poor man accused of some grievous crime and bearing no counsel. She has been counsel to the earth for the better part of three years. Standing in the expansive driveway, identical to every driveway in front of every McMansion from here to the Pacific Coast, she feels herself standing in the belly of a mythical monster who she has fought hard against but lost — in the end swallowed up, eaten whole.

The sun is at its apex and the closeness of its descent anticipates winter. Clouds of dust rise off the hard landscape and she tastes it in her mouth, the destitution of it all, the torn up, unseeded earth. She heads down the far western road, speeding out of the subdivision and past the solar farm and Christ by the Sea. A police car pulls out of the parking lot ahead but she maintains her speed, acts natural, until she sees that it is John Whitney and the sheriff waves to her and then she waves. He squawks his siren and continues on in the opposite direction.

She thinks old habits die hard — she almost made a break for it. Thinking that even if it hadn't been the sheriff, even if it had been an officer she hadn't known, there would have been no reason to run. That even the Bible differentiates between thoughts and deeds, and she hasn't met a person yet who can read minds.

Michigan &
California
1985 – 2002

ONE

A young girl stands in the foreground of a green-cut field. Her hair falls past her shoulders. She is naked, this creature, and barely nubile; in her hands she twirls a silver spaceship. The toy is long in its carriage, with two wide wings affixed to its fuselage and fanning out from the tailfin. Her slightly parted lips are both reverent and pleasantly exhausted — the phallic implications of the photograph are obvious.

Edie recalls this image as her earliest memory. She remembers examining the girl's freckles and then examining her own; she remembers wishing her own hair was like the girl's — the most strawberry blonde. She wondered where the girl lived, what strange place she called home, where the sky was azure and the angle of the horizon lay sharp and steep.

She remembers this photograph and is surprised, years later, to discover it again, although she has not thought of the photograph in years, in a record store under pop/rock. The nameless sylph, with air as her element, gracing the cover of the 1969 album, *Blind Faith*. A girl no older than Shakespeare's Juliet, or Mary, the mother of Jesus, were in their own time — thirteen or fourteen years old.

THE PASTOR'S BOY was shooting a potato gun he had made from PVC piping, an aerosol can, and a barbeque igniter. The other children played in the yard while the adults congregated in the basement where they said no children were allowed. Edie found herself alone in the kitchen with a spread of cream cheese and diced ham and chives, cheddar cheese Combos, smoked beef rounds in a thick gravy, and bottles upon bottles of unopened soda pop. She hefted a two-liter bottle of RC cola to her lips and the carbonation left her breathless. It was not something she was normally allowed to do. Out in the yard again she lost track of the children. The fireflies were coming out with night coming on and nothing around for acres. From somewhere in the half-light came the whoosh and pop and then the long delay before the splatter of Idaho potatoes bursting against the trees.

PUNCH BUGGY.

Where?

Kiss me.

She did. He tasted sweet, like a chocolate milkshake. She was fourteen and out with a boy riding in his car on a Sunday mid-day. It was just after eleven o'clock.

If this is like church, I don't want to go, she said.

It's not like church. It's like a party where everyone is nice.

Do they talk about God?

Another bug. You're terrible at this game. Kiss me.

THE BACKYARD sloped severely toward a thin line of trees and beyond that, cornfields. Night fell. The other children were still outside with their game but when she went outside to find them they were gone. She sensed they were hiding in the shadows. They were hiding as part of their game but she didn't like the sound of it — Ghost in the Graveyard. Instead she carried the empty soda bottle and descended into the yard where hundreds of lights flashed in the grass and in the trees beyond her reach, sailing up toward the moon. She wanted the lights for her own. She moved toward them with one arm outstretched. She felt something in her palm and opening her palm found the insect body lying quiet and black. There were red markings on its wings. She dropped it into her bottle. The lightning bugs moved fast and she chased after them, the sweetness and snacks sloshing in her belly as she turned circles through the dimming yard.

AT THE PARTY where everyone was nice they sat in a circle on the floor and the youth leader talked about God. At the end of his talk they prayed for a long time — they prayed over Edie to receive the gift of tongues.

Don't be embarrassed, said the teacher. This gift is for everyone.

Her eyes were closed and she was listening for the Holy Spirit but inside herself she heard only open space, a rock kicking down a canyon wall.

This is private language, the teacher said, between you and God. It will sound strange to your ears because your soul speaks a language of its own.

She sought more deeply within herself but all she could do was wonder why this boy had brought her here. This must be something that was important to him. He was concerned for her salvation. He was older than she was and she wanted to impress him, or at least for his sake try. She told herself to make it up — just play pretend.

A MOVIE played in the basement. This surprised her because movies weren't allowed. But the adults sat in folding chairs facing the projection screen and no one noticed her slide down each step, clutching the now-radiant bottle of fireflies to her chest. An acidic bubble rose in her throat; the taste that seeped between her lips was the charcoal and the ash of sausage rounds. Her throat was raw from too much cola. She found an empty chair and climbed into it, her feet not long enough to reach the floor. The bottle was perched on her lap and the fireflies lit up the inside of the bottle with their pulsing lights and the man beside her glanced once at the bottle and smiled. She knew him; he was an usher at their church. He sometimes let the children play in the coatroom when the services ran long. She was glad to find a familiar face in the dark. The man looked at the fireflies and then he winked at her once before turning his attention back to the screen. That wink—she felt like an adult for the first time, like a grown-up.

She felt her tongue quiver. She heard words coming out, nonsense syllables. Words strung together and mixed up and muddled like any silly song she might sing as a lullaby—she wondered, should she stop, or was this it? She felt hands on her shoulders and in her hair and the Young Lifers whispered encouraging words as if she had undertaken something arduous or as if from this moment on she would never be the same. She hoped the boy was there—she knew he was. Soon the sounds she made were effortless. She wondered at how easily they fluttered from her lips, like a million snowflakes.

The cover of the eponymous *Blind Faith* lying face-up in the garbage can; her father's entire record collection set out on the street. Her earliest memory: her father deciding to get religious in the early hours of a Thursday morning, before driving her to preschool and continuing to his job at the University.

The faces in the chairs were cast alternately in shades of red and blue. On the projection screen, dark-skinned people, thin as sticks, carried themselves through streets that were mud and the houses were made of mud and the sky was made hard white from the heat. Their skin pulled across their bones and their smiles were caverns rimmed by pinkish gums and the thin leaves they sucked through the sides of their mouths ran green with saliva and pulp. The breasts of the women were like raspberries left too long on the vine. Flies ascended and then danced across the eyes of old men as they lay moaning in their filthy sheets. The flies crawled across the backs of children's hands when they pounded their fists against the bottoms of their supper bowls. A man's voice spoke but she understood very little of what he said. Inside a hut were ten or fifteen people crowded around a boy with many bleeding sores and on the sores were many flies that lifted and then hovered around his ankles and legs. A closer camera shot revealed worms inside the sores and white worms stark against the boy's black skin, caught up in the pockets of flesh. Like one hammerhit upon a steel drum, she felt her stomach contract; she felt a great shifting in her belly. She'd eaten much too quickly.

ANOTHER RECORD ALBUM stuffed inside the trash: On its cover, six young girls pick their way across a landscape that is barren like the stone of ancient ruins. The landscape sweeps slightly up; the girls are naked and the red color of the sky makes their bodies seem overly done, the pink color of boiled shrimp. They seem to crawl out of the sea, these girls, with their baby fat and their strawberry-blonde hair and the softness of their bodies tinted against the landscape of rock and ruin. They have crawled up out of the sea to find this place that is very old; they seem to be drawn to something atop this island in a chain of islands in the middle of the Persian sea.

ON THE PROJECTION SCREEN, a yellow field went on forever. A tiger leapt over fallen trees and dashed across a great expanse of dry grass. Zebras and okapis and water birds in the background as movie extras, watching the tiger but pretending not to, hiding their faces as the camera panned. The film slowed and the muscles on the tiger rippled beneath his fur, inhumanly powerful.

DISCOVERING THIS ALBUM TOO, years later in the same record store: Led Zeppelin, *Houses of the Holy*.

A SHOT RANG OUT. The tiger was lifted into the air and the tiger spun, projected, before landing several yards from where its feet had left the earth. Afterward, it lay still. She felt the back of her tongue swell with saliva and she felt her nose go suddenly dry. Sweat broke out behind her knees and she knew there was no holding it back. The wheel began to turn inside of her; on the projection screen a man with a bone stuck through his nose hung the dead tiger upside down with leather straps, eenie meenie meinie mo, and as the man withdrew his large flat knife she thought, If he hollers, let him go.

O, SPEAK AGAIN, bright angel! For thou art as glorious to this night, being o'er my head, as is a winged messenger of heaven unto the white-upturned wondering eyes of mortals that fall back to gaze on him when he bestrides the lazy-pacing clouds and sails upon the bosom of the air.

THE MAN with his knife split the animal from pelvis to throat and the entrails billowed out and blood ran and the black man pushed past the white fur now dyed red to open wide and pull back the skin. She felt her own insides turn out and she leaned into the aisle, just, before spewing forth a charge of pink foam that splattered across the legs of chairs and purses left on the floor and the bottoms of high-heels crossed beneath the chairs. A rush of sharp cheddar and salt and her own acidic flavors seared the inside of her nose. Below her feet swam half-chewed chunks of smoked sausage and the watermelon she'd made herself eat; the floor around her eddied and swirled and stranded her like an island as the movie shut off and the lights came on and all around her people stared.

Her father's voice: Who in the hell let her downstairs?

And then she was being carried. She didn't know by whom. She didn't care. She thought they were taking her to pray over her and to get rid of whatever sickness had caused her to sin in the basement while the movie played. Her eyes were closed and she might have recognized the smell of the person who carried her, but all she could smell was her own regurgitated odor that seemed to somehow be inside of her and outside on her shirtsleeve and on her wrist.

I THOUGHT I'd find you in here. Care for company?

She made room for him on the bale of hay. She'd gone inside the barn to get away from the party where everyone was nice and to eat her lunch in quiet. He found her though, and she found she didn't mind. His shorts were still wet—he'd just come out of the lake—and she was strangely excited by his white flesh, where his bathing suit sagged below his tan line. He had two chocolate brownies and he gave one to her; she'd missed them on her way through the buffet line. He was days away from leaving for his freshman year at college.

SHE WAS TOO OLD to cry, strapped down in the back seat of her father's car. She'd done something wrong—something sinful. She knew by the way he picked at the steering wheel leather and lit one cigarette after another. She rested her head against the window and the car was thick with smoke and the smell of her own sickness; her left knee was spotted with throw-up and dusted with the windblown ash of her father's cigarettes. They passed dark roads and dark gas stations and the roads were dark and empty on the long drive home.

IN THE BARN, they kissed a little and she let him slide his cold hand beneath the cups of her bathing suit top. Her desire for him coming as a surprise, as did her inevitable request to stop. She always made them stop. She didn't know why. She clung to her virginity not out of some moral or religious obligation but she clung to it. She had been arguing with herself for weeks. She was fourteen. She was old enough not to be a virgin.

They heard voices outside the barn, the other Young Lifers finishing their dinner and heading back into the lake for one last, frigid swim.

Have you been upstairs? he whispered.

He led her by the hand up the wooden steps. The steps were caked with dust. The floorboards sprouted loose nails and wood shavings. He said, Watch your feet. It was much warmer at the top of the stairs than it was in the barn below, all the heat and stuffiness trapped. Both of them knowing. Things that were worth seeing on a summer afternoon, in late August, with already a note of fall blowing across the lake, in the charcoal smell of the fire pit, in the smell of suntan lotion rubbed into the skin.

SHE WOKE LATER that night stripped of her clothes. She woke and found herself in her own bed. Someone had opened the bottle of fireflies and now the fireflies were dancing on the ceiling and on the walls—she'd forgotten about the soda bottle full of lightning bugs. They seemed to be speaking with their lights and she tried to hear what they said to one another, the magical secrets they spoke of, about the mysterious dark basements of the adult world.

THERE WAS ONE window at the far end of the room and its glass was murky with dust and grime. She began to feel dizzy. He asked what was wrong and she said nothing, that she wanted to. On the wall were hung dangerous-looking picks and swivels and farm tools. He led her to a pile of blankets on the floor beneath the window. They stretched out across the quilt. Her clothes were off in no time. She raised her hips slightly to help him slide the bottom of her bathing suit down her legs. He lay down again and his hands roamed across her stomach and her thighs and he grabbed her flesh while she lay mostly still, looking past his ear to the rafters where thick cobwebs were strewn between horseshoes and expired license plates nailed to the wall, the high shadows in the corners that concealed what she didn't know — bats or owls or wolf spiders.

She heard the rustling of his bathing suit and knew then that he was naked and he pressed himself against her leg and then he took her hand and guided it to him. He was mushier than she expected, although perhaps she had expected strength like iron or steel, something unnatural. She felt the bristle of his hair on the back of her hand; his eyes were closed and his fingers parted the shadows between her legs and the feeling of his fingers made her stomach uneasy somehow, and yet the feeling was not altogether bad.

They were lying beside a traveling trunk, the kind a woman of luxury might drag with her on an African safari, in a black and white movie. On the face of the trunk, lovers past had carved their initials: *CFxAT, BBxAA, PSxLV.* She understood then the fortuitous placement of the blankets and the tone of the boyfriend's voice when he asked her to go upstairs. She hadn't understood that they were part of a tradition, a summer ritual, but now she did. She closed her eyes and his fingers pressed farther and she should have felt cheap or sleazy or misled but she hadn't come up to the loft under any other pretense. She was waiting for his fingers to hurt but they hadn't yet.

He knelt before her and pressed himself against her and she reached down to guide him, glad that it was almost finished and wanting it to happen. Her belly felt cold and his face was twisted into a sort of half-grimace, full of concentration.

Again he leaned against her, but she felt nothing down there. She could feel his frustration in the way he adjusted her hips, forcefully with both hands. He pressed again; she heard a sound coming from the corner, behind her head. It was unmistakably the sound of baby birds. A choral chirping, timid but insistent. She heard a fluttering of wings in the high corner above them and thought they had separated the mother from her young.

The boyfriend ground against her and she began to feel badly for him. She wanted to help, but all she could do was hold him weakly and listen to the sound of the birds until she started to laugh. Once she had laughed there was no way to stop—the chirping of the baby birds had revealed a certain artifice like lights coming up over a party.

What's so funny? he wanted to know.

The birds, she said, feeling her body convulse. She tried to stifle the laughter. I just can't concentrate.

Then he was off of her and she knew she had said something wrong. The moment was vapor and then was gone and she knew they would not come back to it again. The boyfriend stood; his hands were on his hips and his penis dangled there like a torn windsock, deflated. The birds were chirping but she sat up and reached for him because she didn't want it to end like that.

Listen to them, she said. It's just funny, that's all.

The boyfriend walked a wide circle around the attic.

Lie down, she asked him. But the birds were chirping now louder and more insistent. She wished the mother would return with food and quiet them. She looked to the rafters, searching for the fluttering of wings. Because as much as she feared leaving the attic a ruined woman, the shame of having gone up there to do just that and failed would be far worse.

Please, she said.

The boyfriend knelt down again and she thought maybe he was going to try. But he leaned past her and fished for something behind the trunk and then he withdrew and he was cupping something in his hands, a baby bird just as she'd thought. Nothing more than pink skin quivering in his palm. She lay on her back, watching him and watching the bird in his hand no bigger than his thumb.

Maybe, the bird moved. She thought she saw it raise its head, strain its neck or stretch out one thin leg. But when the boyfriend, startled, flung the bird side-armed, the sound the bird made against the barn wall was a sickening, wet thud.

The boyfriend wiped his hands on the quilt. And then she was fumbling with her towel and she wrapped the towel around herself, clutching her bathing suit in her hand. She saw the boyfriend reach into the corner again and she yelled for him to stop, or maybe she yelled at him, but she was pushing open the attic door and hurrying down the stairs, not hearing him call after her and not hearing the shifting of the floorboards as he moved the traveling trunk out of the way to get a better angle on the birds.

The rest of the Young Lifers stood on the lakeshore and turned to see her emerge from the barn half-naked beneath her towel. In the center of the yard was a fire pit where the remains of a pig still turned over the coals, a headless but wholly recognizable hog with an iron bar running through its cavity. The teacher who had prayed over her not so long before stood to the side of the fire pit and then he turned to her and made a little gesture with the fork he held, shaved portions of the sticky meat jiggling on his grill fork.

She clutched the slightly damp, now obscene bathing suit parts in one hand and held her towel closed with the other. She vomited into the dry leaves and undergrowth near the side of the barn. She vomited until there was nothing left in her stomach. A few Young Lifers cheered. They would make up gross stories later about her willingness to swallow.

WHEN SHE WOKE the next morning, the sun was bright through the window shades. The black bodies of the fireflies lay dead on the bedroom floor. She found their carcasses for weeks after; they fell behind books or into shoes or littered the space between the headboard and the wall.

READING, in the public library, in summer, how Cleopatra bathed in asses' milk. How the henna she rubbed into her hair attracted suitors from across the ancient world.

EDIE'S OWN HAIR always wavering between strawberry and blonde, so on the night she left for college out west she massaged red dye into her scalp, needing to decide one way or the other, tired of hovering. The bathtub still faintly red when she returned at Christmas break; her hair no longer strawberry but inflamed and rubicund.

REDHEADS SCATTERED throughout the paintings of Dante Gabriel Rossetti, who seems to have known one or two in his lifetime.

CERTAIN COLORS off-limits now: yellow, for example. Her entire wardrobe reduced to blues, greens and patterned grays. Wintry and cool but for her matchstick hair.

SHE MET THE BALINESE in line at the grocery store, at the end of her freshman year. He appeared suddenly behind her and piled twenty tins of wet cat food on the belt. She was not the sort of person to speak to strangers in the checkout line but the cat food was too much for her not to say something.

Expecting a shortage?

They're cheaper in bulk, he said.

He was grungy, an outdoor type, all torn knees and frayed elbows. Not a type she'd been attracted to before. His head was shaped like a ball peen hammer and a five-inch beard sprouted from the point of his narrow chin. The straps of his ski-cap dangled and bounced about his head when he spoke. Although he did not look at her, she saw how blue his eyes were, blue as the sky above the sloping green field in that image from her youth, that portraiture of dim-sighted faith.

She asked, How many cats?

Two. He noticed her finally and seemed to like what he saw. He said, Two strays that I found. Or, that found me.

She handed cash to the girl behind the register. Two cats, with large appetites.

He laughed. She took her bag—brain food to see her through final exams, Funyons and refried bean dip—and waited for him at the end of the checkout. They went to the same university, although they did not know one another. He was working on his Ph.D. He said he'd been there longer than some professors, that if he wasn't careful he'd have tenure.

I think I've heard about you, she said.

Really?

No.

His clothes were obviously discount and purchased at bargain basements but there was something regal in the way he carried himself. His hair was knotted and unwashed and his sneakers were tattered but this could not hide the sapphire of his eyes—they could not hide an intelligence she found unbelievably sexy. The way he spoke, as if a million fragments of painted glass rattled inside his brain and he was trying to select the most pure, the most brilliant, each time he spoke. They emerged together into the parking lot of Safeway Foods and she found herself wondering what he'd scored on his SATs. Higher than she had, probably. It was the kind of thing she wondered about people.

He unloaded the groceries into the trunk of his Pontiac. The car was banged up along one side.

Seriously, she said. What are you going to do with all of that cat food?

THE STORY OF SALOMÉ, when she discarded the last of her seven veils and the sight of her flesh, pale as the moon, and the color of her hair (turned carmine in the torchlight off the palace walls) caused her father King Herod to hear the beating of the wings of the angel of death.

HE DROVE HER across town to an Indian restaurant. He parked around back, near the dumpsters. There were woods nearby and cardboard boxes stacked like stairs. He knelt with the cat food and placed the tins in a circle around him. The cats appeared, slinking out from behind the dumpsters and from underneath the overturned boxes. Soon the ground swarmed with stray cats — twelve and then fifteen kittens and older cats with gray hair, tabbies and muted calicos and black cats with copper markings. Their hair ragged, their coats grown scattershot.

I wish I could take them all home, he said.

There were more places in the city, just like this, where he fed strays. Once he'd found a litter and fed them, he didn't have the heart to stop. There were others who did the same — they recognized one another, sometimes in line at the grocery store. It was an obsession, really. He said sometimes he would be at a party and if he hadn't made his usual rounds, the cats were all he could think about: whether or not they'd found something else to eat or if they were hungry and waiting for him. Sometimes he fed them very late at night, after the party was over and he couldn't sleep for thinking of them. He said he couldn't believe he had told her all of this and thought it would drive her off for good.

But as freshman year came to a close, phone calls with her parents had grown terse. Spend one more summer at home, they said. But she did not want to go home. Already she loved the west coast: The weather, the people, the pace agreed with her.

Where will you live? they asked.

I was hoping you could help with that.

No can do, they told her. We have your brothers to think about.

By the time she met the Balinese, she already had her plane ticket home.

SHE SPENT one night at his apartment and then she was living with him. Her parents screamed, but she told them not to worry, she'd change the plane ticket. Christmas break, maybe. Or Thanksgiving. She'd come for a visit soon.

She found a job with an environmental agency. Six days a week, between three in the afternoon and seven o'clock at night, she rode the Vespa she'd been given as a graduation gift out to the tonier neighborhoods of the East Bay armed with a clipboard and a shade of red on her lips to complement her hair.

The houses she visited were cut from one mold. Mexican laborers mowed or watered pristine lawns and the workers themselves were part of the landscape, part of the natural terrain. In the muggy nights of July and August, neighbors chatted while children bounced on trampolines or rode skateboards down the steep driveways of San Francisco, riding on their bellies with their arms outstretched and their legs lifted up slightly behind them to gather tailwind. It was life just as the developers had planned. Some of the homes she went to were still occupied by their original owners, widowed senior citizens who stood blinking in the entryway, blinded by the light from the outside. They gave her crumpled dollar bills, mistaking her for the paperboy.

OBLIGATED TO MENTION, the face that launched a thousand ships: redhead.

AS SUMMER WANED she talked each night about registering for a dorm room and she weighed the pros and cons of roommates and location. He ignored her, mostly, until one night he put his lighter to her registration form and that was the end of the discussion.

Don't you feel sometimes like we're playing house? she asked.

They made joint purchases. They consulted on grocery lists. Their dirty clothes mixed in the laundry basket and in the heavy-duty washing machines at the laundry mat, where they could sit drinking beer and listen to a live band while they did the wash, the thrumming vibrations of these machines like a fourth or fifth instrument, like experimental noise.

> Lizzie Borden took an axe
> And gave her mother forty whacks.
> When she had saw what she had done
> She gave her father forty-one.

A SECOND TYPE occupied the hillside mansions of Walnut Creek and Pleasanton: working professionals with young children who lived as shining examples of the burgeoning upper-middle class. Their shirtless brats would be spraying each other with the garden hose and their Labrador would be barking and she would walk up the driveway navigating Tonka trucks and Hoola hoops strewn across the pavement. She would ring the bell and the mother would answer. The mother who was no longer young despite her chopped blonde hair and running shorts. The mother who would come to the door cradling the telephone receiver against her ear. When Edie introduced herself, the mother smiled and answered questions as they were posed, as they were scripted, between bursts of conversation with the phone. Edie enjoyed the charade and made it last as long as possible, until the mother raised one finger and disappeared and then returned with her husband in tow, the husband emerging from the darkness of the house having been downstairs smelting weapons or having been in his garage changing the muffler on his Yukon. They too would offer her money to go away. Sometimes she took the money. Her clipboard was not filling up very fast with signatures and the summer was nearly over.

THEY LAY on his old couch with the windows open and two fans blowing over them and she'd never felt a fan blow hot air before but so it was. He wore boxer shorts and she wore a T-shirt of his and they were looking at the course catalog trying to decide what she should take in the fall. She needed to choose a major.

I like what I'm doing, she said. But I wish it were more.

Field Study in Environmental Science.

You have to imagine yourself as a saleswoman, he said.

Environmental Science, Policy and Management L&S C3OU: Americans and the Global Forest.

I just don't see how collecting the signatures of the almost-rich is really going to stop corporations from bottom trawling in deep-sea coral forests. You see? I can't even talk like a normal person anymore.

It doesn't matter what you take. Take Russian. Enroll in glass-blowing. Majors are about as useful as those signatures you've been collecting.

Crime, Detection and Punishment in Literature and Film, also listed as Scandinavian 150.

If I only take three classes, will I still be considered a full-time student?

GROUND-UP BONES of redheaded men as common ingredients for potions and spells. Red hair as the sign of the devil. As the sign of a witch.

JUST BEFORE LABOR DAY, a door slammed in her face for the last time.

We don't support terrorists, the husband shouted, barging down the steps and out of the darkness.

The door slammed and she felt hot tears in her eyes as she hurried away, clutching the stupid clipboard to her chest. She mounted the Vespa and sped from that place, ending her last shift early. Along a wide curve in the road, she flung the clipboard into the ravine, losing all forty-three signatures she'd managed to collect in nearly three months of door-to-door begging.

RED HAIR having once been considered unlucky; redheads having been turned out of Cornish dairies because it was feared they would turn the butter sour.

HE BOUGHT HER a guitar for Christmas. She knew nothing about instruments, but the guitar was made by a company in Nashville that he said handcrafted each model. There was silver on the neck that looked like pearl and the strings were hard and clean and copper. She wanted to learn to play like Joni Mitchell, who only she and the Balinese and maybe her parents listened to anymore. The Balinese taught her chords. The strings buzzed beneath her fingertips and her fingertips throbbed each time she played but he said she would build up calluses and then her fingers wouldn't hurt at all.

JONI MITCHELL with hair the color of wagon rust in Big Sur, California, 1969.

SHE FLEW HOME for the holidays; she caught an early flight back before the New Year. Home was strange to her now. She felt empty on the familiar streets of her old neighborhood and she spent most of winter break in her parents' house, dodging phone calls from old friends. There were two of her, or so it seemed: One in California and one who still lived in Michigan and the two were like siblings who had irreconcilably split. After the New Year, landing at the San Francisco International Airport, she thought it would be a long time before she went home again.

ELIZABETH I, known commonly as the Virgin Queen: redhead.

THE WINTER PASSED, mild and rain-swept. She was elected president of the University's student-run environmental group. She was contacted informally by the leaders of other environmental agencies, for networking, they said. They were stronger if they merged resources from time to time, instead of a hundred small cells fighting and competing with one another for what was ultimately the same goal or the same deep pockets. Instead, they could get together and do one huge thing—and do it effectively. Make a real difference. She went to beach parties and cocktail parties at art galleries and she went to class and learned the science to support her burgeoning sense of social outrage. The waste she saw everywhere around her. Before there had been only her and the Balinese but in the winter and spring of her sophomore year she found others that spoke like-minded thoughts and these people became her friends. Soon the friendships and the work were mixed up beneath a certain momentum they all seemed to generate with little effort. The momentum became unstoppable almost on its own. Increasingly, talk centered around the logging of old growth timber, specifically along the Oregon coast.

ELIZABETH I mixed wood ash with water to bring out the red in her hair. Redheads now permitted to enter dairies due to red hair's soaring popularity among celebrities and socialites in 16th Century England.

SHE FELT SOMETIMES that her only function was to absorb new information. She was a machine: input only. Her worldview changed daily; she finally saw the truths beneath the half-truths she'd been spoon-fed her entire life. And still, the more she learned, the more she vacillated.

Some nights she lay in bed thinking about all that was wrong with the world, the starvation, the irresponsible raping of the land, and she wept. She wept at the devastation and pain and she wept at her own helplessness in the face of it all. She hadn't known she could feel such depth of emotion for anything.

Tuning: Standard (Capo IV)

E   A   E A
Deconstruction and re-use
E   A   E   A
Take something old, make something new

A

It's where you tear me down

E

But don't turn me loose

A

Break it all down, you'll start to see

E

Raw materials and possibilities

E

You can build a table, you can build a chair

B7

Or pile it all together, light a match and start a fire...

RIDING THE BUS IN LATE APRIL, she defaced an advertisement for a sports utility vehicle. She took the scissors from the sewing kit she always carried and swiftly shredded the poster. Nearby passengers moved away and then glanced back at her as if she were one of the criminally insane. But she wasn't insane. She tore the last strands of paper and glue from the wall. Thirteen miles a gallon and a hundred and thirty tons of carbon dioxide—that was insane.

She quit riding the bus and soon it was warm enough to ride the Vespa without gloves. She began trying to live all that she had come to believe. She used baking soda and vinegar as her all-purpose cleaner; she purchased reusable nylon grocery bags and made the long trek across the city to the farmer's market to avoid pesticide-laced produce; she conserved water in the shower and while brushing her teeth; she washed dishes with cold water; she carried not only her own but also her neighbor's recycled goods to the depot on Saturdays; she and the Balinese let their pee lie in the toilet and flushed only once at the end of every day; they ate dinner by candlelight while she turned all that she was learning over in her mind: SUVs dodged emission standards by qualifying as light trucks; unsafe levels of untested phthalate metabolites in hair products and cosmetics caused cancer or interfered with reproduction; the absurdity of clear-cut logging. Understanding finally that the world was a mobile made of paper swans and this mobile was dangled by an unseen hand above the crib of an infant — a diversion to loll the infant to sleep.

He was sitting shirtless on their bed, untying his shoes. She came into the room and sat behind him, to slide her legs around his narrow hips. She was going to Oregon. She had asked him many times to travel with her there, but he refused.

You don't know what you're getting into, he said. It's not a game.

All your talk, and now you're presented with the chance to make a difference and you just sit there, doing nothing.

He stood and crossed the room. No one even knows who this agency is. And you're delusional if you think your little camping trip, this tree-sit, will change anything.

He went to the closet and dropped his jeans to the floor. She watched the two hollow pools at the bottom of his spine. He ran his thumbs along the elastic waistband of his shorts and then he turned out the light.

In the darkness he said, The city is full of kids just like you.

Kids. She laughed, once. She lay down and waited while he fell between the covers. She said, Don't patronize me.

The city is full of kids just like you — except the other kids have nothing to lose.

She ran her fingers through the hair on his chest. She put his fingertips to her mouth and felt the calluses there. She moved her feet along his shins, slippery and smooth.

I can feel you here with my hands, she said. But you're gone.

You're far away.

I can't come with you, Edie.

Tell me something you've never told anyone before.

SALOMÉ DANCED the dance of the seven veils and delivered the head of John the Baptist; Elizabeth I saw her mother's head delivered by her father, Henry VIII. Helen of Troy left her husband, Menelaus, who once offered the cooked limbs of a child to Zeus, as a test—this *decree nisi* ignited the Trojan War; Lizzie Borden hacked her father and her stepmother to pieces with an axe in the farmhouse they shared; General George Armstrong Custer was finally scalped; Vincent van Gogh lost his ear. Redheads connected across millennia by severance and the vermeil lacquer of their hair.

HE TOLD HER he had been to jail once, for a short time. He stole a car and then was caught siphoning gas at a highway exit outside Santa Monica.

Does that scare you? he asked. During his story they had taken off the rest of their clothes to lie naked beneath the cool sheets.

No.

Now tell me something, he said.

I don't have anything like that.

There were voices passing outside the window, boys roaming the intoxicated night. Her hand brushed the hard ridges of his stomach; she bit him softly on the nipple. He wrapped his arms around her and held her close.

She said, Sometimes I wake up in the middle of the night to a strange noise, like an airplane passing overhead, and my first thought is that the Rapture has come. I lie in bed waiting to feel... lifted up. To be suddenly ascending, or taken up into the sky.

He still wore his ski-cap, the perpetual jester.

And not just airplanes, she said. Loud noises. Construction. Thunder. I lie in bed rigid, my hands at my side, waiting for it.

Every night?

There's something else we haven't talked about.

That's kind of fucked, Edie.

I come from money.

I thought maybe you did, from the way you talk sometimes.

All of this…rage. That I feel.

It's not your fault, how you were raised.

Sometimes I feel like where I come from makes my thoughts and passions disingenuous.

You never call them.

What would we talk about?

They lay motionless in the quiet. They could hear the television from next door, through the walls.

She said, But does it make me less real? That's what I want to know.

When you're up there in that forest, he said, you will be a hundred percent on your own. There's no one to come rescue you then, not even me.

GG.

Or Gg.

A question of genetics.

HE VISITED HER every day while she recovered. He lived at a motel nearby. After two months he brought her home and helped her bathe and fed her increasingly complicated foods. Their summer and then their autumn swallowed whole by him caring for her like an invalid. Her baths and then her meals served on a silver platter that was wholly different from the silver platter on which she had been raised.

TWO

At a Persian restaurant in the warehouse district they passed heaping plates of dolmeh and baba ghannouj and ate the tabbouli with their fingers until lime juice ran down their chins. The restaurant had no liquor license but its tables were adorned with hookah pipes; the menu offered seventeen varieties of sheesha.

Edie ignored the open kitchen and the smell of meat and the view their table afforded of the brick oven where long, indefinable carcasses turned on spits, slow-roasted, their flesh charred and red. One of the cooks would pass by and shave portions of the meat as the bodies turned but even this did not bother her: She ate with gusto. Ignoring the Balinese, who took many pictures with a disposable camera he'd found; ignoring even the inattentions of their waitress, a girl their own age who was churlish enough to make the Balinese complain—loud enough for other guests to hear.

But Edie found the waitress amusing and thought her dour edge was all for show. The waitress was an aberration in the otherwise subdued ambiance, barging in and out of the kitchen, her arms loaded with Chilean sea bass or duck breast bathed in plum sauce. Using the width of her backside to open and close the kitchen door, plating their dishes as if it were the one aspect of the job that she despised and not, in fact, her position's sole raison d'être. Where there should have been softness around her body there were only hard, fleshy folds; her eyes and her nose were an afterthought on a human form that was otherwise all arms and feet and locomotion.

It's very European, the Balinese whispered. To treat your customers like shit when they're the ones paying your bills.

Edie was glad to be out on a Thursday night. She enjoyed the feeling of cheating the workweek. If the night went long enough, she would roll into class the next morning still draped in her smoky, fermented clothes, not having slept. It was six months since her accident; it was the New Year. She was only just starting to reduce her medication, to not be left breathless by a walk across campus. In autumn her weight had dipped dangerously below ninety pounds but she had started to gain it back. She felt like she hadn't been out of the house in weeks.

The Balinese said, Did you see the flag when we came in?

No, she said quietly.

A computer printout of the American flag was pasted to the front window.

She wouldn't have been able to find the place on her own. There had been no sign out front and no number, only an eye painted above the door in brisk, loose strokes, a circle between two half-shells. Inside, they sat on cushions at a low table, separated from the dining room by a complicated system of sheer drapes. A cloud of sweet fruit, the fragrance of crabapples left too long on the ground, glided across the floor and curled idly toward the ceiling. A sitar played on the stereo, above the light cadence of silver. Their hookah pipe held caramel tobacco and the coals were smoking through the seams of the tall pipe. Its copper plating was warm to the touch when she turned the pipe and put her lips to the hose. She breathed in, quickly at first, then slowly to fan the coals until she came away with a mouthful of the smoky flavor. The Balinese flashed his camera. She lay back and puffed smoke rings at the curtains.

It was cause and effect. It was two sides to every coin. Her fall and her subsequent recovery had given her plenty of time to consider her nation and her place in it—she saw everywhere an utter lack of irony. But then perhaps great tragedy made irony impossible to digest. She, and her country, were entering a period of mordancy—of unobserved paradox.

It was smoking Arabic tobacco in a Persian restaurant in the wake of 9/11. It was the computer printout of the American flag pasted to the restaurant window, facing the street. It was being Caucasian, and being abused by a Caucasian waitress for no other reason than…what? That they were of a certain type: college liberals. Edie drew from the pipe and lay back against the cushions. She rarely smoked, and the sheesha caused a pleasant, tired feeling.

The waitress returned, balancing the check pad on her hip. Their dishes were empty but she made no move to clear them, not once looking at them but somewhere past the front door and the street beyond.

We have fair trade coffee, she announced. Not that there's anything fair about it.

The Balinese glanced up from his plate. Fair is fair. We pay more so the South American farmer can earn a living.

The waitress cocked her head and smiled for the first time. If we can make you believe that paying a higher price will put an end to child labor, bully for us.

Edie watched the Balinese sift through his pants pocket looking for matches—he was lashing together his thoughts like arrows. She'd witnessed this tic countless times, whenever they argued. At home, it was disagreements between two cooped-up lovers. Here it seemed to be political sparring between two sides of the same ideological front.

Children in these countries may work, the Balinese said, but their labor is voluntary.

There's nothing voluntary about child slavery.

A gross misrepresentation.

The waitress glanced over her shoulder to see if anyone was listening. No one was.

She said, There are corporations acting as middlemen grabbing ten cents on the dollar for negotiating this so-called fair trade between the farmers and a colossus like Starbucks. Not including a ridiculous method of taxation that nations spend as aid but in the end amounts to little more than colonialism under a Samaritan guise.

Consider the alternative. The Balinese rose to his knees. Edie adjusted her pillow and settled in for the lecture. Stroking each word, he said, Let me teach you about economics. An overabundance of supply lowers price. Lower price raises consumer greed. For supply to keep pace, yes, millions of acres of natural habitat are destroyed, the beans are over-harvested, but without fair trade the farmer sees nothing — he sees no profit at all.

One thought flashed through Edie's mind: She wanted the Balinese to be quiet. He owned his opinions and she loved him for them, but as with every opinion he sought the middle ground — the compromise. At least this, if not that. What the waitress argued made sense to Edie; the spurious nature of altruism, of activism.

Again, the Balinese said, I'm not saying fair trade is perfect. But at least the farmer earns a higher salary than the schmuck who still pulls a rickshaw or whatever.

Here's the reality, the waitress returned. Charging more for fair trade coffee soothes the conscience of the American consumer. It allows the American consumer to drink their mocha latte and drive their off-road vehicle knowing at least they paid a little extra to help out the Third World farmers. In truth, the only people profiting are the mega conglomerates that espouse this notion of fair trade. There's absolutely no evidence, and I mean none, that any of this so-called foreign aid is being funneled back to the community that produced it.

The Balinese laughed. Of course it is.

Look it up some time. The waitress shook her head. There's only one way for these Third World countries to improve. The tariffs need to be distributed democratically —

Ah, we return again to democracy as the answer to the world's problems.

Distributed wherever the local government decides. Over time, who knows? Maybe these puissant nations learn to compete in the global economy.

The owner of the restaurant passed by, a short, balding man with glasses. The waitress waved her pen above the check. Can I interest either of you in coffee or dessert?

Coffee please, Edie said without a trace of irony. For two.

When the waitress was gone, the Balinese turned to say something more, but Edie spun the hookah pipe and held the hose to his lips. Breathe, she told him. Breathe deep.

SHE WAS SITTING THINGS out for now. She was taking it easy. Maybe the fall in God's Valley had shaken her more than she let herself believe. Maybe she deserved some rest. She was a semester behind in school; it was all she could do to make it to class; some mornings she awoke feeling so stiff she wondered how she would ever maneuver herself into a standing position. Often during lectures she would stand against the back wall to alleviate the ever-present pain. She propped her notebook in the crook of her arm and wrote down every word until her palm began to sweat and her fingers cramped. But focusing on the words was easier than focusing on the pain that shimmied up her legs scattershot.

The doctors said to give it time. She was not at heart an immobile person, but she let the underclassmen take charge of the student-run environmental group. After a few months, she began to believe she was done with all of that.

THE WAITRESS RETURNED with two Turkish coffees. She left them with the bill. Edie drank from the tiny cup and tasted a faint undertone of what could only be described as bathroom water.

How does yours taste? she asked.

The Balinese smiled. I don't think we've been poisoned.

She was alternately amazed or infuriated by his ability to argue with no hard feelings after. They had the occasional tiff at home — nothing major. But while it took her hours to come down from an argument, to get past her wounded pride or hurt feelings, locked behind the bathroom door sorting it out, when she emerged the Balinese would be waiting for her, as gentle as he'd been before the argument began.

She drained her mug. The coffee left behind a thick, syrupy residue at the bottom of the bowl. He reached for her cup and turned it upside down.

He said, There are women in Persia who make their livings reading coffee mugs.

He righted the cup and showed her where the syrup had run in textured patterns along the concave.

Read my fortune, she said.

He lifted the cup to his eye like a slide-lens. It's very cloudy. Maybe you can't handle defeat. Maybe you're not the type to bounce back after a loss.

Stop it.

It also says you should stay out of trees from now on.

He leaned across the table and kissed her. She took his cup and turned it over. When she turned it over again she peered inside and made a sound through her teeth.

It says you're lucky to have a girlfriend who lets you argue with strangers, she said. Especially over something as meaningless as fair trade. It also says that to apologize you should call in sick to work tomorrow and take this said girlfriend out on the town.

That's what it says?

Yes.

It says all of that in there?

I'm not making it up.

He kissed her again. She tasted the coffee and the flavor of tobacco on his lips, in his beard.

He asked, Are we ready then?

We should split this tab.

He drummed his fingers on the check. I didn't open it. This place is a shit-box, and the waitress was rude. I think this hookah pipe was made in a Chinese sweatshop and I think the prices here are exorbitant. I don't think I'll be back. Ergo, I don't feel obligated to pay.

It did not bother her as much as she would have thought, stepping out of the smoke and the dark and hailing the first taxicab they saw. It was not her job to be everyone's moral compass. She was done with all of that.

IF THE BALINESE minded her near-constant presence in the house, he never said. She was sitting things out. She was learning to fingerpick. When he came home from work, she would be flat on her back stretched out across the living room rug, strumming the guitar, her face to the ceiling. It was hard to sing along with Joni Mitchell. She managed to keep up with less acrobatic songwriters. She learned traditional and bluegrass songs, "A Lonesome Soul Am I." Singing, or thoughtlessly strumming, gave her mind a certain distance. Her emotions sorted out in three-quarter rhythm, the downbeat of the plucked notes, the achingly lonely melodies. *I feel like I'm on my journey home.* The long-ago lyrics somehow standing in for her own yearning, her voice a direct communication with something she'd never tapped into before, call it a higher power. *He saw his son returning back. He looked, he ran, he smiled. And threw his arms around the neck of his rebell'ous child.*

SHE WAS NOT everyone's moral compass. It was not her place in the world. She was done with all of that. But as the days went by, their walking out on the bill began to nibble at the periphery of her conscience. That they had stiffed the waitress bothered her, but more than that she began to mistrust herself in light of her relationship with the Balinese. She thought that the girl who came to California more than two years ago would not have walked out on a bill to impress anyone, if indeed that had been the reason, if she'd given it that much thought. The truth was, she didn't know why she'd let them leave without paying the bill, but the action reeked of the me-first, self-serving attitude she saw in so many of her generation, of everything she hated about her classmates and about the underclassmen who argued more about offices and titles than what the next project would be.

She rode the bus across town. She rode shoulder-to-shoulder with quiet Mexican women and their children; out-of-work blacks with headphones around their ears like barnacles. Certain leaders of political and religious circles claimed America had brought tragedy upon itself, but it was people like these, who she rode the bus with in cold weather, who made her doubt all of that America-as-Sodom-and-Gomorrah chatter. These people had no time for imperialism, worrying about how to pay rent. She disembarked at the bus corral where the still souls of her generation waited for something she wasn't sure what. There were women in business suits and sneakers, skaters kicking their boards around, queens posing, blacks from across the bay, vampiric drifters, schoolgirls with long black coats and shoulder bags, drug pushers—buds, buds, shrooms—and the homeless, always the homeless; after a few false starts, backtracking, she found the eye painted above the restaurant door and found the restaurant open.

It was early even for the lunch crowd, and only one or two tables were filled. Around a table in the back sat several off-duty policemen in their T-shirts and black vests. At the entrance, a girl younger than Edie perched on a stool behind the hostess stand with her legs crossed.

The hostess smacked her gum. Waiting on someone?

Edie reached into her shoulder bag and brought out the envelope stuffed with money. She had sold every one of her books to raise enough to cover the tab.

She said, My boyfriend and I walked out on the bill last Thursday. This is what we owed.

Who was your waitress?

Edie described the waitress as best she could until the owner appeared, the short balding man with wire-rim frames. He asked what the trouble was.

She skipped out on a bill last week, the hostess explained. She wants to make sure Bridget gets her tip.

Good one, said the owner.

Edie pushed the envelope across the hostess stand, trying not to think of the favorite titles she sold — *Jitterbug Perfume* or the entirety of the Orson Scott Card series. The owner shuffled through the bills.

Two entrees, Edie told him. Plus, a pipe.

Kid. He held the envelope away from him as if it were slightly damp. Take this. Please. Buy yourself some new clothes. Buy yourself a bath at the YWCA. I don't want any part of this money, who knows where it came from.

Then she was back on the street, crumpling the envelope in her purse, feeling heat rise in her face and hands. She was caught up in a tidal shame that swelled and then swept her out across the sidewalk, like trash being hosed into the street. The patronizing refusal of a deed done right; she reeked of poverty, of mistrust. The manager had thought the envelope was full of handouts or drug money, marked bills, not trusting there wasn't some other motive. This was how the world saw her—poor, starving, in need of a bath. She couldn't see how these things mattered in regards to honesty. Why her appearance in any retail store drew the attention of the clerk. Not because they thought she had money to spend but because they needed to watch over her like a crook. She found it hard to believe these things mattered—weren't they all appearances? As unreal as expensive price tags on plastic champagne flutes? Then the waitress was right in front of her; they almost missed one another, both walking fast with their heads down, caught up in their own particular anguished thoughts and cursing the wind off the bay. For Edie, there was no mistaking that stride even with the waitresses' hood pulled over her head. She put out a hand and stopped her. She shoved the envelope toward her and held it there until Bridget accepted.

The waitress said, I remember you. Fair Trade Agreement.

I didn't want you to get docked.

Bridget counted the money in the street. I recognize you. I didn't say anything the other night. I didn't want to spoil your date. But you led that protest in Oregon last summer.

I guess.

You were all over the local news.

I don't own a television.

The waitress slid the envelope inside her purse. Did you get them to stop logging?

Edie shook her head.

Lot of good it did, then. Look what all your suffering earned you.

SHE WAS DONE with all of that until the one morning she woke to the sound of chainsaws and the sound of the chainsaws pulled her from her recurring dream. She believed trees wept and she believed that she could sometimes hear them; when she fell sixty feet to the forest floor she heard the trees mourning as one. She dreamt of drifting through that sad music, falling through its complex harmonies and the lowing of the older trees. It was music only—no words could delineate so great a grief. When she woke she lay in bed shaking, remembering the sound of the chainsaws in God's Valley and the sound the branches made as they fell beneath her—until she heard the chainsaws again outside her window and looked into the yard to see three men in a tree that stood on the neighboring property. The men wore white hardhats and one man held a long rod with a saw blade fastened to one end; he used the blade to prod and sever the highest branches. Another man balanced on the garage roof holding onto cables and ties. A third held a chainsaw and lopped off the thick, rounded branches that may or may not have grown precariously close to the power lines.

And then Edie was storming across the backyard in her nightclothes, half-dressed, half-awake, screaming at the men over the sound of the saws and the sound the branches made as they fell to earth. The men looked down and watched her come across the yard but they went on with their work, the one man probing the upper limbs with his spear.

Loose ends of harness cables dangled from the tree and she took several in her hand and yanked them with all of her hundred pounds. She ran with them until the cords pulled taut. But she was not heavy enough—the men simply braced themselves and waited for her to tire as she ran with the cords until she fell weeping and spent into the arms of the Balinese. He had heard her screaming and looked out the window to see her taking off across the yard in her nightclothes. The entire episode lasted ninety seconds.

What were you trying to do? he kept asking her, stroking her hair. You can't go pulling people out of trees.

Trees are windbreaks, she wept. Trees are shade. Trees are canopies and shelter and oxygen — they can't just go cutting them down.

They're just pruning, the Balinese whispered. That's all it is.

THE CALLUSES on her fingertips were hard, white domes. She knew many songs by heart now and could play them with her eyes closed, her fingers finding their own way along the strings. Maybe she had mentioned the guitar, but the waitress invited her to an open mic that was being held at the restaurant. The waitress said there was someone she needed to meet.

Edie left that night without telling the Balinese where she was going. She hadn't told him about returning the money or about the friendship she started with the waitress, the waitress whose name was Bridget and who poured so much cream and sugar into her coffee it tasted like candy and who painted her fingertips electric-blue sometimes with glittering swirls or black spirals etched into the nails. Her personality seemed to vibrate, or to hum, but Edie wanted to keep it separate from her boyfriend, her lover, her caregiver — whatever it was the Balinese had become after caring for her all summer, after washing her and helping her to pee.

In the restaurant, she found the waitress sitting at a back table with another girl their same age who had dark skin and large eyes. Selma bore angular features and straight black hair. She was introduced as the owner's daughter.

Bridget leaned across the table. She's beautiful, isn't she?

By nine o'clock the restaurant was full. College kids crowded the pillows in front of the stage and circulated three hookah pipes among them. Selma cut through the room like a sail, her arms shimmering with silver clasps. On stage, microphone in hand, she cocked her hips and held her elbows out from her side as if she bent against a great headwind. Her lips brushed against the microphone as she delivered, rapid fire: Pond scum! Accentuating her words with gyrating hips, elbows flailing: Do you want some? Of my flotsam? Her entire body metering the measures of rhyme, her tirade lasting three minutes with Edie lost inside the verbiage and the complicated turns of phrase — Thanks, but I've already got some — and it was nothing she had seen or heard before.

When Selma returned to their table, sweating and out of breath, she said, It's better than sex.

On stage, Bridget introduced Edie as the Fall Girl. She thought it was hip in a retro-eighties sort of way. To scattered applause, Edie carried her guitar by the neck and made her way to the front windows. She balanced upon the stool.

Hello. Edie spoke into the microphone. She was surprised at how loud her voice sounded, and she pulled away a little. She said, If you love a redhead, set her free. If she follows you everywhere you go, pitches a tent on your front lawn, and puts your new girlfriend in the hospital, she's yours.

There was some laughter. She strummed her guitar once. Through the P.A. she caught the echo of her voice and of the instrument in her hands. She strummed the guitar again and the guitar felt alive — she could barely control it. She took a deep breath, strumming. She began to play and concentrated on moving her fingers over the strings. Her rhythm plodded. The fingers on her pick-hand felt stiff and unresponsive — nerves. But the notes sounded different to her; more resonant. And as she began to sing, although the words were familiar, she understood the lyrics differently, as if singing them before an audience turned over each lyrical phrase to reveal its brilliance. The strings, for their part, seemed more difficult to command and writhed with their own buzzing.

> Beams and boards, floors and walls
> Every switch gets uninstalled
> It's not a house, not a home
> It's an antique mall

The song never changed tempo, or increased in volume, and it was nothing but the same few chords repeated, but the sound of her voice rose and the lyrics carried until even the kitchen fell quiet. When the song was finished there was a moment before the kids on the pillows and the off-duty cops in the back of the room burst into applause.

She did not remember the walk from the stage to her table. Her entire body filled with rapture unlike any she'd ever felt. Seated again with her new friends, they listened to a boy read a poem about turning twenty-six on the twenty-sixth and all of his candles were black.

They sat at the far end of the room, facing the stage. The off-duty cops were watching the stage and anyway it was too hard to hear above the din. Selma reached into her purse and slid a clear, plastic folder across the tabletop. Edie found, tucked inside, a bumper sticker that read in large black letters: SUV = TERRORISM.

This is…tremendous, she said.

I have thousands, Selma said.

And you put these on cars?

You have no idea how satisfying it is to see a bumper sticker that you yourself have placed, cruising around the city. We put them on the rear bumper, on the passenger's side, so it might be days or weeks before the driver notices. Some soccer mom dropping her kids off at school with this plastered across her car — what must the other parents think?

It's perfect.

I'm glad you like it. Selma returned the bumper sticker to her purse. But it's not quite perfect. They're funny, and sort of smart and ironic, but bumper stickers can be removed. A little soap and water and a little elbow grease.

She folded her hands over the purse in her lap. Bridget told me you worked for Greenpeace.

That's right.

And you were part of the God's Valley protest last summer?

Yes.

How did that go?

Edie was keeping an eye out for the server. She desperately wanted a glass of water. And this girl Selma was sitting too close, speaking too directly in the warm room and the smoke from the tobacco pipes drifting, the smell of cherry and smoldering coals.

Edie said, Nothing happened. I worked all summer and in the end I threw all the signatures I'd collected into a ravine. Last summer, I spent ten days in the top of a redwood, fell sixty feet and broke just about every bone in my body—and nothing changed. They cut the forest down anyway.

How does that make you feel?

Pissed off. Like I can't make a difference. Like I don't matter.

Selma flagged down the server and Edie ordered. When the waitress was gone again, Selma said, Organizations like Greenpeace—they can't function because of the bureaucracy. It's not entirely their fault. Their hearts are in the right place, they just happen to be an enormous organization that takes a long time to get anything done.

Bridget was on stage reading something of her own, a poem or a prose-poem that Edie had a hard time following. It was written with a sort of gothic sensibility, with language that sounded like it had been lifted from vampire books.

Do you know why Bridget wanted us to meet? Selma whispered.

I'm not looking to get involved with anything.

That's something I can respect.

I've devoted every part of myself, all my soul and my entire, broken body, and I haven't accomplished anything.

I can change that for you. Selma touched her hand. Myself, and Bridget, and the organization we represent.

In class she learned about a type of ant that adhered to a strict caste system. The warrior ants, for example, would return from some fierce raid and sit patiently while the smaller-bodied ants cleaned and healed their battle wounds. The smaller-bodied ants were useless on their own, no larger than a thumb screw, but in aggregate they could span a crevice in the earth and form a bridge for the warrior ants to cross. Each ant to his or her own particular duty. And maybe before she had fancied herself a warrior ant, charging into battle on behalf of this cause or that, when in reality she was a worker ant, useful only as part of a ferocious swarm. She thought she could be comfortable with that description of herself — people often said, Just do your part. The trick was devoting herself to the right greater good. No more politics, no more collecting signatures, no more features on the nightly news. She would find the in-between.

She kept the bumper stickers in the front closet, with the winter coats, where the Balinese kept his Ziploc bags that were empty but for seeds and stems. He was too paranoid to throw them away and this peculiar habit drove her crazy. So she hid the bumper stickers Selma had given her there, in the pockets of the winter coats, bound with rubber bands. She took a handful of the bumper stickers when she went running and plastered them on the rear bumpers of Cherokees and Excursions, Yukons and Rodeos, vehicles with naturalistic names that exploited the very heritage they were meant to honor. Meanwhile, she was getting stronger. She was gaining muscle. Her legs became hard and sinewy again, her body lean.

WHAT HAPPENS when you pump a rat's stomach full of soap? Selma asked.

Edie stirred her iced Americano, with room for cream.

Selma answered her own question. They die.

Was that supposed to be funny? she asked.

Bridget said, They'll douse rabbits with chemicals just to watch the effects—just to observe the death throes.

The EPA requires all pesticides, for example, to be tested on something like two hundred rats before they're deemed safe for humans, Selma said.

Keep in mind, no one knows if there's a correlation between animal reaction and human reaction. It's all theoretical.

Big corporations, too. In broad daylight. These are not underground labs. These are tax-paying buildings with parking lots and doors that open when you swipe your badge.

Big corporations is right, Bridget laughed. Our federal government, for one.

DURING HER RECOVERY, the Balinese had made a nest for her on the couch in the living room where she could read or play her guitar and keep her legs elevated. She could fish fresh icepacks out of the mini-fridge when he wasn't home. She could sit up or lay out flat, depending. The couch had a texture like corduroy but softer. There were places in the cushions that had a funny smell, a bad smell like old sex. And there were places in the cushions that smelled like cats. And there were other smells in the cushions, depending on where she put her nose: black cherry cordial ice cream; damp leaves at the bottom of a compost pile; Arm & Hammer baking soda.

Until the September morning her phone rang and it was the Balinese telling her to turn on the television. They didn't own a television, so Edie limped across the hall and knocked on the neighbor's door, the neighbor who ran some kind of marketing firm out of his home and who she sometimes brought lunch to if she got lonely, the two of them eating hummus and green pepper sandwiches on the back patio. She knocked on his door and he let her in and they turned on the television because he hadn't heard anything either. After they watched a little while in silence, they held one another as a pillar of smoke rose out of lower Manhattan. They took turns calling the people they knew who lived there; calling those friends' parents when they couldn't get through and worrying until they heard something either way, until all were accounted for.

In their bedroom, Edie lay on the floor with a map of the city spread out before her. A hot compress balanced on the small of her back.

The Balinese came into the room. Where's the guitar?

She did not answer. She smoothed out a crinkled edge of the map. It had taken him almost a week to notice.

He prodded her with his toe. What happened to the guitar?

Someone borrowed it, she said.

He did not raise his voice. It's worth a thousand bucks. Maybe, two thousand.

She thought of the boxes of Tide, stacked floor to ceiling in the utility closet. She folded the map expertly and rested her head on her arms. She listened as he went into the kitchen. She heard him open the utility closet and drag out the garbage bag she had hidden there. On the bag she'd written *Winter Clothes*.

I'm doing laundry tonight, he called to her. Should I take these too?

She stood, pressing her hands against her lower back, leaning first to the right and then to the left. I don't know what those are. They've been here since I moved in.

This is your handwriting on the bag, he said. Isn't it?

She came into the kitchen and stood watching him. He opened the bag. He withdrew the scraps of cloth she'd collected, the shredded bedsheets, the rolls of bandages. He held up a cloth strip and twirled it in the air like a towel twirling at a sporting event. Then, to be funny, or to be ironic, she wasn't sure, he tied the rag around his head.

You gave the guitar to a friend? he asked.

Trey needed an acoustic for a gig.

A gig? the Balinese said. That's great. We should go.

She leaned against the sink. In the space beneath the sink were two dozen empty wine bottles she had stashed there, along with a plastic bag full of rubber corks. Probably he had found these too.

I don't know, she said. It might've been last night. Come on, it was Trey. Why should I bother him with a million questions?

The Balinese scooped his car keys off the counter. Let's go get it. I feel like playing.

Let's not. Let's get in bed.

But he insisted. He held the door open for her, gesturing, mockingly, like a hotel doorman. She slid into her sandals and past him. He followed her down the porch steps out into the street. Before they reached his car, she stayed him with her hand.

It was mine, she said.

Edie, he said. I spent a shit-ton to buy that guitar.

They stood on the corner. She hardly noticed when a bus pulled up to the curb and passengers stepped around them both to board.

When it was only the two of them, the driver leaned over and put his hand on the knob. You kids riding?

The Balinese waved the driver on. What happened to it?

I sold it, she said.

Look, he said. It doesn't matter. You needed money, fine. It's all just material shit. But you had to get a fair amount of cash for it — where is it all?

She looked toward the road, as if someone or something might come from that direction and save her from answering. Finally she said, Invested.

His laughter seemed compulsory. In what? Options? Gold? Or is that what's inside those detergent boxes, cold hard cash?

He walked a wide circle to the corner and back again. Then he reached out and punched the bus stop sign. The sign shook and the sound of his fist against the sign reverberated for a block in either direction. It made her jump. It made her frightened of him for the first time.

I won't let you do this, he told her.

Date: Thursday 14, Mar 2002 01:25:36 -0400
From: "ACORN" <security-news@actionearth.org >
To: "Edith Clay Aberdeen" < eaberdeen@berkeley.edu >
CC: "Bridget Meadows" < bmeadows@sfsu.edu >
Subject: ACORN

Active Conservation as the Only Recourse for Nature. The newspapers have labeled us "eco-terrorists." But we are different from the 9/11 hijackers, or Japanese militants who drop anthrax from crop dusters. We do not target civilians. We do not take lives. Our aim is economic sabotage because

it is our only recourse—our only way to
be heard. In the hundreds of millions of
dollars we've cost the conglomerates and
the corporations, we've not lost one life.
We at ACORN believe this track record
speaks for itself.

She lay in bed with a body pillow thrust between her knees.
The Balinese was talking to someone on the phone, in the kitchen
pacing. He was calling every friend of theirs, berating them.

You can't do this, he shouted. I'm not saying you did or did not
convince her of anything. But I'm telling you, whatever you were
planning, Edie is out.

But there was no one he could have called. No one he knew
could have told him how she spent her early mornings in the
still-dark towns that outlined San Francisco, or what tools she
used. Later, the Federal Bureau of Investigation would label them
incendiary devices—officially, these devices contained *residual
flammable accelerant*—but between them Edie, Bridget and Selma
called them Cocktails. Laundry detergent sifted into empty
Steelhead Amber beer bottles and rags, first doused in gasoline,
stuffed into the bottles' mouths. The rags lit; the bottles thrown
through windows of sports utility vehicles; the devices firing; the
insides of the gas-guzzling, mass-produced, super-sized vehicles
turning instantaneously torched and black.

Molotov cocktails and cans of spray-paint. Words scrawled
across Hummers and Escalades, Mercedes and Lexus: MURDERER,
SHAME, FUCK SUVS; 14 LIVES PER GALLON; ACORN; POLLUTER; FAT LAZY
AMERICAN; —; JESUS HATES YOUR SUV; SUPER UNPATRIOTIC VEHICLE; IS
YOUR PENIS REALLY THIS SMALL? Over eighty vehicles, all told, along
back streets, in three different car dealerships, at several private
residences in Fremont, Pleasanton and San Jose.

Date: Saturday 20, Apr 2002 11:54:55 -0200
From: "Ninlil" < ninlil101@hotmail.com >
To: "Kevin Holman" < kholman@sacbee.com >
Subject: ACORN Arrests

> To the contrary, there have been few arrests
> (see ACORN home page). None of the major
> players have gone down. As to the fires, I'd
> rather not confirm nor deny anything. Each
> ACORN action is completely independent.
> If I get arrested, I don't want to give the
> Feds anything with which to build a case.

> I will say this: The FBI is in a state of
> disarray. They are embarrassed and
> frustrated by their inability to stop attacks
> from within our borders or from abroad.
> You ask is someone capable of setting these
> fires and not feeling guilt, in light of the
> attacks in New York and Washington D.C.?
> The answer is yes.

SECURITY CAMERAS at the entrance to the University library recorded her coming and going within minutes of her ID card being swiped at the computer lab door; moments later, her password-protected student account was accessed and then incriminating messages were sent from a Hotmail account registered to several of the school's IP addresses. The FBI tallied it all. The websites she visited were all evidence. Security cameras at the car dealerships recorded someone of her stature and build along with two other (possible) females setting fire to vehicle after vehicle and leaving the same outraged, inflammatory graffiti as calling cards.

Date: Wednesday 22, May 2002 07:12:44 -0400
From: "Edith Clay Aberdeen" < eaberdeen@berkeley.edu >
To: "Peter Moran" < balinesestyle@gmail.com >
Subject: …

> I am sick over our argument last night. I
> thought I could open up to you and trust
> you with all of this. I'm heartbroken to
> find you don't condone this. Did you see
> that? I used the word "condone," as if you
> were my parent, which obviously you are
> not. Regardless of your personal feelings,
> I realized today I never swore you to
> secrecy about all that I came clean with (in
> hopes that you would accept me and love
> me still). I hope you still do love me. But
> no matter what ends up happening with
> you and me, you need to promise me that
> everything I said last night dies with you.

SHE WAS ARRESTED crossing the University quadrangle in late afternoon when the angle of the sun threw long shadows across the lawn. At that time of day she walked on the edge of the shadow and the still-light and imagined herself an artist in a high-wire act, challenging herself to keep her line steady for fear of some imaginary consequence if she faltered. She was crossing the quad in this manner, one foot in front of the other, when two men in business suits and two uniformed police officers—the San Francisco Police Department, not college security guards—came up behind her and did not handcuff her but escorted her to a black sedan parked nearby. She was not afraid; she said nothing as they listed the charges against her. *Maliciously damaging or destroying by means of fire a building or vehicle used in interstate commerce or any activity affecting interstate commerce in violation of 17 U.S.C. S 844 (i).*

The police kept a dog and the police had given the dog a scent pad and the dog tracked the scent of her from the car dealership in Pleasanton to the home she shared with the Balinese on Hazel Street. The police also had a tracking device; she had been carrying it on her Vespa for weeks.

They had images of her at the car dealerships and images of her at the school library. They had emails traced to many of the library's IP addresses. It was all circumstantial; they let her go after three days. But not before letting her read a sworn statement given by the Balinese only one day prior:

> My name is Peter Gregory Moran. My date of birth is June 2, 1972. I have voluntarily spoken to members of the FBI and the San Francisco Police Department. The questions I have answered pertain to an investigation concerning the arson and graffiti of SUVs. These incidents occurred on March 27, 2002. I currently reside with Edie Aberdeen and have spoken with her about these incidents on numerous occasions. She spoke to me in the UC Berkeley library, in our apartment on Hazel Street, in my car and in other unrecalled specific locations. I looked at four photographs shown to me by the FBI. In photograph #1, the person on the left reminds me of Edie. I initialed and dated

the bottom of the photograph. I was not personally involved with the incident on March 27, 2002. I have told the truth as best as I can recall.

THREE

The Balinese was not asleep, and Edie no longer lay beside him. She was getting dressed in the dark. An arm's reach away, she leaned against the wall for balance, slipping into her pants and fastening them. He listened as she opened the closet door and knocked against the wooden hangers. The door pushed along the carpet as she closed the closet and went into the bathroom and shut herself there.

The alarm clock read 1:16 A.M. He heard her come out of the bathroom and hurry into the kitchen. The hall closet opened and shut. He listened as she gathered her house keys from the basket on the kitchen counter; he heard the front door open and close. He listened, and he did not move to stop her. He released her tie line, as maybe he already had when he spoke to the police, already a week ago now, when they exhibited the evidence mounted against her — she who he had loved with his entire being. There was nothing for him to do but tell the authorities, Yes, she's the one you're looking for. All of what you say is true.

He felt like she had somehow played him, but for what, he didn't know. There was his career to think of, the necessity of maintaining his name. He couldn't have his name in the papers alongside a felon. Not with one arrest already on his record.

But Edie's actions were more than criminal: she was a terrorist. And he argued against terrorism whenever he could, whenever he was met with one of the radicals. Violence had never once produced lasting results; violence begat violence, end of story. And this, what Edie was engaged in, was terrorism in its most pure form — domestic terror where fear and moral outrage became one.

Radical activism: He knew these people and loathed them. They were little more than a nuisance, something on the fringe, like any gutter trash armed with cans of spray paint tagging the face of a new condominium, or skateboarding in herds through the park. A pestering force, at most. But in light of the current climate, considering the global forces at play.... Edie's actions were unconscionable. To carry on this deranged plot while the nation mourned the loss of nearly three thousand of its own....These were not the actions of the lonely freshman he'd met in the grocery store three years before. This was not the person he shared his apartment with, who he shared his bed with, who once wept when a sparrow broke its neck against the kitchen window. He had watched the change come over her and he had done nothing to stop it. He tried to give her space after the injuries she suffered, after her failure in the Oregon woods. And in the space he granted grew a monster that now vandalized property and crept through the city streets at late hours insidious and sly. Perhaps he was an accomplice after all. By taking no action he had only let her wade deeper into the abyss.

He rose from bed hearing a noise in the backyard. He parted the curtains to see Edie crouched near the garbage cans alongside the house. She wore a watch-cap and she squatted in the shadows. She wore her hiking pack and the green pack loomed over her like a second figure leaning in from the yard. Seeing her there, the Balinese had the feeling no less than of watching her drown.

He went through the house, checking closets and cabinets. The boxes of laundry detergent were gone from the hall, as were the rubber corks, as were the wine bottles below the sink. He heard a car in the driveway; he went out and stood on the front stoop, below the porch light. A sedan he did not recognize sat idling. Edie emerged from the side of the house and climbed into the back seat of the car. There were two others inside the car and he recognized their shapes, shifting and half-obscured by shadow — the same two that had been in the surveillance tapes he'd screened at the police station, the same two who had been with Edie at the car dealerships. The police and the FBI thought they were female. He wasn't sure, and he didn't know if they saw him standing there, then. He didn't know if she would have cared. The car backed out of the driveway and sped southwest toward downtown.

Inside the house again, he snatched his car keys from the counter. He fumbled into his work boots and did not bother to tie them. He was like some tragic clown, or a vagrant, wearing his knit cap, his boxer shorts, and a flannel shirt thrown over his shoulders unbuttoned as he tumbled down the front steps and across the lawn. Hurrying to his car, where a late frost shone on the glass, he started the engine and peeled away in the direction of pursuit. Fog on his windshield retreated from the hot air blowing up from the vents. He brought nothing with him. No wallet, no phone, no money. He drove by instinct, as if there were flares laid out for him in advance, a hallucinatory path that illuminated the most direct route to her, through the pockmarked city, as his Pontiac blew through stop signs and red lights, remembering to look for police cars only after the fact, wanting to attract the police cars maybe, to have them follow him gliding through intersections like the blade of an ice skate glides across a frozen lake.

The night opened up; the city was lit before him. He heard a rattling in the passenger's side vent and slammed his hand against the vent so the rattling ceased. He was not alone in the city, but almost. He caught air on the crests of hills and his tires squealed. Cars loaded with teenagers drifted out of all-night diners; a city bus nosed its way from empty stop to empty stop. The city slept while he gripped his steering wheel and each mile carried him farther from his home and his exhaustion came apart like a cigarette thrown from a moving car, the sparks and ashes scattering. At the top of another hill, car dealerships and sit-down restaurants lay quiet and dark, the parking lots lit but the buildings empty. Behind chain-link fencing sat new and used vehicles, spotless and cool beneath the lights and the ambiance from the billboards overhead. Driving this stretch of road he thought this was how terrorism acted, that terrorism moved in opposition to routine. Predawn was the silence that evil was permitted to move through.

Past the dealerships and restaurants, he rounded a curve and found himself on an industrial drive. Low buildings sat off from the road, their parking lots divided by strips of grass and some semblance of landscaping that made it feel less like what it was — a maze of cubicles for tech companies and medical equipment suppliers. Toward the end of the cul-de-sac sat a nondescript concrete building with a sign out front that read, *Med-Safe, Inc.* He recognized the name from something Edie had recently said. He cut his headlights and eased his car down the drive. The research center was to his left and to his right were storage units and two buildings that were quiet and dark. He parked along the median dividing the lots. He cut the engine. He listened for a time and heard nothing. He thought maybe he had guessed wrong until a set of headlights bounded toward him and pulled into the entrance of the lab. He hunkered behind the steering wheel. It was the same maroon sedan that had sat outside his house; the car passed the enclave of trees and drove toward the back of the lot. He saw Edie's face like the pale moon passing behind a cloud, consumed with something in the back seat of the car that he could not see.

Out of his car now, he crossed the median and made his way along the research center, keeping to the sidewalk and out of view of the road. The back parking lot was lit like daylight. Across the lot was a trailer and the trailer backed up to the highway. It was like watching a movie and then waking a week later to find himself inside the film; the scene before him might have been footage from any of the police tapes. A heavyset girl was dousing a pile of cloth strips with gasoline; a taller woman moved across the lot toward the trailer, a bolt cutter in her hands. The women wore gloves and masks and the doors of the sedan were flung open and the car's engine idled, seeping exhaust fumes into the air with the smell of gasoline rising and the power-washed walls and the nose-tickling fragrance everywhere of laundry detergent. The heavyset woman stuffed doused rags into the mouths of the bottles and Edie stood facing the Balinese from across a great distance. He paused at the corner of the building and she could not see him, bathed as she was in light and him in shadow. She reared back with one bottle already in hand and heaved the bottle skyward. End over end the bottle turned and the bottle unlit shattered the laboratory window and the bottle was swallowed by the jagged hole it made.

Propelled — not thinking, but moving — the Balinese dashed into the light. The heavyset woman saw him first and shouted something he could not distinguish over the rush of blood into his face, through his ears. Across the lot, Edie dumped bottles that were not yet lit through the gaping hole, laying an incendiary groundwork. The Balinese ran toward her, his clothes flying everywhere loose, the laces of his boots flailing.

He kicked at the empty gasoline can. Terrorists!

He passed the heavyset girl and brushed against the sedan and made straight for Edie where she stood against the black mouth of the window. He did not hear his own screaming or his accusations of terror — the face of his angel had turned horrible. It was not Edie he made for, not the girl he had fallen in love with over tins of cat food in a back alley so long ago. At that moment, beside the empty highway, he was heading for a criminal, a terrorist, a witch who flickered against a backdrop of smoke and flame. She needed his rescue; she needed him, and he would help her through this, just as he had nursed her back to health after her fall. It hadn't been her family, or her friends at her bedside, washing her, feeding her. It had been him. He would take her in his arms and carry her away. His arms were outstretched. He stumbled toward her, garish in his windblown clothes like some risen half-dead. He moved for her and she swung at him and in her hand was a blunt object, a glass bottle that she swung in reaction to him and not, he believed, with intent, but he felt the bottle against his skull and felt his feet go out from under him like a cartoon, a hobo slipping on a banana peel, before he was blinded by a rush of color and then a singular clarity that brought with it a burnished, garnet-colored dark.

For Edie, all sound flushed from the night, compressed and finally muted. The Balinese lay crumpled on the ground, blood and mush burbling up through his beautiful black hair, his ski-cap on the ground and its straps caught up in the mess and curls. She was overcome with the sensation of standing in a long, clean hall full of doors that were suddenly shut in quick succession, a rush of air as each door swung closed and then only the reality of herself for miles in any direction. She felt the pavement spin as if she were the handle of a Chinese yo-yo—flimsy and brightly colored paper twirling in a child's hand.

Get in the fucking car.

Bridget was already in the car, pounding her fists against the steering wheel. The bottle Edie held was taken from her hand and Selma held the bottle then, the bloody weapon. Her own hands hung uselessly at her sides while Selma lit the rag and held the bottle away from herself until the smoke curled seductively up the length of her arm. She reared back and flung the bottle through the laboratory window. Air forced itself into Edie's lungs and she gulped the air and choked on the sulfur, suddenly not able to swallow enough. She fell to her knees, grasping at her chest, unable to breathe deeply or to quiet the panic that beat like wings inside her gut, down deeper than her soul. The bottle was lit aflame and the bottle spun through the air and disappeared into the darkness and the smoke. When it finally fired, bursts of flame shattered windows along the façade and the sky rained burning plastic and glass. Edie felt the power of the heat through her clothes.

Then all was still. When she looked up again, the car was gone. The Balinese lay where he had fallen. It was only the two of them in the night, until she saw movement to her left and saw the trailer door open and saw two dogs emerge and behind them rabbits skittering their way across the lot. Grief welled up inside of her; something tragic about the way the animals made their way into the shadows and then were gone, something heartbreaking about their newfound freedom. Something forlorn and helpless about the shards of glass that lay about her and glistened in Peter's hair and in the weave of his knit cap as she took the hat in her hands.

Sirens. Her body tensed, listening. They were coming closer. On her knees still, she dug into the shirt pocket of the Balinese. His car keys were there. She did not touch him otherwise, to check his breath, or to wait for his pulse—she would not. On her feet again, she ran toward the cul-de-sac, knowing the Pontiac would be parked somewhere close by. She found it on the grass median between lots. She fumbled with the car keys as she ran and she found the driver's side door unlocked. Three bells chimed as she opened the door and fell in. Headlights bore down on her and the headlights swung into the parking lot, followed by three or four more sets of headlights and their madly spinning sirens, the red and blue strobes ensnaring her only chance for escape.

Then she was out of the car again. Three police cruisers to the right; another to her left blocked her access to the main road. Their flashing lights marked each interminable second. She stumbled into the parking lot again, bathed beneath a spotlight crashing over her like a wave breaking. Flames roared from the laboratory windows and curled back on themselves and bent across the roof. Someone yelled for her to stop, to drop, to freeze. There was no real time and there was no color either. Already she was rendered in red and black newspaper ink, a criminal on the front page news.

She tripped over her hiker's pack. She wove her hand through its straps. And then she was on her feet again, sprinting toward the trailer and past the trailer toward the highway lit by the long necks of streetlights bowing their heads in mourning.

Already she was halfway across the lot. She waited to feel the hands of someone dragging her to the ground. She waited to suddenly change direction, for a single bullet to rip through her backpack and clothes and pierce her empty heart. She almost pleaded for it, but nothing came. All that drove her legs across the parking lot was the desire to flee; the parts of her body were motion spurred by fear. She closed her eyes, waiting for the grip of retribution that would drag her kicking and screaming into hell.

But her hands caught the chain-link fence and then she was scaling the fence quicker and more nimbly than she would have thought herself able. She dropped down the other side, moving without thought, down a muddy embankment, even as a single gunshot tore the night. She did not turn her head to see if anyone followed. She kept low to the ground and darted into the highway. Across the empty highway and up the far embankment into a network of side streets and alleyways that she followed to a frontage road and then to where the interstate bent back on itself and she could drop below an overpass. The farther she ran the less she felt the pull of pursuit. When after several miles she allowed herself to glance back, she found herself completely alone.

FOUR

A car window folded; not shattered but stripped and peeled back on itself; not one break, but thousands of invisible breaks that spread across the broken glass, spidery and white as lace lay over the blue-tinted pane. She once saw this on a car — how the empty window, the negative space, told the story, and not the substance of the glass window itself which had been pulled back like a freshness seal. How the air between the glass and the top of the window enhanced the sense of loss, absence as the essence. She would have thought the glass would shatter instead of fracture and peel, she herself either shattering or peeling back endlessly in that night now nearly morning, when she woke behind a dumpster where she'd managed to sleep for an hour or two before dawn.

All night she moved from alleyway to alleyway and avoided the main streets, crouching in doorways while cars passed, pacing dizzying circles across the city. Sometimes backtracking in the event the police still followed. Sometimes lost or disoriented in her exhaustion. Her old injuries flared into liquid pain across her shoulders and smoldered on the points of her hips. Her skin was sticky with the grime and the filth of the city streets and she tasted the saltiness of her skin and sweat.

She melted into the street and folded her edges and came back in on herself and then she was sitting up without meaning to.

Her head pulsed: a scattered network of pain. An experiment in science class, testing electricity, lighting up a circuit of small bulbs in succession, each bulb urging her to flee. She stood, the electricity pulsing stronger now and with more current buzzing behind her eyes.

She staggered onto the sidewalk. A crowd of Mexican men waited to be driven to a job somewhere. She turned left; past the barred windows of storefronts displaying watches and jewelry alongside electronic devices she'd never found use for; past carry-out Thai; past a coffee shop where inside the barista was taking down chairs; past a bank; past a shop that sold eclectic clothing and collectibles. All were dark. Several joggers passed by, men and women about her own age. She might have been one of them if not for her clothes and her ridiculous hiker's pack. She might have been any college girl out for a morning run, looking forward to a summer abroad or an internship somewhere, her thoughts full of her boyfriend or her sorority sisters or maybe her mind would be free of any thought whatsoever, the mindlessness of youth. But those things belonged to someone she would never be again.

She caught her reflection in a shop window. She tried to match her eyes to someone she knew from long ago—the same pupils but a different face, or the same apparent void behind new eyes, the irises cut with imperfections. It was impossible to pin those eyes on any other face but the one she saw then in the mirror, a thousand power grids away from the eyes that once wept over a dead bird or shuttered open at loud noises in the night, expecting the end of the world. Conversely expecting a new world. Those eyes now belonged to a killer if the Balinese was dead. She was repulsed by her reflection, turning from it as she might turn away from a sickly passenger on the bus, afraid to catch the poverty or the misery or the infection of the insane.

Her pallid reflection said to keep moving: Flee.

She ran. The pale sidewalks felt loose and the streetlights burned through the cool morning air. Gone was the adrenaline that had propelled her the night before. In its place was the weight of lead in her gut, the weight of guilt. Her mind was calm, her thoughts lucid. But gone were sharp edges and fine detail. In their place were buffered angles and runny lines and she thought she could move through this kind of world; she found in herself an undiscovered resolve. Everything she loved was gone from her and in its place was the city grid and beyond the city still more danger and still more paths but also the certainty that if she chose correctly she would remain free.

Canada was the closest border but its proximity worried her — they'd be waiting for her there, or so she believed. To the east was wilderness, the beginning of wildfire season, and mountains she'd never be able to cross. West, of course, was ocean. She turned her thoughts south.

She traveled by foot until she found a bicycle, unlocked and leaning against a fence. She rode this bicycle with the white basket on the front for the next hundred miles, until its front tire went flat. She had in her possession two hundred dollars, an allowance that relegated her to a single meal each day — she didn't know how much money she might eventually need at some undefined moment in the future. She filled a water bottle in public restrooms as the streets of her adopted city became the streets of smaller towns down the Cabrillo Highway. Clapboard houses sat askance on mud hills that were spotted with palms and always the sound of the surf breaking like white noise, perpetual. She'd dreamed of visiting this part of California but now she barely noticed it — she did not track her progress or the medley of broken days, borrowing rides from strangers, washing herself in the swimming pools of anonymous backyards or beneath the showerhead at the beach with browned, shirtless children weaving through her legs and splashing in the standing water and the sand. If she slept, she did not mean to. In Salinas, she allowed herself to buy a one-way bus ticket to San Diego. She was thinking of crossing the border; she was thinking of Mexico.

But stationed at the Mexican border were police officers and federal agents and in the town of Chula Vista were armed militia with their hunting rifles and fold-out lawn chairs and their pick-up trucks. They were not looking for her of course, but their presence sealed the border. In the end, she lacked the courage to try the crossing; she did not trust herself, if pressed, not to tell the truth.

She wondered about truth as she headed east through bus stations in Yuma, then Scottsdale, and finally Tucson, Arizona. At each station she watched the same coyote work the rows of benches that were like pews for desperate immigrants caught in limbo, penniless and wilting in the desert heat. She had heard about men who rustled illegals and packed them onto trucks and drove them across the country to work the harvest seasons up and down the eastern seaboard. She had always wondered what fear or what circumstance could drive a man to risk so much. Maybe she finally knew. Desperation was also a kind of truth.

In Tucson, she purchased a bottle of bleach and in the bathroom of the bus station rinsed her hair in the sink and washed it with the bleach until her fingers and scalp burned from the chemicals. When she looked at herself in the mirror again the eyes were the same but her hair had turned white as fireworks in a night sky. In the bus terminal she stood near the entrance and watched the same coyote work the length of the room. He seemed to be gaining converts. She did not have the money for bus fare to take her as far as she needed to go.

She trailed the coyote into a diner, where he sat at a table across from a muscular white man. Edie hovered near the checkout counter, concealed by a plastic jar filled with water and coins heaped up along its bottom. The coyote spoke Spanish to the white man and the white man didn't say much, but tore the crust from his toast and tossed the crust on the floor. When finally she began to draw the attention of the waitstaff, Edie crossed the restaurant and sat down beside the men.

She was blonde. She was attractive. She was filthy and rough-cut. Even still, they did not agree to carry her until she agreed to pay. They were going to Florida and they still had room but they were suspicious of the gringo. They doubted she had the stamina for such a long trip. They had never carried a woman before and they thought it might disturb the men. But she placed fifty dollars on the table and promised the rest to be paid upon delivery.

She was cargo. The last to be placed in the back of the truck with those sweltering bodies and a smell like nothing could ever be clean again, the sounds that men make without women there, although she was there, huddled in the corner at the tailgate, consumed by discomfort and self-pity. I-10 plowed through Texas and Louisiana, became beautiful estates along the Mississippi shore, became the Florida panhandle, became I-75 southbound, past dog tracks and jai-alai frontons that made the men talk excitedly for the first time, became a road in the center of the sunshine state, became that same road in a downpour and her alone upon it, became a million words she'd counted and repeated silently to herself in a language she didn't understand as she swam amidst the negative space through octaves of counterpoint, ever east.

Florida
2002 – 2003

ONE

Stars play like silver lilies on the pond. The water is still and the night is cool and quiet; it is good to be outside, inside the screened porch where citronella candles waver and their shifting casts an otherworldly glow, devious. In this untrustworthy light, curled on the wicker loveseat, the girl wears the soft, reposed expression of someone just out in the world. Mae thinks she must be twenty or twenty-one, no older, although the way she carries herself makes her seem three times that. The great effort of simple actions, her strained expression rising from a chair—Mae can only guess the reasons why the girl moves crooked-backed through cool mornings. The stiff and arthritic sounds her body makes cause Mae to guess at so many things. There is the question of the girl's history; her eerie watchfulness; her monkish devotion to routine.

In conversation they speak perfunctorily, like office workers who share a cubicle wall—obligatory conversations not wanting to seem rude. When Mae comes home she finds her boys asleep, their homework finished, the dishes stacked and dried. Weeks pass when she thinks she and the girl have not spoken at all. They never leave notes or speak on the phone. There is only what needs to be done and the doing of the thing.

She is thankful for the blessing of this girl. The house is tidier beneath Edie's watch. Sometimes she does not even have the thought to buy more Tide or replace the light bulb in the garage before the errand is done. Sometimes the girl's efficiency frightens her, Edie's preternatural ability to anticipate her needs.

In autumn the leaves do not fall and there is no crispness in the air to warn of the changing season, only Arcadia's population swelling with snowbirds down from their northern retreats. On Saturdays, Mae makes the family breakfast like her grandmother once did. Waking, Edie slide-steps into the kitchen to pour herself coffee and to pour more juice for the boys; she takes her usual place at the table. Mae slides eggs over-easy onto four plates. She shuffles rye toast and bowls of sliced honeydew and cantaloupe. Edie sits at the table making eyes at the boys and laughing with them at some private joke they shared the night before, or the night before that. Something Mae is shut out of this morning, every morning.

They hold hands around the table but Edie does not close her eyes. She prays with her eyes open, as if she is afraid to miss something fleeting. Or as if she fears what she might see by closing them — Mae can't decide. She does not think the girl prays on her own, or if she does, she does not pray out loud. Only once, when the cats got to a rabbit near the septic tank and Evan found it bleeding and hobbled in the yard; Edie wrapped a towel around the creature and carried it to the porch.

Lord, make this bunny feel better, she said in a voice straight as a ruler.

Mae supposes that was a sort of prayer. She asked her boys if they said their prayers at night even when she wasn't home. They told her yes, but that Edie does not pray but stands in the center of their bedroom listening.

We listen to sounds, Troy said. And then we try to figure out what they might be.

When Mae is home, Edie is gone for hours, off on the bicycle she found somewhere in the garage. Why the girl won't just drive and save herself time, Mae doesn't know. From John Whitney she learns the girl feeds stray cats behind the Chinese Fortune and behind the high school, different places. Hearing this, she understands the girl better. Edie is someone who feels more comfortable in nature than with people. Mae knows there were saints who felt the same. The girl shows great compassion and Mae prays it holds the promise of a deeper witness.

SHE WAS GETTING dressed for church when the Holy Ghost told her to invite the girl along. Edie slept late on Sunday mornings, as was her right, and Mae had never invited her before; she never thought to ask. But she heard the voice and she thought back on her first time at Christ by the Sea, how overwhelming it had been—overwhelming but exciting too. Had she not invited the girl because she was afraid of how the service might be perceived? Or was she fearful of what judgment an outsider might bring?

Easing open the bedroom door, she found Edie still asleep. The girl's knees were propped over one pillow and her head was thrown back against the bedspread, the sheets discarded sometime in the night. Mae remembered when she herself slept like that, with total abandon. Surrendering herself at day's end. She sat at the foot of the bed, remembering how she learned to sleep anywhere growing up—how she needed to. How jealous she had been of children who had one bedroom to themselves, one bed. All she remembers of her childhood is a series of beds in a series of apartments and trailer homes, falling asleep in the backs of cars or on blankets spread across the floor; bunched into a twin bed with a sister on either side. How it hadn't mattered to her then—she learned to block out the shuffling between homes and the sounds that followed, nights her father came home late if he came home at all, if he wasn't gone for weeks. She chose sleep as a second skin because sleep was the only place where frightening words and harsh things did not find her. Given this, she wonders how she ever learned to go any way but slumbering through the world.

A fluttering of the girl's eyelids; Mae wondered at her dreams or what they would reveal if she could view them like a movie. How little she knew of the girl in the bed, the girl she trusted her children to each day. Nothing of her past, only facts grounded in the present. No meat—not even fish—and no smoking. Instead, her only apparent vice was an adherence to routine that was clocklike in its mechanism. And there was the matter of the girl's age—when Mae was that young she was taking care of her grandmother, had never even left the county.

She reached out to wake the girl but hesitated, wanting the touch to be familiar but not forward. She shook the girl's foot gently and spoke her name. Edie opened her eyes and did not seem angry or particularly surprised to see her perched on the foot of the twin bed. She wiped her mouth and managed to smile and then to sit up against the headboard.

It's Sunday, Mae said, not knowing where to begin. I was wondering if you'd like to come to church.

Edie rubbed her face and straightened one strap of her undershirt. I don't have anything to wear.

Mae laughed. The Lord don't care what you come to church in. You could wear your birthday suit for all he cares—he just wants you in the pew.

The woman rose and the bed rose with her, relieved of her weight. She ran her finger along the footboard, the white-painted, wooden slats. A floral design was etched there—it was the bed of a little girl. It was only owing to Edie's diminutive size that she managed to fit in the bed at all.

This twin can't be too comfortable, she said.

I'm grateful for it, all the same.

I wasn't sure whether or not to invite you. I didn't want you to think we didn't want you to come.

The girl leaned forward and wrapped her hands around her heels. Her spine pulled itself flat as an ironing board, a hundred creaking joints.

We'll look for something bigger, Mae said. Something a little more grown-up.

Driving to church felt like a family with Edie in the front seat and the boys seated properly across the back. Singing along to praise tapes, although Edie did not sing—she didn't know the words. But the girl smiled and looked very pretty, done up for Sunday service with a touch of makeup and her black slacks picked clean of cat hair and lint. In Scripture, God promised glory to the widows and the orphans; Mae was the widow, Edie the orphan.

Edie did not know the words to the songs in praise and worship either but she followed the white letters that scrolled across the television screens. She did not flinch when Mae pulled the tambourine from her knit bag and hammered it against her hip; her expression never changed when the worship leaders prayed in tongues and the congregation hollered back, Hallelujah.

Pastor Reginald Dancer said, The voice of the Lord. The voice of God. Even the angels acknowledge His all-encompassing glory. And the day will come, so says the Lord, when His voice will shake the wilderness. His voice will lash and splinter the cedars of Lebanon and strip the trees bare. His voice. Will strip the trees bare. Until everyone and every living thing under creation cries out glory.

Walk in the land of the living in the face of the Lord.

And our enemies make for us a smooth path. Our enemies may pronounce peace, but evil is in their hearts. But God will give them according to the work of their hands and He will not build them up. He will tear them down.

His voice strips the cedars bare. His voice makes the deer give birth.

You've seen it with your own eyes. I don't have to paint the picture for you. You only have to walk out the back doors here and stand a little while in that muddy expanse we call a back lawn — and we're working on that, we truly are — to see the mansions going up. Close your eyes and you'll hear the buzz saws and the great movers of earth, smoothing out a place for the almost-rich. That's right: you heard me correctly. The almost-rich. Maybe there's some in the congregation that plan on moving into one of those glamour homes, those starter castles. Go right ahead. Be our guest. But they will not make you a rich man.

The voice of the Lord shakes the desert and strikes with flashes of lightning.

Because those starter castles are not the mansions of Heaven, the mansions that are being prepared for us right this very moment in his heavenly kingdom. They have streets in that subdivision behind us, but they are not paved in gold. And every stone they overturn, every tree they fell, every molecule of dirt they move in the name of progress will lift their voices to praise him upon his return. The very stars will sing out. The very earth — all the beautiful lilies of the field.

Until the voice of the Lord divides the flames of fire.

When the sermon ended, Edie did not go forward for the altar call. At the front of the church, women lay prone across the steps, weeping. Men fell down slain in the Spirit. The organ played dissonant chords and the pastor spoke in a harsh whisper as he laid his hands upon the congregation.

Most of the chairs were empty. Many in the congregation lay sprawled across the carpet or stood in line to receive a blessing. Some were calling out praises or tongues from the corners. Others knelt beside those slain and prayed over them. The smell of hibiscus drifted from the candle pillars and the drummer rolled his cymbal and rattled the rim of his snare.

An usher touched Edie on the arm. Do you know Jesus Christ?

Mae watched the exchange. She thought if the girl went forward she would know the Lord was telling her what to do. The answer seemed to come as Edie followed the usher into the aisle and toward the front of the church, as calm amidst the chaos as someone tying up the trash.

Mae watched it all and gave praise to the Lord. Edie stood at the altar and the pastor moved quickly to her and placed one hand upon her head. Mae knew what that hand felt like, knowing that hand held the power of Jehovah. She prayed over the girl too, focusing her energy toward the front of the sanctuary. She prayed for Edie's heart to open. She prayed that she would be a positive influence on her boys; that God would bring an end to Evan's self-imposed silence; that even Vester might find peace, wherever he was.

The pastor took his hand away and said, Praise Jesus! and then the flat of his hand fell like an anvil and Edie staggered backward before her legs gave way and two ushers on either side of her lay her out flat across the floor.

AFTER THE SERVICE, Mae waited for Edie. The girl had been held back by the pastor. Mae moved to the corner of the reception hall because she didn't like to stand in the middle of the room like a car wreck in the center lane of rush hour traffic. She balanced her orange juice and a flimsy plate and she folded the plate to bite at the donut it held.

She wanted Edie to appear so that she could sweep her home and sit down at the kitchen table and witness to her at length, to assure her what happened at the altar was God's will, a cause for celebration. Keep the girl's mind out of it and focus on how she felt—find out where her heart was. John Whitney came by and said a few nice things but he couldn't stay long—he wanted to get home for the Dolphins' game.

Her boys darted through the room, past table legs and the legs of chairs and past long skirts that fluttered as if lifted by a breeze. She grabbed Troy on his next turn past and told him to wait for her by the front doors. He heard her, or he didn't; he was off again while she navigated her way like a cruise ship through glacial shards into the calmer waters of the hall.

The glass vestibule ran the length of the church and wrapped around the sanctuary and back on itself, framing the atrium and providing a view of the parking lot, through the east doors, or the muddy backyard to the west. Behind the church a rolling, brown moonscape, undeveloped, and beyond this the new subdivision, separated from church property by a buckling orange-plastic fence.

At the fence line she spotted Edie and the pastor. As soon as she stepped outside and the door slammed she regretted making her presence known—she thought she had intruded upon something private.

There you are. Edie lifted one heel and then her other, checking for mud.

The pastor took the girl by the arm and helped her across the muck. His white teeth shone behind his sun-tanned skin. Mae thought she saw him run his hand quickly through the girl's hair as he said, Edie has agreed to do a little yard work for us.

Praise the Lord, Mae said.

I know you need her in the evenings. But mornings, while the boys are at school, she's mine. Is it a deal?

Mae could only laugh and allow the reverend to pass the girl from his arm to hers. She pulled Edie close. Oh honey, the Lord has a plan for you. Yes he does. And I'm not going to stand in his way.

SHE WENT TO WORK that night and for the week following. She no longer worried about the influence the girl might be having on her boys. The Lord was working on Edie Richards and that was enough for her — she asked only that she be made an instrument. And if the girl's past remained a mystery, she decided to judge only by the fruits of her present labor. Her sons came home with report cards trending in the right direction; Troy said it had been nearly a month since Evan suffered one of his terrors. The boys were clean and her house was clean and she gave thanks daily to the Lord for sending her the girl, what a difference she had made. And Mae was in no position to cast the first stone, given her own checkered past and the past of the only man she ever loved. In the end, she decided there wasn't much Edie could have done that would have changed her mind anyhow. She decided, as Troy might say, to zip it.

Near Thanksgiving, on her way home from work one morning, she drove to Christ by the Sea and parked in the back lot with the engine running. Mulch piles spotted the yard; stacks of perennials leaned against the wall. Christmas carols played on her car stereo and she felt a deep pride in what Edie had already accomplished — a line of budding trees ran the length of the church and around them were small, white garden stones. But the true testament to the girl's labor was the low-lying wall silhouetting the hill. For now the wall rose only a foot or so high, but piled before it were concrete throw-aways of various shapes and sizes: square slabs that were cleaved at their corners; gray shards with rebar poking out; and broken pieces smaller than a case of beer. Back-breaking work, the way Edie had scavenged these from neighbors' yards, industrial sites, and Kevin Boyd Excavating out on 769. There were damaged bricks too, and rinds of asphalt, but Mae saw it all suddenly brought to fruition — how the wall would provide an aesthetic defense against the new development, how it might buffer some of the noise. Edie wanted biblical flora planted in the yard, the entire enterprise founded in Scripture, and the wall that would be built from recycled refuse and debris was part of this: the stones that the builder rejected. She fished a napkin from her glove compartment.

She saw clearly the Lord's hand in all of it. How he guided Edie to them. Now the garden would flourish and her work would carve out a place in the community: a garden for spring coffee hours, a tranquil place to spend time in prayer and contemplation. And how much it weighed upon Edie's future here—it would cause her to be recognized. It would pull her out of her shell and cause her to put down roots.

She blew her nose, surprised at how much she'd already fallen for the girl—like one of her own blood.

AT HOME, she found the house dark. She set her purse on the kitchen counter and continued toward the back. One light shone from behind the half-open bathroom door. She called out for the girl and heard no answer. She called out again, rapping her knuckles on the door and heard distinctly the sound of weeping from within.

Edie sat cross-legged on the floor amidst piles of her own hair. Clippers hung limp from one hand, dangling by their cord. The scissors in her other hand were still. All around her clusters of peroxide hair floated like pollen. Her head was shaved; two dark patches ran behind each ear and a thin line of blood ran down her scalp, turning the shaving cream residue an off-pink.

I'm making a mess, Edie wept.

The bathroom was ungodly warm. The shower heater was on and it lit the room like the nocturnal house at the zoo, faintly orange and predatory. The heater buzzed, ticking off the minutes. Mae ran a razor blade beneath the faucet and cleaned up patches of hair Edie had missed. Before long the girl's scalp was smooth and pink as a chicken neck. She stretched the skin to pull it taut and snip the last stubborn whiskers—the patches soft as down. She wrapped the girl's head up in a towel and dried her with it, drying between her ears and around her eyes. When she removed the towel there were no more tears, only the whiteness of her scalp stark against her sunburned brow.

The women sat at the kitchen table after, Edie warming her hands on a cup of coffee. Her scalp was spotted by where they had stuck tissue to the scratches and nicks. She said she needed a fresh start—something clean. Think of the money she would save on haircuts and shampoo.

I'm done with the person I was, she said. I want to forget that person. I want to become someone new.

She said she wasn't from Tallahassee, but California. That she had fled a bad situation there; that she had gone to college and would have graduated in December. She had no desire to speak with her parents, who she hadn't contacted in a year or more. She said she felt like she was establishing some new identity and didn't want to lose momentum by bringing up ancient shipwrecks from the watery depths of her past.

But please keep this between us, she said. No one else needs to know.

Mae agreed. Bit by bit the girl was opening up to her. She realized all she needed to do was wait for it and encourage the girl to open up a little more each time she gave a sign.

It's peaceful here, Edie said. Things are simpler—less charged with electricity. Somewhere I've always imagined myself living. A place like this.

Mae went to the freezer. She removed a pack of cigarettes from the carton there. It's peaceful now, sure. But it wasn't always like this.

She knocked the cigarette pack against the heel of her hand. She unpeeled the plastic and the foil. She said, You say this bad thing happened to you out in California? Well, Vester was the bad thing that happened to me.

Vester Carson came to her without a past and she sees now that he came to her with no certain future. This is what drew her to him. She carried her own past like a suit of armor, an unyielding and inflexible weight. But in those first heady weeks or months, in their first year, they never spoke about the past and they never planned for the future. The fantasy they both clung to—that one day they fell weightless into one another's arms—was the sustaining myth that supported their devotion.

That which he chose to reveal came to her in pieces. A childhood spent in Upper Darby, Pennsylvania; some ambiguity as to whether or not he finished high school or if one day he simply left home to join the United States Marine Corps, which must have seemed as far away as possible from the Amish country of his youth. Basic training in Fort Bragg; straightaway placed aboard a carrier and sent to the Persian Gulf until Operation Desert Shield turned into Desert Storm, became vaccinations against unnamed threats that seemed to remake his insides, became weapon-grade uranium and uranium lodged inside his bronchi, became uranium body armor he wore to protect himself against stray bullets, bullets that never seemed to come and if they did, were so far off-target they seemed to be fired randomly or by chance.

More murkiness after: a reprimand or a self-inflicted discharge. Either way, he was sent back to the States.

But of mementos there were none. No pictures or souvenirs. He arrived in Arcadia wearing a flannel shirt and jeans and the wallet in his back pocket and nothing else. Living day to day, picking up odd jobs where he could.

One incident he told her about: Outside a rock concert in Asheville, North Carolina, shortly after being discharged from the Corps, he found himself with a spare ticket. While Vester worked the sidewalk, looking for a buyer, the lead singer of the band happened outside. The singer took exception to Vester's trying to scalp the ticket; words were exchanged. The argument escalated into a brawl. Vester was arrested but years later maintained he was calm, that he gave no thought to fighting the man until he noticed the T-shirt the singer wore, a screen-painted caricature of a U.S. soldier pissing on the American flag.

Once the boys were born, Veteran's Day and Memorial Day were kept as holidays in their household, attending parades and making the celebrations into day-long affairs, which is how it should be, she supposes — most people give no thought to veterans or what they're owed. He taught Troy to salute when he was only two years old. This is something the boy still does any time he passes a serviceman in the street.

Despite this, there was a great deal wrong and it actualized in his excessive drinking. The alcoholism owed its roots to something more than addiction; the cause of his trouble seemed to be physical but hidden even from him — ailments with no cause, side effects with no source. Something that had nestled itself inside of him and occasionally, always violently, bloomed.

Nights she found him in front of their bathroom mirror, shirtless, wearing a brilliant red rash like welts across his shoulders and along the lengths of his arms. The headaches so bad he stayed in bed all day with the shades drawn and a cool rag over his head, what he described as iron rails being driven into his legs. In the end, he drank to make the pain go away; he drank to steady his hands that began to shake not long after Evan was born.

What continues to surprise her, when she lets herself consider it, which is more often than she'd like to admit, is how long it took for her to understand the crisis of their relationship, how long it took for her to comprehend the terror she allowed into her home, the menace she trusted her children to. She thinks the realization should have come hard and fast, a sudden and irreversible change of heart, but instead it was misery poured slowly over ice, across a number of years, weighing the good days against the bad until the bad days were all they shared. Until she left her boys in his care one night and he abandoned them in a bar—until he abandoned all of them for good.

Even now, the memories soothe the bad patches. She reminds herself what it was truly like those last few years. She reminds herself too of what was planted in him, the pharmaceuticals he ingested under orders, the drugs meant to protect him, yet short-sighted in their aim. No one knew what might one day happen to those who served. Least of all, her. She had only to live with the results, to try and raise her boys under the manifestations of the desert sickness borne back with him across the ocean, the desert-blooming virus he'd carry to the end of his days.

They have heard from him twice since he left:

The first time he was in North Carolina.

It was him for certain, John Whitney said. The sheriff had gone up to Yanceyville to see what he could learn from their penitentiary labor force, to install something similar in Arcadia. Whitney sat at Mae's kitchen table, not tasting but inhaling the steam rising from his coffee cup. Mae fought the urge to lay her head down on the table and weep for everything she had lost.

He was picking up trash alongside the highway, the sheriff allowed. Which is a technological innovation in my mind—trash that collects itself.

What was he in for? she asked.

It's a funny story once you get over the sadness of it. Whitney fished for his pack of cigarettes, caught in the front pocket of his uniform. According to the warden, he beat up some old crow in an apartment complex. This woman was old, understand. A senior citizen. Vester was driving through the complex one morning, driving too fast to see this family of geese crossing the road.

Mae slid the butter across the table and the sheriff took time slathering his toast and licking the knife clean. He kept his cigarette balanced between his fingers.

He said, Vester wound up hitting one of them geese, killing it with his car. But he had the decency to stop when it happened, and to get out of the car to see what might be done. Well this old woman was right there, saw the whole thing. She was bent on feeding them geese like she probably did every morning. She starts giving Vester a hard time, slapping him on his back and on his arms, talking about the geese like they was family. Saying he killed her children. According to Vester all he did was push on her a little bit, just to get her off him. But he ended up knocking her down, and she rolled down a hill and broke both wrists and her hip.

That temper, Mae said. I always told him.

A resident witnessed the event and wrote down Vester's license plate. I suppose it should be noted that he stopped for the dead goose, but let the old woman lie there at the bottom of the hill. Vester was on probation, of course. So he went back to the slammer.

She told the sheriff, We ain't getting checks from him or nothing.

The last time she saw Vester she heard him before she saw him sledging through the pond outside the house. She was watching TV when she heard shouting and went to the window and saw her husband waist-deep in water, waving his arms as if some airborne menace might swoop down to pluck him out of the mud. Although she had been advised, Mae had not changed her place of residence—had refused to talk about it. When she saw Vester out in the pond she held her youngest son up to the window and said, That is your father. I want you to remember him just like this. He's soaking wet.

Vester was shouting nonsense. Words like *disgrace* and on and on about being only half-human now, a medical accident. Words that meant nothing. He tore off his T-shirt and whirled it through the air. He yelled about being cheated and when he lost the shirt finally he submerged and came up sputtering. He shouted, I'm a mutant. Mae remembers this. She didn't know what the word meant. She had to look it up in a dictionary later. He kept hollering, Mutant.

She might have rushed outside, flung open the doors and dragged him from the pond and laid him out across her bed; undressed him, cleaned him, spoke soothing words to him until he sobered. Or she might have done what she did in fact choose to do: draw the curtains, lock the doors, and phone the police.

She waited on the couch and her boys sat beside her until they heard the sirens screaming up the drive and they saw the headlights pull into her yard. But she did not move; she would not stand witness. Through the drawn curtains the spotlights changed the color of the living room. She listened to car doors slam and to the police yelling for Vester to come out of the pond. When he refused, cursing them, she heard men enter the water and drag him back to dry land. Whitney came to the door soon after, to make sure they were all right; angry and wet up to his shoulders, pissed-off at how his night was spoiled.

And then Vester was gone. They have not seen or heard from him since. Whitney said he released him a few days later. He escorted him personally to the county line. Mae has not bothered to go to court for a restraining order; she knows she will not see her husband again. Evan has not spoken since that night when he saw his father floundering in the dark water outside their home, and when she is honest with herself she cannot shake the feeling that his terrors and his silence were provoked by the prevailing image from that night—his raving father. She wonders if she should have spared her children the sight of that. She does not want their last memory of him to be the one of him raging and sick but she wanted that image of him to be burned upon their consciousness — she wanted them to carry the memory forward like a brand. So that when she is gone, when she has finally gone home to be with Jesus, and they ask each other why they never heard from their father again, or why they only carry vague memories of him from their childhoods, they will remember the image, although perhaps they will not know whether it is from a memory or from a dream. Maybe then they will forgive her for the severance she caused, and if not forgive her then maybe at least they will understand. She doesn't let herself hope for more.

She tells Edie all of this, sitting on the back porch late into evening. Mae cannot see the girl's face but she is like an aesthete with her bald head and an afghan pulled to her chin, hovering there, flickering between the shadows and the dancing stars. Her own voice drips like candle wax across the water.

He was so violent, she says. And his mood swings were so brutish. A hundred percent man. I thought that I could soften him, or cool those things that seemed to set him off. The most insignificant things sometimes.

I don't understand why you let him run all over you, Edie says. Or why he was allowed so many chances.

You talk about putting down roots, Mae says. Plants have roots, plants and trees. My sisters and I were succulents—rootless. Always changing schools. So that even now I don't know how much learning we missed. We'd be on the verge of studying grammar at one school and then move somewhere else where they had just finished grammar. So we never learned. And we never thought about the reasons why. Our mother made a game of it. We never thought of it as strange. Looking back, I don't know if we got evicted from those places or if my father was in some kind of trouble.

She says, I'm not one to make excuses. And I don't think it's healthy to blame your past for all of your present troubles. But it was particularly hard on me, all the moving around, because of my weight. For a fat girl like me—and I was fat even back then—my only chance was to ride out all the snide remarks and the meanness until the other kids got bored. But we never lived anywhere long enough.

I don't say this to gain your sympathy, and there's no way for you to know what it's like. You can reason all you like about beauty being skin-deep: that's the depth that matters most. Especially growing up.

Not that having friends helped my self-esteem. Having friends created a whole host of problems. A girlfriend would invite me down to the beach. Most girls don't think about it twice—just put on your bathing suit and head out to the water. But for me there were considerations. That I wore a one-piece bathing suit goes without saying; I've never owned a bikini. But do I wear a T-shirt, too? Would it hide anything? It may only draw attention. Or you see young girls sometimes, heavy girls like I was, wearing a two-piece. And I can't think of anything more pathetic or shameful than hearing complete strangers whisper to one another how much they admire the girl's confidence. Good for her, they'll say, as if wearing a bikini is a victory for fat girls everywhere. It makes me sick. And the same logic applied in the shower, in locker rooms or at camp—a whole host of problems.

I did manage to go to the same school for most of fifth grade.

It was a privilege for the fifth graders, who were the oldest in the building, to go away to camp for one week during the school year. The entire class together. The girls had their cabins, the boys had theirs.

I was assigned to a cabin with the clique of popular girls—some sick psychiatric experiment by the school counselor. Maybe she thought it would give me the chance to show the girls I was just as cool as they were, even if I outweighed them by a hundred pounds.

We would wake up to reveille and trudge down to breakfast. One morning we saw someone's underwear run up the flagpole. Word spread they belonged to one of the boys. I don't remember his name. The counselors stole his underwear and ran them up the flagpole. The kids thought it was pretty funny, but I remember being glad they weren't mine. I slept with my underwear beneath my pillow for the rest of the week.

Some girls got homesick. But not me. Anywhere was better than home—at least at camp I had my own bed. And that was the first time I started thinking I could one day leave home, that maybe my situation wasn't forever. That some day I wouldn't have to shuttle around so much, that I could live in one place without all the craziness.

I'd brought a box of tarot cards and before lights out I'd read the girls' fortunes. The women in my family always read tarot cards around the dinner table. It was just something I knew how to do. Now of course I know it's the work of the devil, and I haven't touched those sinful things in years. I still remember the major and minor Arcana—you can't always help what you remember. Some of the girls were scared of the cards, pictures of skeletons or whatnot, even though I left out all the bad news and told them only the good. And wouldn't you know it, the popular girls were more interested than anyone.

On the last night, as we were getting ready for bed, one of the girls told me to keep my clothes on, to just pretend like I was going to sleep. So I got under the covers all excited, happy to be part of their secret. Maybe I let myself believe the school counselor was right, that all the girls needed was to spend a little time with me to realize I was no different from them on the inside. Once our chaperone was gone, we climbed out of our bunks. One of the girls held a flashlight underneath her chin so her face lit up like a Halloween skull. She said, The time has come for you to join our sacred ritual. We belong to a girl tribe whose rites and membership are older than America. The time has come for you to be initiated. Well, it seemed my dreams were coming true. It was beyond my wildest hopes. But I kept cool. I told them, I would like very much to be a member of your girl tribe. And then we all filed out the cabin door.

The moon was out. In the other cabins, our classmates slept. We were doing what most people only talked about doing.

We followed a trail into the woods. Along the trail were monkey bars or tires and two-by-fours set against each other at strange angles—a fitness trail. We were hidden from the moon. Every sound made us jump. I thought about what our teacher had said the night before, on a nighttime walk. There's nothing to fear out here but man. Other kids seemed to take comfort in that, but for me, if there was one thing I feared, it was man. Rapists. Murderers. Saying there was nothing to fear but man only proved my point. But we plunged on, deeper into the woods, until we reached the fire pit where we held nightly sing-alongs and the teachers told stories about Indians. The ashes still smoldered from that night's fire. We took our places around the circle. The leader of the girls, her name was Trina. She touched my arm and took me into the center. She brought out a bandana and draped it over my eyes. She knotted it like a blindfold, saying, No matter what happens, all of us have gone through this before.

I couldn't see nothing. I felt fingers on the buttons of my shirt. On my jeans. Trina said, You must enter the girl tribe the way you entered the world. When I was standing in my underwear they told me to take those off, too. Whenever I reached for the blindfold they slapped my hands away. Trina said, We promise not to laugh. And that was the right thing to say — laughter was the one thing I'd been afraid of all along. So I took off my underwear and stood in the middle of the circle wearing only what God gave me. I didn't hear one person laugh. But someone started to hum, sort of, and I can hear the melody even now, drifting hmm-hm, hm-hmmm back and forth between two notes. So primal and yet magical at the same time. I felt something thin and hard against my skin. Trina said, It is now our duty to give you tribal tattoos. All of us were given tattoos once. We now give you yours. The girls passed a marker back and forth and they drew designs on my stomach and on my legs and on my feet. My face. They kept up the humming and Trina said, We anoint you Starborn. Someone told me to march and I put one foot forward and someone else took my hand and we all began running together, away from the fire pit toward the woods.

I still wore the blindfold. I could hear the other girls running beside me. I could hear the way they breathed through their noses. I felt the lawn become wood chips along the path. I felt us moving uphill. All the while, the girls were saying things like, Almost there and Don't give up. Trina was close by. She said, We run to channel the woodland spirit, the wild-woman spirit in all of us. Someone else said, Don't worry about your clothes, I have them.

All at once the girls were quiet and we stood absolutely still. They led me by the hand and I knew we were in the courtyard between the cabins. I was worried about someone seeing us. Hands began spinning me around until I was dizzy. They backed me up against something cool and metal and I felt my hands being stretched behind my back and then someone tied rope around my wrists. For you to be initiated in the girl tribe, said Trina, you must die and be reborn. We are tying you here so that you can die. You must be silent. Don't say a word until we untie you. Then you will be Starborn.

I couldn't move. There was a long moment when I felt the breeze across my legs and I could smell that muddy grass, that smell of trampled grass that smells like the underbelly of the earth. And then, just as clear, I heard the sound of sixteen footsteps running away.

My hands went numb. My wrists burned. I stood there hoping this was still part of the ritual—that any minute Trina would untie my hands and tell me that I had been reborn. Flies landed on my skin. My heels sunk into the mud.

I stood there all night.

Maybe I slept.

The next thing I heard was a hundred voices. My classmates woke up that morning, put on their shoes, slogged to breakfast, and found me on their way to mess hall—I don't know how long I stood there. Hours. And the only thing I thought was that I had pubic hair and no one else did. I prayed they wouldn't make fun of me for that. I stood there enduring the jeers and the mean words and all the mean things kids say. Until a teacher—it was the school counselor, come to think of it, she was there—untied me and threw her coat over me and sent the other kids along to breakfast. The counselor walked with me back to my cabin and waited for me to dress. When I took off the coat I saw that instead of tribal tattoos, the girls had circled every pocket of flab on my body—along my wrist and between my thighs. Over my belly. On my elbows. Circles and arrows. Nasty words written. I couldn't even look at the counselor. I just wanted to get dressed and go to breakfast and be a normal kid.

In the cafeteria, all the seats were taken at the popular-girl table. But I paused there and said to Trina, I did it. I stood out there all night. She looked at me, and I can still remember that look. She said, What do you want? A gold star? And all the girls burst into laughter. But the thing was, until that very moment, I had thought it was all part of their initiation. Everything, from the nakedness to the markers to the tying me up for everyone to see, I thought it was all an actual rite of their sacred girl tribe. That in the end, I'd be popular too. I never questioned it—not until I saw their faces and heard the hatred behind their laughter, hating me for no reason I could ever understand.

SOMETHING LIVING laps across the surface of the pond. She can feel Edie watching her. She is nervous but also relieved to have told the story.

She says, Maybe that sounds crazy. But that's why I let him hang around—if you'd ever truly loved someone you would know.

I have loved someone, Edie says.

When was the last time you spoke to your parents?

Two years. Longer.

If you had ever really been in love, Mae says, if you had ever truly loved someone, you would call them right this instant and let them know you're alive.

Edie leans her head back. If I haven't ever loved, I've spent a whole lot of time and energy on nothing.

Mae stands. She reaches up with both arms to stretch. Why do I let him come back? It's because I look at those boys, all of our soldiers heading overseas, and I see Vester in every last one. Vester is a lot of things, but he is a hero for serving his country. For defending those poor Kuwaitis when they couldn't defend themselves. And after that, something changed inside of him. Something even he don't understand. Something in his brain or in his body. The doctors don't know. He don't know. The Bible says we aren't given nothing more than we can handle. I truly believe that. So, I can handle Vester. I can handle raising two boys on my own, with your help now especially. I just wish that God, if He's designed it this way, would make it a little easier sometimes. That's all. I just wish He'd ease up, just a little bit, every once in a while.

TWO

As a child Edie resisted sleep and fled from her parents who called her to it. Their pronouncing bedtime sent her tearing through the house to hide in closets or below the stairs; or into the yard where she would wait until her father emerged from the sliding glass door and let the flashlight he carried drive each shadow from the yard until, inevitably it seemed, no matter where she hid, the light would find her. Then he would carry her back inside, she wailing and squirming and struggling against his strength, against the nightly routine of washing and undressing and finally being forced between the sheets. It was being sent to bed with no alternative; it was the seemingly arbitrary ending to the night brought upon by the mindless clock. She was too young then to make decisions on her own and that is why she struggled — it should have been of her own choosing.

And so she imagines her life as a story told to her by a distant relative, as if it were someone else's life, and not her own, being disclosed. She feels no ownership of her past. What might be called her history might also have been experienced by a stranger, so little thought she remembers giving to its doing and so little has she examined the results. The results add up to nothing; they point toward a living purgatory, a sloshing existence where if she could gather the many aspects of her life and, matching one jagged edge to another, fit them together like broken glass, might understand its full scope—she might do something of her own choosing. But she doubts her life has been anything but reaction to outside forces. That is why it feels as though nothing belongs to her. That is why she feels her life might have gone any direction and it just so happened to go the way it did.

Her shaved head is part of this lack of ownership. She loves the way it feels to run her hand over bare skin where there should be hair, the way her nerve endings tingle in their own complicated nexus, all over her scalp, whenever she wears a baseball cap, which she does each day to keep her head from getting sunburned. She can feel the way her skin clings to her skull. She is pleasantly surprised each time she catches her reflection in a window or mirror. From strawberry-blonde to red, to peroxide blonde to no hair at all. Though meager, it is and has always been the one aspect of her life over which she has complete control.

She keeps to her routine. She wakes at five-thirty to pack brownbag lunches and walk her charges to the bus stop, where the school bus turns onto their road and stops and exhales and then swallows the boys with a snap of its folded doors. And then the boys are gone. Not bothering to shower, she is at the church by seven-thirty, biking the four miles in her ragged T-shirt and overalls or in her hiking shorts flecked with paint and the deeper, impossible-to-remove stains of gravel and sand and red clay. Cars pass by the church and the cars honk their horns and she feels that the finished landscape will signify in some archaic but present and meaningful way her validation in the community, her acceptance as one of Arcadia's own.

Sometimes she passes Mae on her way to work the graveyard shift. Most often, not. Home again, Edie showers and changes her clothes and then walks to the end of the driveway to wait again for the school bus; to wait for the children it carries; the children who are not hers but who seem to become hers more and more each day. Homework at the kitchen table, the boys immersed in study while she cooks, explaining long division between the simmering pots or describing for them fossilization, remembering out loud her college lectures, her small voice echoing in the broiler. After dinner, they watch one hour of television. Then bed.

The boys do not fight her on this point, not like she did as a child, and it is not long before she also tries to sleep, her muscles worn but growing more powerful than they've ever been, her skin warm and taut from the sun. She does not resist sleep now that she's older and would instead plunge headlong into its depths. But now, sleep resists her. It does not struggle, as she did against it so long ago. Its elusions are wilier and quick, a slippery something just beyond her reach that finally surrenders as daylight breaks, leaving her a few brief hours before returning to the metered pace of the day.

The women see one another on Saturdays and this is when Mae recalls the platitudes of her week. Edie forces herself to do the same and finds it's easier if she focuses on the boys, or the banality of her labor at the church—the zoning permits and so forth, or how the pastor, offering assistance one afternoon, hadn't known how to turn on the outside spigot. She chooses things that will make the woman laugh; she keeps a running list in her head so that she has something to share on these Saturday mornings when they break down one another's week as if to understand their own better. As if to comprehend the fullness of the roles they play in one another's lives. At night, with the boys asleep, with the house and the acres of swampland to herself, Edie stands on the back porch overlooking the pond and sees the premonition of movement in the water, not something that might bubble forth or skitter across the break but something drowning beneath the scum-covered surface. This is not her life—no aspect of it belongs to her. She longs for something familiar. She does not belong to the mild temperatures, the palmetto bugs, the meaningless events she recites over coffee cake and chocolate milk and the cigarettes, beneath the ever-present, nicotine-tinged haze on Saturday mornings.

She considers the last few years wasted. She no longer believes in goodness. The churchgoers she's met take for granted the inherent goodness of every living thing. She believes this is a fatal weakness. She feels herself recoil from their congregational embrace; each time Mae puts her arm around her, she shudders. She wants to destroy this goodness, whatever it is. She can't see what their intentions are or what they hope to gain by their kindness.

And the god they worship, so like her parents' god, spewing fire and ash. The deafening worship and its breakneck pace, as if the parishioners fear silence or cling to primitive superstitions and would clatter pots and pans to ward off evil. And every Sunday the tambourine — she can hardly stand the sound of Mae's tambourine or the entire magisterial clattering of her person, like a gypsy cart on a rock-strewn road. Her perspiration, her wobbling embrace, the moisture on her upper lip — and her granting every coincidence the weight of God's providential hand. Edie wonders if it's providence the way her employer collapses in her chair each night, leaving a cigarette burning in the dish; alone but for the television's blue light. Where in that tableau might be found a benevolent, merciful god? Where, Providence?

ALREADY THE HARVEST festival has passed. The town is swept along by a quick succession of holidays. Poinsettias and garland replace pumpkins and gourds: the suggestion of lonely autumn, a certain melancholy. She feels this even here, where no leaves cover the ground and there is no wind to strip the trees and no boxes of winter clothes to drag up from basements — there aren't any basements. And yet she notices all around her, despite the sun-drenched days, a ritualistic adherence to the changing seasons, when a note of cool air blows down from the north, slipping perhaps from a suitcase carried by a retiree, of which several thousand seem to one day appear, tripling Arcadia's population, to hang Christmas lights from eaves and street lamps; to play carols on radios in every store; to carry on with the rituals of Holiday; rituals still upheld in northern cities but that here somehow lose their frame of reference; no one bothers to close their swimming pool and the weather each afternoon is exactly the same as the last—blue skies with a slight breeze. Where Edie grew up, the birds clear out this time of year, the skies suddenly muted. Here the birds arrive to perch and preen above intersections clogged with Cadillacs, or outside restaurants crowded with blue hair and bridge lingo and the faint odor of baby powder everywhere about the place. Arcadia's livelihood depends on this migration, but at what cost, she wonders. The character of the town changes completely. She watches these newcomers, wrapped against the elements in their windbreakers and parkas although the temperature has not dipped below seventy degrees. She believes they are waiting for something, just as her own generation waits in bus corrals or subway platforms—a generation raised to wait in line at music venues, sitting on the sidewalk, on the ground waiting like birds before a storm; a generation raised to wait in traffic jams or elevators and so waits for everything else— for some notion of what to do with their lives. But she sees for the first time how they all wait for the same thing, an interlude that spans generations. Whether in the waiting room at the obstetrician or in the workplace waiting for the coffee pot to brew; whether waiting for their partner to preemptive bid or waiting for their lover to call; whether waiting for grandchildren or waiting on children until their career is settled, they are waiting to be lifted from their steadfast routine: the mind-numbing banality of living. Death, at last, as a reprieve from sultry October days, from the outpouring sun in November, from clear skies and calm seas that stretch on ad infinitum like rows of royal palms lining the flat, sea-town boulevards, this premeditated and still somehow thoughtless coastal expanse.

She divides her time between home and church. In the churchyard she leans against the fence and the stakes it wraps around that have been hammered into the mud. She stands in the shadow of the new development, halfway impressed at the speed in which these mansions are built. A new one sprouts each day.

It's what people have come to expect. Pastor Reginald Dancer joins her in the yard one morning. Homes built by assembly line and dropped on indistinguishable streets. Everyone feels entitled to such a home and seeks the same familiar, homogenous qualities everywhere. This is the American Dream: The Home Depot. McDonald's. Starbucks. Like snails who carry with them all the conveniences of home—everyone affluent and vaguely vanilla.

It gives people comfort, she offers. The idea of blending in with the crowd.

One shouldn't stand out too much, Dancer grins. That's what they always told me. But I never did a very good job of blending in. I believe that progress is one thing. Progress as new construction, as new technology, as peace. But progress without morals, without conscience, isn't progress at all.

It's heartless.

It's perversion, but it may be the future.

Edie and the pastor often talk like this. She is glad for someone to talk to about these things, someone whose cynicism is only romanticism thinly veiled. Their conversations meander and then he takes his leave, retreating to his office or driving out into the far reaches of DeSoto County to drop in on the house-bound and the sick.

Each afternoon, when the construction crew breaks for lunch, she crosses the orange fence line and trolls the subdivision, alone among the wide thoroughfares and the narrow back alleys. She has begun to stockpile equipment, mindlessly at first, and then with more purpose. A pair of pliers she found lying on the ground, a bundle of electrical cord. More and more daring each time. She swiped nearly three hundred yards of PVC piping; she crept into the trailer office and stole the telephone. She keeps these things hidden with her landscaping supplies, in the storage shed at the church. She does not worry about being discovered, just as she did not worry about the Balinese finding her bumper stickers tucked in the pockets of their winter coats in the house they shared on Hazel Street, long ago in California.

Their winter coats — she wonders what happened to them. Who came to clean them out. Whether his parents drove up from Sacramento to claim his things. Whether they gave the coats to Goodwill and whether a junkie somewhere on Market Street is wearing the camelhair coat she always pictures him in, when she allows herself to think of the Balinese, which she does not allow herself to do very much.

She sees herself tuning up some great, stringed instrument to play the same sad song again. She feeds a litter of stray cats behind a restaurant and she wonders at the litters they fed in Berkeley and whether they now go hungry. If they sometimes hunker down below the dumpster and wait for the headlights on the Pontiac he always drove; whether they wait for him to appear, whether they fall asleep waiting, and wake in the morning to find another night has passed and the Balinese has not come. She wonders if cats hope, and if they've given up the hope of ever seeing him again by now.

EDIE COMES HOME on Saturday afternoon to find the family in the kitchen. There is newspaper spread over the tabletop and the boys lay damp towels across the printed pages. Mae slides two pans out of the oven. The aroma of baked goods, cinnamon and molasses; Mae lays the baking sheets across the towels and the baking sheets display square gingerbread walls with cutout windows and gingerbread awnings and panels of triangular roofs. Piled on the table and the countertops are packages of gumdrops and marzipan, wafers and cinnamon star cookies.

Troy mixes a bowl of icing, holding the bowl in the crook of his arm like cranking a worm gear. He asks her, What do you want for Christmas?

A pile of cardboard cutouts sits off to the side and she thumbs through the stencils, assembling the architecture in her mind. The house will have a certain modern edge, with a long roof sloping severely toward the ground. She doesn't know the last time someone asked what she wanted for Christmas—she and the Balinese ignored the holidays mostly.

She says brightly, World peace?

Come on, Edie. The boy shakes his head.

Whirled peas? Mae trims a doughy edge with an Exacto knife and flicks away the thin excess. That's a strange thing to ask for.

Don't forget the skylight, Troy says.

Edie snips the corners from the candy bags, dropping a marshmallow into her mouth and letting Evan see her do it. The boy smiles, nothing else. She says, We always decorated first where I grew up.

Then we'll decorate first, Mae says. She drops spoonfuls of icing into separate bowls and mixes in each a different color dye.

She says, I think you'll really like how our church celebrates Christmas.

The Celebration Christmas Tree, Troy says.

Like a pageant? Edie asks. She is flattening the pastry bags before Mae fills them.

Mae explains that people come from all over to see it, that the

Celebration Christmas Tree is a tradition with their church and has been for years.

Although this year will be different, she says. Sheila Thomas broke both of her legs last week, falling off that pedigree horse of hers.

Edie learns the Celebration Christmas Tree is a set piece that consumes the church altar, rising up to the ceiling. Choir members fill in along the rows, their pale faces scattered like popcorn strings across the boughs. The crest of the tree has been occupied by Sheila Thomas for the past several advents. She is small and spry for her age and weighs nothing at all. This seems to be the only prerequisite for occupying what they've taken to calling the Star of Bethlehem position, front and center, top of the tree.

Mae squeezes perfect green trim along one of the gingerbread windows. Alan mentioned your name as a replacement.

Edie recalls Alan as the music director, although they have not exchanged more than three words. She immediately sounds retreat.

But why not? Mae grins. I've heard you sing. You've got a nice little voice.

Troy is laying dollops of icing across the V-shaped roof. Evan fills in behind him with lengths of red licorice. She knows they want her to do this thing but all she can think is that she should have left weeks ago. It is terrible of her, and so she says nothing out of fear for how the family might react. She doesn't want them to feel abandoned again, especially the boys, and especially since she has not firmly settled the matter for herself. On the one hand, she could spend the rest of her life in this place and no one would find her. But she has never been part of a family that hasn't, in the end, let her down.

I think my days of scaling heights are long over, she says.

What heights? Mae says. You'll be twenty feet off the ground.

But when you've fallen sixty feet, she thinks, twenty is plenty high enough.

THE RUMOR about Sheila Thomas is printed beneath the prayer requests in this week's bulletin. It confirms the story about the horse and that the pinnacle of the Celebration Christmas Tree — the Star of Bethlehem position — is vacant. The Celebration Christmas Tree, Edie believes, is closer to three-stories high — thirty feet — than to two. Its wooden skeleton tapers steeply on both sides and its scaffolding supports eight levels of two-by-fours on which the choir members stand. There are twelve carolers on the lowest rung and two upon the second-from-the-top; the choir members lean against synthetic rails of evergreen for balance. When they sing, their bodies disappear against the dark backdrop so the effect is of a giant evergreen housing tens of beaming faces which bellow out great hymns and deafening carols. There are lights nestled within the branches that can be set for various colors and patterns and these lights flash, run or blink on cue. It is altogether impressive, reverent, entertaining and terrifying.

After the service, Edie is cornered by the music director. Alan thanks her profusely for offering to step in. She watches the hairs above his mouth bounce like tinsel and feels not fear or stage fright but that she should have expected this all along and been more adamant from the start. She has not said yes, but here she stands listening to him describe the Christmas Eve service and how this year will be the grandest yet — she has not said yes and she sees just as clearly that she can't say no. She nods and smiles and even manages to generate some enthusiasm, remembering to thank him graciously for including her, acting flattered to be offered the Star of Bethlehem position in the largest festival of the year. Alan mentions, in a conspiring whisper, the very real possibility of this being the last pageant at Christ by the Sea, that come this time next year the church and its remaining property might be the newest addition to Windfall Estates.

And then Alan is handing her a rehearsal schedule and leading her around back of the scaffolding and pointing out for her the ladder she will climb and the tiny space allotted for her feet up there, behind the rail. He laughs and says he admires her courage. He asks would she like to give it a try. She puts one hand on the bottom rung and immediately her old injuries flare across her back and shoulders, a feeling like too much liquor searing the inside of her gut. She puts one hand and then the other on the ladder and pulls herself forward, dragging her feet behind, ascending. At the top, she wedges herself between the branches and the rail, enough space for her to stand with her legs together and her feet slightly turned out. She lifts her arm and puts the flat of her hand on the popcorn ceiling. She thinks about asbestos and removes her hand. Far down below she sees the empty rows of chairs where Mae stands at the lip of the stage, shading her eyes to gaze skyward. Edie feels very distant. She feels volunteered by proxy. Now would be a good time to run—now before she finds herself caring for these people. But the thought is meaningless, just as this time of year is void of meaning in a place where the leaves don't fall and winter never really comes although everyone waits for it, waiting for the weather to catch up to the calendar that marches defiantly on. Waiting for a change in season and when it doesn't come, going through the motions anyway. Edie knows she is part of this family now, irrevocably part of it.

DECEMBER. Now is the time to go—when the boys are home from school and Mae has time to find someone to replace her. She goes to choir practice and stands with the altos; the altos complain about their monotonous harmony. She sings, and as she sings she thinks about the Florida Keys and their proximity to even warmer climes, how in that place there might be someone willing to take her on a boat somewhere—she is thinking of deporting herself.

The choir gathers around the piano. Edie is the youngest by twenty years. She does not feel at all compared to Sheila Thomas, whoever she is. She stands at the edge of the baby grand and rests her music on it. This way, she can watch the other choir members sing. People are never more beautiful to her than when they are singing. There is something about the voice that portrays the true essence of a person—she can see it in their faces when they open their mouths and produce sound. Earnest and concentrated: how they never get to be during the day. She is thinking mostly of men, but women carry it too—it is only that women are slightly more refined perhaps, or show emotion more naturally. The change is not as dramatic for women, unlike the men, the husky basses booming out the low notes or the tenors struggling to support the upper echelons with breath.

She looks forward to their practices, but Alan is quick to correct her: choirs rehearse. Caught up in the center of their sound, adding to it her own strained efforts, is the only time she feels as though she is the watcher and not the observed, the spied-upon, the criminal. That no one is waiting for her, after all. That she is as far from home as she can possibly be and still find herself in America, and aren't criminals always apprehended when they finally go home? She has no home—no home but the very place she happens to find herself in.

ANOTHER WEEK passes. The weather finally turns and choir members admit with some shame that already they've turned on their heat. They say it's surprising how quickly one acclimates to the climate in Florida, that where they came from, be it Wisconsin or Ohio, they held out until the last possible moment each winter. They attribute it to the certain knowledge that winter—if they can really call it that, nothing like the winter of '77 for example if you were living in Pennsylvania at the time—will come and then quickly pass. How much you're willing to tolerate the cold is directly related to how long you anticipate the cold will last.

By that rationale, and they say this quieter, on break, out of earshot from Alan or other members of the Church Council, this year's pageant should be the most glorious yet. Because no one knows for sure if there will ever be another. Precisely because they don't know how many more pageants there will be, they will remind themselves to savor it—to somehow both celebrate and mourn its passing.

At night, Edie sleeps with her window open, letting the smell of the cool air carry her north. There, Lake Erie would already be starting to freeze—it's hard for her to imagine now that anywhere people suffer temperatures worse than an air-conditioned chill. She did not think of home so much when she lived in California, but increasingly home is all she thinks about—she misses the seasons.

She wonders at the assurance Troy and Evan must draw from waking up with one another each day—waking up across from the only other person in the world on whom they can rely. She wakes each morning with only herself, who is nothing if not unreliable.

EDIE FOLLOWS her routine more carefully than before. The only variation is the care she takes in her appearance, cleaning her cuticles and scrubbing herself clean each night before rehearsing for the Celebration Christmas Tree. She is close to leaving; she can feel the wanderlust like warmth in her body and limbs. She is surprised to find that when she thinks of flight, she sees Evan and Troy and knows how hard it will be to separate herself from them, how much she's come to care for them. After rehearsal she hurries home before they fall asleep—Troy is old enough to watch Evan for the few hours each week she is away. And if at first she had been thankful that Mae's home was a place where she could recover her strength, against her will she feels herself putting down roots, or sees her own wiry roots becoming entangled with the deeper, stronger and more complicated roots of the Carson home.

She is also afraid; she who up until now has been defined by no one else. Her own self whom she imagined as the glass inside a picture frame, without fingerprints or smears and unmuddied by the complications of others, now tangled and twisted and defined only by its contribution to some greater whole.

This fear is directly linked to the breathlessness she feels staring up at the Celebration Christmas Tree. Ascending the ladder to the crow's nest, she worries that the weight of the choir amassed inside the tree will topple it like a fly swatter. Her white robe is several sizes too big. The gold glitter on the sleeves sparkles beneath the stage lights—the par cans and six-by-nines that are close enough for her to feel their heat. The spotlights shining back at her are the searchlights that were mounted to the beds of the government trucks, lights that created a canopy of daylight in the Oregon woods. Gazing over the empty house now it reaches up at her—the hunger and desperation and abject fear of those ten days spent in God's Valley, the terror of her ordeal. She concentrates instead on the darkness and the void that hovers hazily on the periphery of the lights but she hears a sound in the darkness that is not part of the orchestra—the sound of a shutter being pulled and then released. Someone taking pictures. Most of the house is cast in shadow but on stage Alan leans against the upright, looking pleased. The sound again—a flash—they took pictures in Oregon too, a crowd of newspapermen gathered at the base of her tree calling up to her. One spotlight sweeps over her and hovers there and she feels its heat and she feels sweat on her arms and between her shoulders. They are rehearsing the final cue and someone in the house is taking photographs. The flashes strobe first in one corner, then the next. On the platform in God's Valley she thought the sun was close enough to wrap her arms around. Here there are pictures being taken and there is a piano playing. Both spotlights on the tree, the heat of the sunlight on her face: The pageant's wonder-filled culmination where Edie Richards will light up like a Christmas tree angel — the goodwill messenger of the Lord.

AFTER THE DRESS rehearsal she sits on the fountain wall waiting for Mae to pass through the atrium. Mae appears and Edie takes one of the bags she carries, a garbage bag over-stuffed with choir robes needing repair. They walk together into the parking lot and the boys run ahead and clamber into the back seat of the car.

Mae drops the garbage bags into the trunk and then remembers something she needs; she opens the trunk again and brings with her a shopping bag. In the car, she drops the bag in Edie's lap. Edie opens the bag and shakes out several books, finding not books but catalogs — recruitment tools from colleges scattered across south Florida.

Pastor was kind enough to let us borrow these, Mae says.

She guides the car onto Roan Street. The boys seem to have lost all of their energy at once and slump in the back seat motionless, the streetlights streaming across their faces like a train passing over railroad tracks.

I've already been, Edie says.

Pastor says our church has its own scholarship to get us started. As far as the rest is concerned, I imagine we'll qualify for financial aid just about anywhere, don't you?

She doesn't smile. It's probably too late to apply for winter — we'd have to wait until spring.

Winter or spring, there's one hitch.

Edie feels both the car and the road turning as if they are caught up in some great flood. They turn end over end through the swift water. She should have left by now; she should be long gone. Now the woman is hopelessly and irreversibly invested.

I'd have to become your legal guardian, Mae says. And then you can earn your degree. Economics. Business. Pre-med. Real money.

I don't remember what school is like.

School sucks, Troy says from the back seat.

Watch that mouth, his mother warns.

Edie touches her own face and her face is hot—fevered. I can't believe you'd want me as part of your family. It's so generous. And kind.

Mae smiles into the rearview mirror. The boys have been telling me they wouldn't mind a sister.

But Edie is swept up by a tumult of water, spinning past debris, fighting against the current. She rifles through the literature: The college brochures hide as much as they reveal. They are careful to portray their campus grounds from very specific camera angles and at the most idyllic times of day. Inside, the photographs are stagey and even-handed in their cross-cultural appeal. The white male athlete, the Indian female chemist, the black ballerina, the Cuban boy whose major is still undecided—all smiling. All of them getting along fabulously within the confines of South Central Everglade Christian College, Florida International University, or the New College of Florida. When she finally speaks, she cannot filter the words, although she regrets them as soon as they've been pronounced.

I don't want a family, she says.

Only the world outside moves. The car is silent. They are sealed inside the four dented doors, carried like something fragile within the rusted machine frame. She picks up the catalogs. She flings them across the dash. Mae turns the wheel and the car swerves, the driver startled by the flutter and the snap of the pages.

Edie says, Let's say, for a lark, I wanted to go back to school. Don't you think I would have done it already? Instead of hanging around here with you?

Mae seems to test the sound of her own voice. I hate to see you going to waste.

Stop this car, she says. Do it now.

The car stops. She throws open the door but does not move to get out. I've done everything you've asked. I've gone to church every week. I've spent more time in church than I have in my entire life—I'm talking cumulative. I agreed to be the top of the Celebration Christmas Tree, and I can't even sing for Christsake.

Not in front of my boys, the woman says.

She pulls herself out of the car, leaving the mess of catalogs and course guides behind. For once, Mae, please—mind your own business. Mind your own damn life.

With her foot, she slams the door. Mae's voice through the sealed window asks, What, are you going to walk then?

But she moves to the side of the road and dismisses them with a wave of her hand. When the car drives off, Evan's face in the back window watches her recede. And then she is alone on the dark road again—alone and still.

She listens to the audience hurry inside from the outside, where a slight chill in the air suggests a season that might be Christmas. Ushers greet each guest and hand out programs and help older patrons to their seats. Edie parts the backstage curtain and peers out. There are well-dressed children and fathers in sports coats and mothers in a little number they picked up at Dillard's; there are older men wearing ties; she smells perfume and wintergreen and beneath it all a sour note of booze—she notices several faces are a little more rosy than usual. Everyone chatters happily, their bellies full, and takes one another firmly by the hand: Good cheer,

Merry Christmas. The house swells to capacity and Edie feels the ballooning of the holiday — the night filled to bursting.

Someone posted a review of the show on the wall in the wing stage left. The review appeared on the front page of the *Sun Herald* with a photograph of Alan conducting the orchestra. Edie had pulled the newspaper from the wall and scoured the picture until she was sure that she appeared nowhere in the frame. She hadn't considered newspapers. In truth she hadn't considered the audience before tonight. Of course people would come to see the show but she hadn't considered the reality of strangers filling the auditorium or the intrusiveness of their six thousand eyes upon her. The danger they would represent. The danger they represented now with no one certain to protect her — not after the way she treated Mae.

The woman had already left the house when Edie woke. She has not spoken to her since last night when she acted badly and stranded herself on the side of the road. Edie walked the entire way home to find the door unlocked and a cellophane-wrapped dinner waiting for her in the fridge. The woman's capacity to forgive sometimes overwhelms her.

The house lights dim. Darkness falls backstage and in the dark house there are feet shuffling and the rustling of winter coats being removed, the crinkle of plastic candy wrappers, the mellow-chime of cell phones powering down, the polite apologies of someone squeezing past legs to find their seat, a program folded, a child's voice asks a question and no one quite catches it — the child's mother responds and the girl is hushed. The piano strikes a bright chord and begins a trilling melody that is shortly joined by the listing drag of the snare. Then Edie is moving, trailing the choir members to their positions in the Celebration Christmas Tree. She sings and she doesn't have to think about the words as she climbs the stairs that are more ladder than stairs, to the top of the tree. She braces herself in her roost. When she looks out over the expanse, the packed house takes her breath away.

Two, maybe three thousand faces shine back at her. The carols flow one into the next and the program seems to move faster than it ever did in rehearsal—she feels slightly disconnected from the music and from the faces below, her feet splayed against the iron framework. Harmonies rise quickly like heat inside her chest, like melted butterscotch running with sonorous music. A warbling soprano on her right; the fat basses at the bottom of the tree squeezed into place and are stuck there now, arms pinned to their sides, their voices felt by the other choir members through their feet. In churches across the country these very same words are being sung and believers are filled with the same Spirit. Below her, out there, the faces of the congregation dissolve beneath a wall of sound that fissures out from the towering structure made of plastic and metal and the lights all timed and flashing.

She monitors her breath, waiting for panic to set in. And yet she feels at ease, her mind clear, her voice steady. If she feels disconnected from the service, from the music and from her hands that grip the rail, she also feels disconnected from her past. There is only her present self astride the top of a fiber-optic Christmas tree where there is no chance of falling and thousands of eyes staring up at her do not bother her at all.

A tableau enters stage right. A girl dressed as Mary and her husband, Joseph, trailing. They pantomime. The boy looks out to the audience, shielding his eyes, and the girl takes him by the hand. Perfectly on cue. Shepherds enter, carrying plastic sheep. Behind them wise men with swirling-patterned robes and ornate turbans. Children dressed as animals filter in and Mary is suddenly holding a baby doll and rocking it in her arms.

The back of the auditorium is lined with red, unblinking eyes: parents filming footage that will be played again at high school graduations, at rehearsal dinners, at retirement parties, and at random intervals throughout their children's lives, shown to a new girlfriend brought home from college, or watched alone in their children's adult lives, awed by the child they were and wistful for the simplicity of that faith. The stage falls dark and a clattering of bass keys is followed by an elongated blast from the trumpet. The music swells and Edie feels the heat of the spotlights on her face — she hears the spotlights thrum. The manger scene en mass gazes up at her; there are silver-glittered wings clipped to her robe and her place on the Celebration Christmas Tree is even higher than the cross hangs on Sunday mornings. But she leans out and reaches up so her hands nearly brush the ceiling. She spreads her arms as directed. The stage lights and their blue-amber gels shimmy along her wings. She wears a white wig that is blindingly lit. Her skin tingles with a sensation she has not felt before, as if it has been pleasantly singed to the roots. The lights reflect from the white of her robe and her silver wings but she feels as if she is the source of the light, the source of the glory. That the light generates from her, not reflected but poured out. And the sounds from the audience are the most telling worship — there is no sound at all. The angel Gabriel hovers above the crèche. The music lowers and drains into a flourishing decrescendo.

Do not be afraid, she says. I am bringing you good news of great joy for all the people.

AND THEN she is gasping for air, pressed against Mae's bosom. The woman clutches her there in the parking lot long after the service has ended. The woman weeps. When Edie frees herself, Mae's shirt is covered with glitter and fake snow and strands of white hair from the wig.

I'm so proud, Mae says. I can't help it. All around me people were asking who you were, but I held my tongue. I just knew inside my heart—that's our Edie.

Troy tugs on her finger. Was it scary being up so high?

She smiles and shakes her head. They settle into the car. They drive the back roads home.

And you were such a pretty thing, Mae says. Lit up, wig and all.

Troy says quietly, Santa's coming tonight, Evan. Did you hear me? Santa Claus.

Mae clears her throat and begins to sing a Christmas carol, urging the boys, finger wagging, to watch out and not to cry.

The boys sing back at her, and so does Edie, who rolls her window down and reaches out to cup her hand against the wind, against the resistance of the air on her palm, thinking that the calendar might say Christmas but the air says late September.

Every other house, or so it seems, is decorated for the holidays. Some light their front windows with tasteful white candles; others string blinking, colored bulbs across their gutters and entwine their potted palms. Wire-frame reindeer litter front lawns and she thinks about how far the reindeer are from home in this wet land, their hooves and thick fur useless in the sand and heat.

She sings the lyrics that describe how old St. Nick watches her when she is both sleeping and awake and decides there is something queer about Santa Claus, something nefarious she has not noticed before in the words. Something unwelcoming in an all-seeing entity who studies her most private moments and keeps a running tally of her wrongs—or rights. Slinking outside her window at night until she falls asleep—the lyrics begging her to be good while hinting at some sort of punishment too terrible to name, only to be inferred like a persistent terror that cannot be spoken of out loud.

But these are thoughts too dark for Christmas Eve. Mae pulls the car into the driveway and the path home is shrouded by the low boughs of willows on either side. They enter a patch of darkness, past the pond and the low embankment and the thick undergrowth along the property line. The car tires crunch gravel as they roll past the water, where the headlights skim the surface leaves and refract through water that is lethal and still as black ice. They have been singing together, but now Mae falls quiet. Edie carries on, turned halfway around in the seat, facing the boys. She doesn't notice the quiet or the unease falling over the driver.

The moon peers through the line of trees. There is a car in the driveway that Edie does not recognize.

Daddy, says Troy.

Vester Carson leans against the trunk of a beat-up Cadillac, looking exactly as Edie imagined him. Tight stonewashed jeans that bulge around the crotch; a worn leather jacket thrown over a work shirt faded beyond color; greasy tangles of black hair. Mae stops the car and no one moves. They just sit staring at one another through the glass, across the night air lit by the high beams.

Vester comes toward the car. He carries a small Christmas tree and grins like someone who has won a great prize.

Merry Christmas baby, he says. I couldn't let my family have no Christmas tree, could I? Could I? Get out of that car baby and give your honey bear a kiss.

THREE

Vester drags the Christmas tree behind him like it's some thing he's killed. Edie follows in his wake, drifting in the smell of Old Spice and cigarette smoke and the tree-sap smell of his leather jacket. In the living room, he props his dwarf tree against the wall, beside the Christmas tree that already stands decorated in the front window, the tree that she eventually felt sorry for and purchased even though it was scraggly in places and had a large hole on one side, its trunk bent like a bow. She watches Vester Carson remove his jacket and sling it across the sofa: the carelessness of a man returning to claim what he rightfully owns.

The boys play in the living room while the three adults congregate at the kitchen table. Vester sits with hands folded; Mae offers him nothing to eat or drink. His fingernails are black underneath, oil or grease. Edie brings him up to speed, her coming on as a nanny for the boys—outlining the last few months. He listens and watches her talk and seems to study the way her lips move. She's never been more aware of her own mouth. His stubble is days old and the skin on his face is darker than the skin on his neck and hands.

I'm back for good, he says. I'm back to stay.

Mae studies him for a long time before she says, We're comfortable. We're doing just fine now—we've got no need for you.

Sober now six weeks, he says. I've cleaned up. You can smell my breath if you want—smell me all over.

Those boys think they don't have a father, she says. It's been so long since we last seen you.

He puts his hands flat on the table. Set out in the open like this his hands tremble; his fingers keep their own unsteady rhythm. I know what I've done. I've been…unreliable.

Mae's words clatter across the tabletop like dice. You've been out of touch for more than a year.

Edie rises and offers them both something to drink. He declines; Mae asks for scotch. Edie crosses the kitchen and brings down a highball glass from the cupboard. She fills it with ice, listening but also trying to—wanting to—disappear.

He says, I don't want to bring any of my trouble here. I haven't seen my boys for so long. I don't want to bring nothing here that will trouble them.

She pours the scotch over ice and delivers it to Mae, who stirs it once with her finger before setting it on the table. The glass sits untouched, an arm's reach from Vester, but he seems not to notice. His eyes don't waver. Only his fingers which seem to move to their own peculiar, internal rhythm, as if rustled by the slightest draft.

He says, I spent a long time not listening to anybody. If I've caused trouble before—and I know I have—I want a chance to make it right.

A whole year, Mae says. Things ain't the same as they was.

Things we can do, make it work.

Where you been, Vester?

Locked up. North Carolina. Dan River.

Things different now.

We'll take it slow. I'll sleep on the couch.

One whiff of you drinking—

You can't be out here all on your own.

We're doing just fine.

I won't drink.

I don't know that we can be man and wife again.

We are man and wife.

Edie, the woman says. Edie is surprised to hear her name in the exchange. Take a fresh pair of sheets down from the closet. And a blanket. Set him up with a place on the couch.

Thank you, he says.

It's only on account of it being Christmas Eve, Mae tells him. The boys should have their father home on Christmas. One night is all — after breakfast tomorrow you got to be out of here. I'll call the sheriff otherwise, I promise.

Do me one favor, Edie says. She pauses at the archway and waits until Vester looks up. Move that tree of yours out to the porch. It may still have critters, and we've let in enough critters for one night.

She makes for him a bed on the couch. She is expert at making couches into perfect harbors of sleep. She wraps the sheets tight around the cushions, the powder blue sheets and the extra blanket that is worn in places, thin enough to see her hand through the print, the face of a lioness in the underbrush. Vester holds his forearm up to the blanket and compares the print on the fabric with the Bengal tiger inked into his skin. He growls, and then laughs.

Mean kitties, he says.

She says, Let me find a towel on the off-chance you want to shower in the morning.

She feels his eyes on her. She turns, clutching the unsheeted pillow to her chest. But his gaze is not prurient — not in the way boys have of undressing girls with their eyes. His head bobs a little, like a cat, his eyes large and watchful.

He asks, Do I know you from somewhere?

Edie pauses, considers, but decides to take the question at face value. We don't know one another.

Then why are you giving me such a hard time? You've been busting my balls ever since I got here.

Edie only shrugs, but she is relieved that it is her manners he's concerned with and not some notion of her criminal past. She says, Take your shoes off. We just had the carpets cleaned.

The boys have been messing around with cardboard blocks painted to look like bricks. There are two shapes: rectangle and square. In a spirit of competition, they have arranged the blocks into two neighboring structures. Troy crosses the room and takes his father by the arm.

These are our factories, he says. Which is better?

Edie returns with the towel and a wash cloth neatly folded and sets them on the chair. She stands to the side, watching this stranger interact with the boys she feels are now more her own sons than they are his. Vester examines the factories. Troy's design is palatial, with windows and inner rooms and a handwritten sign propped against the building: *Carson Steel*. Across the way, his younger brother has built what looks to be a bomb shelter. The majority of his bricks form the foundation; the foundation supports a one-story building stretching across the carpet like a low, immovable shell.

I think Evan has you beat, Vester says.

That's impossible, Troy says. Evan's building is boring. He doesn't have a sign out front or nothing.

Vester kneels on the floor and peers through the front door of both designs. He settles on Evan's, the low-lying shelter, and flicks his finger against it. Nothing on the building moves—not one brick. At Troy's factory he puts his ear to the roof as if listening for a heartbeat. His breath blows the sign down from the façade and he replaces the sign before backing up a little and glancing once more through the entrance.

You have a lot of rooms in here, he tells him.

Eight rooms, the eldest son says.

Vester lifts his index finger and exhibits it for the boys. He taps against the front wall of Troy's building. Then he flicks his finger once against the outer wall with no more force than he used with Evan. The front wall of the factory buckles as if someone has kicked it in. Each wall collapses in quick succession, toppling the second story in a great calamity of cardboard blocks.

That's not fair, Troy says.

Doesn't matter how nice your place looks. Vester musses the boy's hair. It's gotta weather storms.

Mae emerges from the bathroom, shutting off lights as she moves toward the back of the house. Too much laughter out here, she says. It's bedtime.

We're on our way, Edie says, but Mae has already closed her bedroom door.

Like a general, Edie thinks, who knows she is badly outnumbered, but who still must fight tomorrow in the coming of the bloody dawn.

EDIE IS AWAKE. She hears Troy shouting for her and calling her by name. Her first reaction—Vester. Then she is up and moving down the dark hall; she is at their bedroom door before she has fully opened her eyes. She navigates the star-cast patterns on the floor and she knows now where the lamp chain falls; she finds it in the dark. But she pulls the chain and the light comes on and she discovers only Troy sitting up in bed and cowering against the headboard. Evan is nowhere to be seen—not under the desk or behind the bed when she throws back the covers and finds only his socks where they were pulled off and discarded in the night.

She yells at the older boy. Where's your brother?

But she is already moving through the bedroom door and then

out into the hall, not yet thinking to call for him, to call his name into the darkness, only moving in the direction of pursuit. She runs headlong into Vester, who has slipped from Mae's bedroom to collide with her in the shadows. She feels his bare chest and his bare arms around her and she fights back — instantly transported to the highway and the coyote and the hands reaching out for her from the darkness of the truck. She might scream, but she won't give him that satisfaction. She struggles and finally he lets her go.

Relax, he says. It's just me.

She backs against the wall, waiting for her eyes to adjust. She feels instantly foolish. I thought you were sleeping on the couch.

Evan? he whispers.

Sleepwalking, she says. He's never left his bedroom before.

Vester sweeps the house but finds nothing. Edie brings the flashlight down from the hall closet and miraculously the flashlight discharges a bright fluorescent beam. The family always prepared for catastrophe, as she herself was when she lived in California. There, the danger was earthquakes. Here, hurricanes.

And then she is hurrying into the yard, Vester at her side, where the cool night air dissipates the sleepy smells that surround them both, where the breeze and the dark sky make them feel undressed and vulnerable. She pauses at the footpath and her flashlight brightens the yard in places, defining the depth of the wilderness where before there were only indistinguishable shapes.

As her own father did, standing on their back porch in Michigan. Calling for her in a night drained of sleep. The way the lights shone through the trees in Oregon and made the leaves look frozen as if by a deadly frost; like spotlights mounted on the cars of the San Francisco police, chasing her into the murderous night.

When she woke, she thought that Vester was harming the boys. Then she thought he had taken the youngest boy, Evan. She wonders if she always expected the worst from people or if this is some new development, characteristic of adulthood, something she recently learned.

And then Vester emerges from the darkness, cradling the boy in his arms. Evan is asleep and there is no struggle—there are no words exchanged as they head back inside the house and quietly close the door. She moves a kitchen chair below the doorknob, not to keep intruders out but to keep the boy in. She thinks they must sell special locks in hardware stores for a problem such as this.

In the bedroom again she watches Vester lay his son down and speak softly to him words she cannot hear. It is only in the blue-cast light of the room she sees the network of red lines running across Vester's shoulders and arms, down the pronounced dorsal fins on his back. Long lashes of crimson, raised like a rash. She moves to the older brother and tucks him into bed. Soothing him with quiet words, whispering him into sleep.

In the predawn light of the hallway, Vester asks, He do this a lot?

Not for a long time, she says. When I first came here, it seemed like every night.

He tilts his head toward Mae's room. She don't do nothing?

We're hoping he outgrows it.

He walks with her into the living room. The bedding on the couch is untouched. The VCR says 4:30.

What time does Santa Claus come around here? he asks.

Pretty soon, I think.

Hardly seems worth going back to bed.

Once I'm awake—that's it.

She leans against the wall between the hallway and the living room. Vester reaches up and touches the top of the arch. His chest is covered in tight black curls and beneath the hair the rash or irritation of the skin that is raised and clearly visible in the dim light of the hall.

Hell. He lifts himself on tiptoes and presses the flat of his hand against the ceiling. I can't ever sleep. Too many thoughts and things I'd rather not be thinking of.

I never sleep, she says, unless it's light.

They say you can't sleep with a guilty conscience.

Maybe you and I have something in common then.

He laughs and then covers it. You're too young to feel guilty about things. You cheat on your boyfriend once or something like that?

Go on thinking that way, she tells him. The less you know about me, the better.

But in her case it's more than just something to say or a half-hearted attempt at humor: ambiguity and deceit are her only allies. How little any of them know — of her or her past. She turns up the burner on the stove and sets the kettle there, watching the now fully-dressed Vester arrange and rearrange the boys' presents beneath the tree. It is hard for her to pair the man in the living room with the man from Mae's stories — the difference seems to be the essence of the question as to whether or not people change.

He sticks his head into the kitchen, shaking a small gift bag. I think this one's for you. Sounds expensive. You must have been a very good girl this year.

Better than some. She lifts the kettle from the stove before it whistles. She pours two mugs. The glass mugs are stenciled with snowmen. How strange, she thinks, for the boys to have grown up never having seen snow — real snow, anyway. White crystals falling from the sky are as mystical to them as wood elves or space travel. Space travel probably seems more real.

She drops a tea bag into each mug and presses each tea bag with the back of her spoon. She says, There's sugar in the cabinet, cream in the fridge.

Vester says, Black for me thanks. I'm a man of simple tastes.

Vanilla ice cream, she says. She pours three tablespoons of sugar into her own tea and floats the creamer, turning the liquid a delicious tan. Plain waffles.

That's why you never sleep. He nods toward her cup. All that sugar.

Cheers, she says and they clink tea mugs. Merry Christmas.

They sit together on the back porch watching the darkness lift from the edges of the pond, soaking in the quiet between the going to bed of the night and the waking day. It seems they belong to both worlds, and to neither. Curled up in her place along the wicker loveseat, she studies the way he slouches in the armchair with his legs stretched out; and the way he drums his fingers on the armrest as if adding percussive fills to a song only he can hear. Something obvious and visceral, she decides: Van Halen perhaps.

I love it out here. He tilts his head back against the seat. From her perspective his face is all nostrils and lips. It's warm all year 'round.

I find myself missing the seasons, she says.

Seasons. He folds his hands across his stomach and for a moment their persistent tremor is quieted. There's seasons down here. You just don't notice them much.

A breeze moves through the screen. Vester is silent for so long she suspects he's fallen asleep. Until he says, This business with Evan is strange. I've only seen something like that once before, back when I was in Salisbury. A boy had his arms blown off at Medina Ridge. He was going to live, but nobody knew if he'd ever sleep again. They kept him on a steady drip and it made no difference. Every night he was up screaming nonsense. Nothing happening anywhere, except inside his head. Sometimes he'd roll off the bed and smash his face against the floor. Then his nose would be bleeding over everything and him trying to push himself up against the wall or pull himself back into bed by his teeth—a fucking mess. But this business with Evan—it's not right.

His schooling is fine, Edie says quietly.

He don't talk there either. Am I right?

A loon comes screaming across the pond, pounding its wings over the house. It startles them both. Edie laughs. Daylight sifts over the tops of the trees and across the road the outline of the water tower glows faintly.

He can speak, she says. I've heard him. At night when he has his terrors. He can talk perfectly fine.

He just don't want to, Vester says.

Rebellion maybe.

I remember his first word, he says. Then, as if refusing to lead or to be lead through a series of painful memories he says, This is all my fault. I probably fucked both of those boys up good.

He gropes for cigarettes, finds them in his shirt pocket. He lights one cigarette with the butt of another. She hears the sizzle of tobacco; the smoke exhaled gets hung up in the screen and hovers there. She stands and pulls the ceiling fan chain.

He says, Anyway, they ain't gonna have one parent anymore. They gonna have two.

Water runs inside the house: One of the boys is awake. They wait in quiet until the water shuts off and the house is silent again.

He asks, So what's your story?

My story?

The lies you tell yourself so that your life makes sense.

Maybe I don't lie to myself at all.

Don't give me that. He reaches for the ashtray and draws in the ashes before stamping out his cigarette. Smoke drifts from his nose, when he speaks. We all lie to ourselves. Now a girl as young as you, pretty as you are—don't take that the wrong way, you're not my type—on her own down here, what, killing time?

I'm not from here.

You've come here from somewhere else. This I already determined. And people only come to Florida for two reasons. They come here to die, if they're old. Or they come here to hide, to reinvent themselves, usually because they're running from the law. That's the history of this state. Like it or not. And since you're not old, I must assume you're on the run. That pretty, bald head of yours tells me all I need to know.

Maybe I'm dying of cancer for all you know.

He fixes her with a hard stare—she immediately regrets her words. He says, We all die. As a great man once said, those who ain't busy being born—

Are busy dying.

She decides she was right about his internal soundtrack—he's a rocker. He quotes Bob Dylan. And he's a criminal. And from what Mae has told her, he's not to be trusted. But then she herself is all these things. He's figured most of it out anyway in a short amount of time.

You're watching my kids is all, he says. Every day my wife leaves our children in your care. I'd like to know the things you're teaching them. What kind of influence you're having. And to know the answers to these things, I need to know your story. What's your story, Edie Richards? Where do you come from?

California, she says. Mae knows everything—I'm not telling you anything she doesn't know. But we keep it between us, because, people talk. And no one else really needs to know.

Two life stories. He whistles, acting impressed. That's a lot to keep straight.

Like having two wives? she says.

She has the thought that he might hit her—it comes to her suddenly but not for any reason that she can see: Vester doesn't move. A twitch in his cheek maybe, a flick of his fingernail against the filter of a fresh cigarette.

Not two wives, he says. Children by two different women. Mae is my only wife. My only love. You and I might keep on lying to each other for the rest of the night, but that right there is the truth.

Their shapes become more defined, light seeping in now through the screen. She breathes and smells the evergreen from the Christmas tree he dragged inside and then outside to the porch because she told him to. His obedience makes her smile.

She ventures a question. What happened to you so that you were in the hospital?

Gulf War. He picks at something on his tattoo. Operation Desert Storm. Marines.

I admire that, she says.

He waves her sentiment away. It's already a footnote now. Hardly worth remembering.

That's not true, she says.

He coughs into his shirt. Listen. All that shit you hear about flag-waving and old women crying in the streets—that's what's not true. We barely saw anyone. I'd look to my right and I'd look to my left and on every horizon was smoke, thick as a blast wall. At night, all we could see was oil fires burning, bursts of flame, that hot burn that tends to collapse on itself even as it rises. I'd go to bed and imagine a perfect pillar of black smoke coming out of my mouth, from my lungs, where all that junk tended to dig in good and deep. Breathing oil for months. Oil—and who knows what else. Stuff they never told us about. Burning.

Whenever it would rain, we'd take a couple chairs out back of the warehouse. We'd sit and watch the storm and let a bucket fill with rainwater. The rain was black and the water inside the bucket was thick and black. Raining oil.

After things settled down I was stationed in Al Burgan. We hadn't occupied Kuwait for three weeks when Greenpeace arrived.

Those people — spectacled granola types. An international coalition of tree-huggers. There we were, we'd just finished fighting a war, liberating a country, and those people climbed off their rusted ship and right away started griping about the environmental hazards, the damage those burning oil wells were doing to the water and the land. As if we'd started those fires. As if somehow, we were to blame.

But it was our job to escort them to the oil fields, while they ran tests and sampled the soil and more or less spent the entire time shaking their heads and looking horrified. None of them seen a war zone before. But I saw a lot of things traveling with that particular caravan. I saw a herd of camel laying dead, incinerated to ash. Daytime turned to night — we thought we were caught up in some Biblical plague. Signs from God were everywhere, if we looked. Pillars of fire and new lakes forming every day. The land running over with oil.

War is good for business, she says.

He nods his head. Good for business. Hard on the body. My body has never been right, since. Little stuff you'd expect. Nightmares. Or that my sense of smell is no good anymore. But I'm sick, have been since the day I got back. That's why I was in Salisbury — trying to find some cure for whatever is eating away my body.

There is nothing she can say, no way to follow up. Her own cache of experiences, a few days in the Oregon woods, nighttime raids on stationary SUVs that never fired back — what were they compared to service like his? Silence fills the back porch and buffers the memories that hang everywhere thick as the rainwater he described.

Merry Christmas, she tells him. But he has already fallen asleep.

FOUR

He is trying at least. This is as much as Mae can say for her husband — and as little.

Christmas morning saw Vester Carson shuttling presents back and forth from underneath the tree to where Troy and Evan waited for them, arms outstretched; him more excited than either of his boys, tickled with the way they tore at the brown-paper wrapping (Edie insisting on recycled paper, bellyaching on all the consumer waste brought on by the holidays) and cast it aside, long sheaves of the stuff, the racket of the crinkling paper being torn and pulled and balled up and shaken out, a piece of tape sticking to the finger of the youngest boy and him flicking it once, twice, before the adhesive released and the paper fluttered up and then floated down. Vester scurried for a new pair of gifts while Edie gathered the wrapping paper in her arms and pressed it tight against her, compacting it, pressing the air out of the creases and folds, dead set on re-using it all next year probably instead of throwing it away. Mae herself in her La-Z-Boy, legs covered by an afghan, lighting one cigarette after another (a Christmas indulgence she allowed herself, this chain-smoking), just watching it all beneath the smoke that drifted up into the lampshade and hung there and billowed out the top like something simmering, the lampshade a glowing, ominous Vesuvius.

She was waiting for it, all through opening the gifts; all through the dinner she prepared (something called a Turducken that a co-worker told her about, and a tofu steak for Edie); all that night after the boys went to bed and the three adults sat around the kitchen table playing canasta and drinking hot cider; all the next day and the days that followed until here it is New Year's Eve and not one sign of him drinking or carousing and not one flare-up of his terrible temper.

She keeps expecting to see it. He almost isn't himself without it. Instead, he's like a Vester out of some dream of hers, a good dream and not the nightmares she wakes up from sweating after, recalling him in his worst rages, but a dream she might have allowed herself many years ago when his misbehavior started—the Vester she imagines he could be and yes, would create if the Lord ever gave her the chance to pick and choose her husband's good points and bad.

THE FIRST DAY after Christmas, Vester and the boys and Edie cleaned out the front room of all the boxes she had saved up across so many years: stacks of paper goods, take-out menus, and outdated travel books—stuff she kept because she wanted to remember one thing or another. All those boxes hit the curb, and when she came home from work the sun was pouring in the front room like it hadn't since her grandmother was alive. The quality of the light that came in—she felt like a little girl again.

The boxes were one thing and the window screens another. It was such a nice time of year to have the windows open. Vester removed each screen and cleaned them with alcohol and cotton swabs and re-wired those that had been torn or frayed before putting each one back up tight into their frames so the air could move through the house and not let the bugs in.

And the next morning when she came home from work and the sun was shining through the living room windows and the windows were open and a breeze blew through she saw the light fell directly on where her husband slept, there on the couch. He stirred and then he saw her and then he rose from the cushions — the rest of the house still dark — and followed her into her bedroom and shut the door softly behind them like closing the door on a sacred place. And maybe she let him into her bed, again, still surprised at how their bodies immediately recognized one another like two things meant to complement, scotch and soda, falling desperately and hopelessly into one another until she feared their lovemaking would shake the drywall, rattle the nails and joists and pop the window screens back out from their frames. It was never quiet with Vester. But she told herself so what — it had been so long.

I GOT A JOB, he told her on the third morning after Christmas. They lay in bed, smoking, their ashtrays, one for each of them, between their naked thighs on the bedspread. His ashtray showed the Hawaiian Islands. Hers said simply, *Sin*-cinnati.

The news played on the television and the television was on mute and it was all stories she was only half-interested in — she figured it was a slow news week between Christmas and the New Year. In New York, the EPA announced that pollution from the World Trade Center collapse wouldn't cause chronic illness in all that many lower-Manhattan residents.

Did you hear? Vester said again. I found work.

Who would ever hire you? she said.

They needed somebody out there at the solar farm, to keep an eye on the place.

Like what, she snickered, some kind of security?

He rolled away from her and covered up with a corner of the sheet, as if he were put off. She couldn't help but reach out and touch his shoulder, wanting his nakedness back. Beneath her touch were places of irritation on his skin, lashings almost, and she remembered the unexplained rashes as part of him, inseparable.

They give you a uniform? she needled. They give you a badge?

Nah, he said. I don't even get a gun. Anything happens, I'm just supposed to call the police.

A glorified janitor was what the job sounded like to her, but she managed to bite her tongue—he had found a job. Something he'd never done in all the years she'd known him.

A job, huh? She reached over and touched the lobe of his right ear.

He glanced at her sidelong. The sheet covering him moved a little.

They paying me and everything, he said.

He and Edie got along—that much was plain. Not at all in a romantic way, but in a brother-and-sister kind of way she found endearing. They were a lot alike: quick-tongued, short-tempered. Their senses of humor dry as foot powder. Edie gave it to him and he gave it right back.

The whole family was sitting around the kitchen table the next evening, before Mae left for work. Edie asked, an edge to her voice, Do I see a glass of water out there in the living room?

The boys hunkered down and stole glances at one another, giggling, knowing what was about to come. Knowing it wasn't them Edie was set on reprimanding.

That so? Vester took a bite real casual, twirling a little bit on the end of his fork.

Funny, Edie said. I don't remember leaving my glass out there.

Then she asked each of the boys if they'd left a glass in the living room and of course they hadn't. She asked Mae and Mae played along, shaking her head and hiding a little behind her napkin. Then Edie pretended to get real angry, setting the flats of her hands on the table and whipping her head toward Vester like a viper.

You! she said in the lowest, meanest voice Mae had ever heard her use. You must have left that glass in the living room!

The boys bust up laughing and Mae laughed and Vester pretended to cower in fear before he slithered out of his chair and out of the room. He retrieved his water glass and set it in the sink. He found his chair again, head hanging low. He made an expression like he was ashamed and made sure his boys saw it. It was all for their benefit anyway.

They were a pair of cut-ups them two. They made sure Mae never had a dull moment.

IN THESE JOY-FILLED passages she could almost forget what life with Vester had been like. She did forget—she gave herself to him again and again. Sometimes she couldn't believe it herself: Vester at her kitchen table made animal puppets with his hands, while his two beautiful sons laughed until they choked, until their bellies hurt, until they pleaded for mercy. And Edie, if not approving, then also did not disapprove. She took no side in the matter but simply absorbed his presence there and made his demands upon her time which were additional now to what she'd become used to, some new thing she now had to navigate, just another part of her unbending routine.

It was not in the happy moments when Mae harbored doubts but on her drives to work or at the hospital thinking it through in the nurses' lounge or at church with her hands clasped and eyes closed—these were the times she remembered what Vester had been. She hated herself for being so weak-willed. She pleaded with God: Make me strong. Take away my weakness. Give me a heart brave enough to stand up to Vester and the courage to raise those boys without him. He had sewn himself upon their lives again like a worn-out patch on a jacket they just couldn't lose.

She knew it better than she knew the patterns his sickness made on the small of his back: He had to go. It was only a matter of time before he made her regret letting him in so easily. It was a matter of a certain risk he still presented to her boys and also a certain matter of pride—her allowing him to become part of their family again after all he'd put them through. She reminded herself, as midnight passed on the fourth day after Christmas, as she held the hand of a patient who'd been brought in, just as Vester once had been, sick with the taste for alcohol, there was a reason, many reasons, she'd driven him out in the first place.

She and Vester were in Albertsons shopping for groceries. They would spend New Year's Eve at home with Edie and the boys. The Carson tradition was pimiento cheese spread and Coca-Cola out of little glass bottles. Also, they always had the television on late in the afternoon so they could watch New Year's Eve happening in places around the world, as the celebrations marched westward from Melbourne to Mumbai to fireworks streaming from the London Bridge, to Buenos Aires and finally New York City, the Big Apple. A twenty-four hour cycle of New Year's Eve so that when Mae popped the sparkling grape juice it was already lunchtime in the Philippines. Like spinning a globe, waiting for her finger to land somewhere: They would travel to many different places by the time the night was through. That's what she told her boys. She told them to use their imaginations.

At the grocery store she filled her cart with the snacks and party foods they ate every year, the ham and cream cheese pinwheels, the economy-sized bag of peanut M&M's. But Vester kept adding stuff she hadn't put on the list, expensive stuff. And she was okay with this at first, an item here or there, something that might make the night special for him—she wanted him to feel like it was his New Year's too. But after shrimp cocktail came marinated steak tips that he said he'd fire up on the grill (which meant hickory woodchips and charcoal briquettes and lighter fluid, along with a grilling fork he swore he had to have), and then dark chocolate truffles and a canister of mixed nuts that must've been from Africa or somewhere because the label read twelve dollars a can.

Vester, she said. Twelve dollars for a can of nuts?

He held the canister, turned it over, read out loud the mix— macadamia, cashew, filbert.

Who's paying for them? she wanted to know. When he didn't answer she said, Put 'em back.

Loosen up, Mae. He dropped the canister into the shopping cart. Everything don't have to be so uptight all the time.

The maple-syrup quality of Vester's voice and seeing that fancy can of nuts sitting there in her cart after she'd asked him not to buy it were too much—it was like a geyser that had been capped off inside her, long ago, finally blew. She reached across the shopping cart and snatched the nuts and hit Vester with them.

You know how hard I work, she shouted. You know good and well how every penny is accounted for.

She thought of his military pension, spoken for by some unwed mother he'd knocked up, wherever she was. Meanwhile, his legitimate sons hadn't seen a dime from him the entire time he'd been gone. And here he was putting a twelve-dollar can of legumes into her cart? She hit him again. Here he was sleeping on her couch, smoking her cigarettes? She rooted through the shopping basket for other stuff he'd picked up, the grilling fork and the dusty bag of charcoal. Here he was after all these years still the only lover she'd ever had—it made her sick. She flung his items down the aisle, sending tumbling wheels of shrimp and flaccid beef points smacking against shelves and sliding past the feet of patrons who, turning into the row and seeing Mae, pivoted their carts the opposite direction. Loosen up? She'd loosen his head from his neck if he so much as touched anything else before they left the store.

But he knew better. He carried the grocery bags from the checkout to her car. He held the door open for her. He didn't say nothing until finally he said, Did you know Edie feeds cats?

The sound of his voice made her start feeling all worked up again — she'd almost forgotten he was there. Her pack of cigarettes had slipped between the cup holder and the seat, and she groped for them while she drove.

Edie, he went on. She feeds strays. Out where all them restaurants are. She took us there yesterday. She must feed twenty cats.

She couldn't quite reach the cigarettes. She rolled her window down. She could smell his aftershave, and it was making her stomach upset. She knew about the cats, of course.

She's full of surprises, that one, he said.

She glanced at him, wondering what he meant by that. He slid his hand down under the seat and came up with the pack.

He shook two free, put one in her mouth and one in his own. Why do you think she does that?

Feels bad for them probably, she said.

Some of those cats can barely walk. Some of them — you can see their bones. Most of them are as good as dead.

That don't mean there's no point taking care of them, she said.

The car lighter popped, and he put it to her cigarette and then to his. I don't know.

Just because they're dying? She looked at him. She didn't know why he was talking about all this now. She wished he'd be quiet. She was starting to be annoyed by the way he never bothered taking the cigarette from his mouth between drags; instead he let it smolder on his lips, the smoke jerking up and getting itself sucked out the crack in the window.

I'm dying, Mae. He did not look at her, but kept on looking straight ahead. I just thought you should know.

IN KREMLIN SQUARE, revelers wave national flags at the foot of candy-striped minarets. White-trimmed towers glow beneath the fireworks and floodlights. Troy suggests next year they make a gingerbread Kremlin: The real thing looks good enough to eat.

At Camp Doha in Kuwait, U.S. soldiers dance to hip-hop music and let the fronts of their fatigues hang open. The television host says 25,000 troops are prepared for possible deployment. The soldiers flash peace signs at the camera. Vester shakes his head and says he wishes they'd finished the job the first time.

In a park in San Francisco, the party hasn't really begun, but a big band entertains the young families gathered there. A mother dances with her daughter. The girl perches on the tops of her mother's feet, swinging first to the right and then to the left, squealing, clinging to her mother's hands. Edie says she celebrated New Year's in San Francisco once—that she paddled a kayak out into the bay and watched the fireworks from the water.

Mae loves all the different places they show on television, all the crazy ways people ring in the New Year. Each celebration is so different, and yet they share the same hope: That this year, this next year, will not only be new, but better.

And then January 1 is only fifteen minutes away. Troy's eyes are glued to the telecast. Evan, curled in Edie's arms, rubs his eyes and tries to stay awake. He's never stayed up for midnight before—fifteen minutes and he'll make it.

Okay, Baldy, Vester says. He calls the girl this, sometimes. What's your New Year's resolution?

I don't do resolutions, she says. Then, ribbing him, I don't need to.

He whistles, curling an eyebrow, skeptical.

How can you improve upon perfection? she asks. You can't.

What about you, Mae? He is lying on the floor, on his side. He says the hardness of the floor makes his muscles feel better, his bones.

I resolve to no longer take the Lord's name in vain, Mae says. I slip up sometimes, and I don't think it's right.

I shoulda known it would be something religious.

She adjusts her position in the chair, kicking the footrest down into place. And what's your resolution, I'd like to know?

He coughs into his fist. The sound is deep and dry, a hollowed-out tree being shaken by percussions in the earth.

Eyes watering, he says, I resolve to take the Lord's name in vain a little more often. Pick up your slack.

Troy laughs at this, but Mae shushes him. I live with a bunch of heathens. Like David among the Philistines.

Vester rolls onto his back. He picks up the pack of cigarettes by his elbow and drops one into his mouth. C'mon, Mae. Give the Bible talk a rest for one night.

I will not, she says. This is my house. And there's nothing more important.

I thought it was our house.

It's not. She allows a moment to pass with no one saying anything. It's mine.

Troy reaches for the television and turns up the volume. Ten seconds to midnight. The red ball begins its stuttering descent. Thousands — millions? — of partygoers shout each successive number. Her oldest boy joins the counting and so does Edie.

Mae wants to say something more, to let Vester have it here in front of their family, her family, but instead she only watches the screen. She can't have it out with him now he's told her he's dying. If he even is.

Every year, every ball-drop, she swears this resolution or that. With the turn of the calendar comes a chance to start again, or so she's always believed, except that an entire year passes and she forgets about the resolution she made. Most years, there's plenty to resolve. But not this year. This year she wants things to keep on going just as they are — she and Edie and the boys. Or as they were before Vester came around again.

Vester is back, she thinks. Vester is dying. Vester who she could never stop obsessing over, but now that he's here, on her floor, watching her television, can't soon enough be gone.

She decides this year she will not offer a resolution, but a restoration. She has her household to protect. And they were doing fine — better than fine, they were doing great — before he showed.

She offers a silent prayer: Lord, forgive me for having no pity for a dying man.

The red ball lands, her family cheers. Vester slides four long, black wires from the pocket of his jeans and divides them between his sons. They hold the wires with both hands. He lights the ends and the wires burst into white, sparkling lights.

Edie herds the boys toward the front door. Not in the house.

The room fills with a sulfur smell. Evan follows his older brother tumbling into the yard. They shout Happy New Year! at the night. Mae rouses herself and goes to the front closet. She brings down the tambourine she takes each Sunday to church, then goes to stand on the porch steps. She watches her sons fly across the yard, four miniature, streaking comets. She shakes her tambourine and shouts, Happy New Year! The darkness swallows her sons and then gives them back and then takes them in again; soon they are so far away that all she can see are two pairs of spitting white sparks somewhere in the blackness. She beats her tambourine. She calls out, Happy New Year! Knowing this is what raising children means: equipping them with light before they flee from you. Shaking a tambourine as you watch them race to meet the unseen world, as if the sound of it might echo in their ears long after they've gone from you. As if you might speed their flight. As if they'll ever realize all you did was dream about them, root for them, live for them.

One by one the sparklers fizzle and extinguish. She watches them drop off, and then she hears the breathlessness of her boys running back to her, toward the light of the doorway behind her, toward the safety of the house.

Her resolution is this: She will not allow her husband to pick up parenting so easily, as if picking up a long-forgotten game of chess. To waltz back in after so many years as if nothing had happened. Despite his health, despite all they've shared, good and bad, she is going to have to find the strength to put him out.

FIVE

Christmas has come and gone and with it, the New Year. The sense of having reached a summit with no memory of the ascent and no pride of accomplishment — only the uncertain winter ahead. A musical term describes the sensation of void where there should be pride, when an orchestra pauses and leaves an aural passage wide enough to fall through. Pastor Reginald Dancer remembers the term: grand pause. Outside his window falls a steady rain, the gray sky thick and close. In the half-daylight, the sign fronting Roan Street has yet to flicker on and so the yard lies dark and flat.

Thanks for meeting me so late in the day, the sheriff says.

I'm always here, he says.

Something weighs on the sheriff's mind. He seems to simmer, but the simmering is practiced, the countenance reserved. There is a patient sort of concentration Dancer has not noticed in this man before now. He notices the sheriff's swollen knuckles and the dark half-moons beneath his eyes that sit just a little too close to the nose — a nose that has been broken more than once. His bearing this afternoon has a sense of martyrdom, almost. That is the word the pastor settles on — martyr. The penitence of someone set before a predetermined and unfortunate labor. He recognizes with almost nothing being said that there is no getting around what the sheriff has come to tell him — his words are as inevitable as blood from a razor cut.

Whitney says, I've come to talk about Edie Richards. She's been working out here, I know.

The church is looking truly grand, the pastor says but thinks, Grand pause, grand churchyard, several hundred thousand grand in debt. He wonders if it is not the end of Advent he feels but the winding down of his ministry. Adaptability as an evolutionary necessity — one he never learned.

The sheriff holds a black binder and draws from it a sheet of paper. He slides the page across the desk where it settles among the pastor's sermon notes, the margins of which are scribbled with half-realized mathematical equations and financial ledgers. Dancer does not reach for the sheet but leans over it, reading. The page has been printed from the Internet, an article from the *Sun Herald* web site dated yesterday. An electronic version of the article that ran in the local paper, announcing the Tenth Annual Celebration Christmas Tree. With one difference. When the story ran it carried a picture of the musical director and a few of the cast members gathered around him. But the on-line photograph is of Edie, lit gloriously atop the Celebration Christmas Tree. Dancer has not seen this picture before but finds it stunning. Her downcast eyes imply devotion; her face seems to generate its own brilliant light. She might contain the Incarnation, the holy embodiment of the season.

A nice photograph, he says.

Not so nice. The sheriff removes a second page from his binder and exhibits it as evidence. This fax came in today. Tell me if you see the resemblance.

The second photograph reveals a girl who very much resembles Edie, sitting at a restaurant table where perhaps the food has just been served. The picture is black and white. Her hair is long and the girl is thinner than Edie now but it is certainly a picture of Edie Richards from some prior life. Trails of smoke curl up from the floor in a piece of photographic trickery. She wears a ragged blazer over a T-shirt that reads *Pixie*. Half-smiling, her lips pursed, she is caught mid-motion, pulling herself closer to the table or smoothing the napkin in her lap.

Who sent this?

Whitney slides one last page across the desk. Dancer does not reach for it, but bows his head over the printed words and offers a whispered prayer. The header reads clearly *Most Wanted by the FBI* in capital letters. Below this, in smaller type: *Unlawful Flight to Avoid Prosecution – Maliciously Damaging and Destroying by Means of Explosives Buildings and Other Property – Second Degree Murder.*

At the bottom of the page are three photographs of Edie, including a cropped shot of her face in the restaurant. Her name is spelled out in bold. Not quite her name, but almost: Edie Aberdeen.

Dancer doesn't bother to read the rest. He says, A fake. A practical joke.

I called the office in San Jose as soon as it came in. It's legit.

You have to be shitting me.

I wish I was—shitting you. I'd rather be shitting on you than telling you one of the most active members of your congregation is a felon.

She's been watching those boys at the Carson place for months.

I'm only just starting to get my mind around it myself. How this girl who can't weigh more than a hundred pounds could be…I can't even bring myself to say this girl killed someone. A boy apparently, in California.

The FBI….

They're waiting for confirmation. I wanted to see you first. I wanted to talk it out with someone. These people she was running with, nothing but dykes and kids who stutter. Social retards. Hard to believe the girl we know was ever involved with lowlifes like these—cowards and dropouts.

Dancer scans the summary of her criminal history. Arson at several car dealerships, a protest somewhere called God's Valley, Oregon. There are the words printed on the page and the story behind the words but he gets no sense of the true story or its worth—the spirit of the thing remains elusive.

These are hard times, he says, almost to himself. Hard times. We are living in a new era built entirely on fear. No doubt we'd prefer to be remembered as the age of technology, as the age of computers. But I believe this is the age of terror. There is an entire generation of children being born who flinch whenever they hear an airplane overhead. They are suspicious of men with dark skin, or beards, or religious robes, just as we were suspicious of communists. It seems ludicrous now—almost quaint. When we were their age, darkness meant safety—entire towns blacked out during air raid drills. But our children—our children have every right to fear the dark.

Dancer pushes back from the desk. He wipes at something there and then stands. It's something we share. All of us. We fear the things we cannot see. And we pass our fears down through generations, through our genetic memory. You show me these pictures, and this flyer transmitted from thousands of miles away, and I'm left speechless. In awe of our technology and in awe of the indecency of man, the terrible things we are capable of. Edie Richards—our Edie—is no more a terrorist than this photograph of her, in this restaurant, is the actual experience of eating.

Whitney says, Terror thrives on fear. Fear serves its purpose.

And we make our play, the pastor says, even when every logical part of ourselves, any sensible person, would lock themselves in the basement of their home and never come out again. We enjoy today only as much as we fear today might be our last.

Whitney settles back in his chair. He reaches for the cigarettes nestled in his shirt pocket, but seems to remember where he is and stops himself.

He says, This would have never fallen to us before. But now every county sheriff is in touch with Homeland Security. They rely on us to take care of things that used to get handled by the feds. You remember what it was like down here. Anthrax scares up and down the coast. We rounded up every adult male who looked like he might be a Muslim and brought him in for questioning. Community member or not. Churchgoer or not. School board members and soccer coaches. Friends of mine. Friends of people in the department.

I remember.

People think of terror as something that happens in desert towns and seedy motel rooms. But it's right here, staring us in the face. Right here in this fax.

And when your country calls....

You respond. Whitney makes some small movement with his nose. We're going to take her down.

When?

As soon as the feds come up from Miami. Tomorrow morning latest.

You've got your duty, Sheriff. I'm just a humble man of the cloth.

EDIE SEES the two men emerge and stand beneath the awning, far across the muted parking lot where rain cuts divots in puddles. She watches the pastor swipe a bit of something from the sheriff's shoulder. The sheriff hurries into the rain.

She spent the morning slathering thinset between pieces of concrete and brick that have taken her weeks now to arrange. The wall stands six feet tall along the property line. She watches the sheriff climb into his car and turn onto Roan Street. And then he is gone.

The pastor also watches the car until it disappears. Then he turns in her direction and, noticing her there, approaches unhurried. She considers the sheriff's stopping by: either he has come for Vester or he has come for her. Trailing behind him a marauding band of criminal sins. Things that need to be accounted for. Across the parking lot in the opposite direction she sees Vester's sedan and the front gate of the solar farm swinging closed. He has recently been employed as watchman, on her recommendation to the pastor and a plea to his notions of forgiveness and second chances.

The Cadillac pulls out. The pastor is still some ways off. The sedan comes toward her. She tilts her Dolphins cap and removes her work gloves. She has not spoken to the pastor since the night in his office, only a week ago now, or less — time having lost all meaning. The night she discovered the pastor kept secrets too.

She had gone into his office looking for him, to see if he had keys to the back door. She was ready to go home; light was failing and she was spent. She found his office door open but no one inside. A sermon was being read on the radio. One lamp was lit and she stood at his desk looking over the pages spread across it, the ledgers and balances of which she understood very little. That the church faced certain financial challenges was no great secret, even among parishioners who, like her, were not among the inner circle. But judging from the slew of negative numbers that infected the pages, the confused and timid math that often ended abruptly, abandoned, the crisis was worse than most suspected.

It never occurred to her that she might be snooping. As part of her employment there she came and went as she pleased and no one asked questions. She had the run of the place; that night she needed only to find the keys and then she would be gone. She opened and closed his desk drawers, not digging but giving each a cursory glance, finding nothing. She turned to the bookcase, to the trinkets and gifts that had been collected over a quarter century, the imposing material and very real gravity of things acquired by power. Well-intentioned gifts that developed a certain obligation over time but also bled into the woodwork until they became part of their surroundings, an extension of their owner. Along the bottom of the bookcase were long, thin drawers and she pulled one drawer open with minimal interest in its contents, looking only for the keys.

Museums or conservatories might display similar drawers with butterflies or beetles pinned to the white boards under glass. But in the pastor's office, there were not insects but single hairs fastened to the matte, each one numbered. Human hairs, black and blonde and strands of red hair that flashed when she pulled open the drawers. That a sample of her own might be hidden somewhere in the collection occurred to her only later, and anyway it was impossible to tell without the number key. But there were hundreds. Meticulously aligned and coded. Some dark magic or voodoo: Their sheer volume made her uneasy. She was closing the last drawer, hurrying to leave, when she felt the pastor's presence — felt him before she turned to see him enter the office and close the door behind him.

Thirty years, he said. Not everyone I've ever met, but almost.

Edie stepped away from the bookcase. She felt shame although her intentions had been mostly honest.

Have a seat, the pastor said.

Now she stands with him at the foot of the new development and feels her time in Arcadia siphoning like the last dusting of grain. When he reaches her, he is soaked to the skin. She shakes his hand but his touch is distant. She knows the essence of his words without being told. It is what she has been waiting for these many months.

Real progress is being made here, he says.

She explains, quick and unprompted, how one day the ivy will cover the face of the wall and the rock bed will carry runoff. She can't plant grass seed until the weather warms, but this time next year he can expect his own Garden of Eden, his own contemplative retreat.

But he isn't listening. His shoes sink into the mud and his blue suit hangs limp and heavy.

He holds out his hand as if measuring the rain. If you have a moment, I thought we might walk.

Wonderful day for it, she says, and tosses her gloves to the ground.

They walk along the wall and find the frontage road. Turning left, they make their way toward the entrance of Windfall Estates. More houses have recently appeared, some still with masking tape on the front windows. Very few have planted yards. Brick piles and cement bags are stacked across the sidewalks. The streets are inscribed with spray-painted symbols and clipped code, the written language of construction. A billboard sign offers model tours. Edie and the pastor pause to take in the palm-lined boulevard, afraid or unwilling to walk farther.

Mae tells me you're starting school, the pastor says.

One class, she says. Just to get back into the routine.

That's good. Finish college. Don't end up like so many around here. The pastor tilts his head in the direction of the sedan, where Vester idles a football field away. You know who I mean.

Vester works hard. I think he wants to make amends.

Forgive thy neighbor, the pastor says. It's what I've been saying to Mae for years.

A machine starts up in the distance, somewhere back of the development. Then a bulldozer turns onto their street and passes.

All of this was ours, the pastor tells her. Three hundred acres.

We never thought of this land as ever being developed. We thought the Lord blessed us with the cheapest land that he could find. But even God can't stand in the way of man's progress.

A car door slams. She sees Vester outside the car now, fussing with something on the windshield, a loose wiper probably.

The pastor says, When Moses stood on the banks of the Red Sea, imagining the depths of that water, hearing the cries of women and children as Pharaoh bore down on them, what was it he felt, do you think?

I know what he felt, she says. He felt there was no escape.

She folds her arms. She takes three steps to her right, to keep her feet from sinking into the mud. She is certain now the sheriff came to ask about her.

She says, You didn't bring me out here for a sermon.

The pastor displays for her one finger. A strand of hair is wrapped around it.

A new one for the collection, he says.

What was John Whitney doing out here in weather like this?

He's received some information which weighs directly on your situation here.

She wants him to say it so that they can stop the charade. How much the pastor knows is irrelevant—if the sheriff is involved it means her troubles have come to roost.

Does the name Peter Moran mean anything to you? the pastor asks.

He was my boyfriend.

Where was this?

She knows her answer will take her one of two directions. She can maintain the façade or she can come clean to this man of the cloth, this collector of souls. She may have no other friend.

California, she says.

I'm starting to get the feeling there's a lot we don't know about you, Ms. Aberdeen. That's your real name isn't it? Not Richards. But Aberdeen.

Down the road she hears the Cadillac again and watches it roll toward them, its headlights cutting through the mist. The pastor says, There is a warrant for your arrest. I expect it will be served before this time tomorrow. I'm only telling you out of gratitude for what you've done for the church.

She wonders what he knows, or to what extent. She has questions, of course, but they seem irrelevant, the hows or whys. Hearing her last name for the first time in months — she should feel fear, or shame, but she feels only relief. A return to the one purpose she's ever really known: forward motion. She's tired of keeping lies separated from truth.

I don't imagine you'll be with us much longer, he says.

I don't see how I can stay.

That may be the first honest word you've said to me.

The sedan pulls up beside them. Vester climbs out carrying a flashlight and pulling his poncho over his head.

Dancer says, We're full of secrets, you and I. And as far as anyone else is concerned, we've never had this conversation. But I can offer you a chance to escape — one chance. It would mean a new life for the church, a second chance for you.

I'm listening.

Were something to befall this development, were it to be rendered suddenly unable to move forward, the land would revert back to the church.

The rain picks up and she catches only every other word. Vester approaches, his flashlight bouncing.

The pastor speaks quick and low. A loophole. A glitch in an agreement that was, at heart, an agreement between lovers. Were this project to suddenly disappear, enveloped in a pillar of flame.... The church would suddenly find itself on solid ground.

Each organism has its role to play, she thinks. A sacrifice to make for its community, for its family, for its home.

Dancer says, Fire might consume an entire home—or a subdivision of newly constructed, uninhabited homes.

I don't know anything about fire.

But I do, Vester says. He has been standing there listening.

The pastor looks at him. Haven't seen you in Sunday service.

I've had enough service for one lifetime, I think.

God wants you in the pew.

They're not pews. They're cushioned chairs, Edie says without thinking. She doesn't know why she's defending Vester, or why she put herself on the line to get him this job. She doesn't particularly care for the pastor either but she needs his help. And he needs hers. She says, People worship in different ways.

It's the community of church that's important, the pastor says. Gathered together in his name.

Anyway. Vester steps closer. What was John doing out here? Sticking his nose where it don't belong.

It's a private matter, the pastor says.

There's nothing private with John and me, he says. He looks toward Edie. You've been found out. He's on to you.

There is a divide between her past and present. Speaking of it for the first time does nothing to bridge the gap between her past wrongs and the carefully-crafted person she's become. She has said nothing to Vester and yet he knows, somehow, not the specifics, probably, he could never guess those, but it is clear to him that she is on the run. He sees the myth she's built around herself for what it is: for its transparency.

If you know what's at stake, the pastor says, then you'll be willing to help. All of our livelihoods depend on it. What we've taken years to build. Maybe it's asking too much for you to sympathize. But if you stand here one minute longer you'll be irrevocably involved.

Vester shifts his weight from one leg to the other. He lifts his hands, palms out, the skin there so much paler than the rest of him, and then shoves them deep into his pockets. Reginald Dancer shakes his head. He wipes his face with the hem of his suit jacket. The whole world feels saturated with rainwater and guilt and the cloudiness of days to come.

Do you remember little Fay Capron? the pastor asks. Do you remember where she's buried? It was long ago.

Joshua Creek, Vester says. Down on 760. Mae used to go there sometimes with the mother, what's her name. Katharine Anne.

That poor girl, Edie says.

Then you're familiar with the story. The pastor turns to her and she sees the flicker of his white teeth through the rain. The girl you replaced when you lived with Cyrus and his wife.

I didn't replace anyone.

Oh, but you did. The pastor draws closer to her and for the first time she fears him a little. She tries to take a step back but her feet stick in the mud and it feels like too much work to shake them out. Vester moves toward her as well — she doesn't know why men always move to protect her.

She can help us, the pastor says. She can return the favor — and replace you.

I don't understand, Edie says.

When your work here is done, when Windfall Estates has been reduced to cinder and ash, will my word be good enough to ensure your escape? With only Vester as witness?

No one takes my word, Vester says.

The pastor asks her, How long did you wear her clothes?

I wore the clothes the Caprons gave to me, she says. They were hers once, I guess. I didn't think about it.

You are the same size as that poor dead girl, dead now nine

years.

They'll be nothing left of her, Vester says.

The pastor nods and pulls the collar of his jacket around his ears. Nothing left of her but the bones.

SIX

In the courtyard of his apartment complex, lawn chairs stack ten or eleven high around the pool, their legs bent, their white straps weather-stained. A tarp covers the pool and the tarp gathers rainwater and petals in its folds. John Whitney paces the perimeter of the pool's kidney shape and stands along the five-foot mark, inhaling the last of his cigarette. The tops of the palm trees are dark and lights flicker on in the apartments around him, blue television lights behind half-drawn shades.

A baby cries behind one of these. Whitney turns his back to the sound. He is thinking of the phone calls he must make, to the Osceola Sheriff's Department, for one. His own pared-down force will need backup in the morning when the FBI arrive, when they start breaking heads. In all his years of law enforcement he has never come across a case like this—he is amazed at the way the girl ingratiated herself within the town and threaded herself into its very fibers. The takedown must be quiet, at the Carson place, preferably, with no witnesses other than the mother and that man, Vester, who has returned and now acts like he's some kind of husband to them, some kind of father.

Not like his own father, Whitney thinks. Murdered on a routine traffic stop outside Boca Raton. Gunned down by the worst kind of lowlife. Leaving the younger Whitney, at twelve years old, to look after his mother. His mother barely spoke English; his father had more or less plucked her off a life raft and married her. Producing one child with tainted blood — half American, half Cuban, possessing two spirits.

The child cries louder now. The sound of its wailing is amplified inside the courtyard, bouncing back and forth between the cement stairs and walkways. A door is open on the bottom floor and the wailing comes from behind the door — the child sounds marginally human, its cry more like the distressed call of an exotic bird. The shrieking runs shivers down Whitney's arms. The longer he listens, the more he believes the wailing is that of an ill-behaved child and not a newborn as he first thought.

A man appears at the door. He steps into the night and crosses the courtyard, lugging a garbage bag in one hand and working a cigarette in his other. He is younger than the sheriff, heavily tattooed and muscular. He tosses his cigarette into a planter urn, into the white stones. He disappears beneath the walkway, heading out for beer or cigarettes or evaporated milk. At the open door the wife appears, hoisting a wailing toddler on her hip. She is young and her hips are wide and loose. The toddler buries its face in her neck and claws at her breasts through the shirt she wears.

She calls out across the courtyard. El tiene una fiebre terrible.

Her husband yells something back, in English, but unintelligible. Their voices, their call and response, threaten to shatter the tile and the stones.

Driven from his place of solace, Whitney returns to his apartment. The child screams again and the weeping fills the night like a siren. His own life delineated by alarms, the arc of their sound and their slow, tonal descent. He remembers when as a child he would watch fire engines pass. He remembers riding on his father's lap, in the squad car, when his father let him push the button and blast the piercing whistle and horn. The emergency sounds of crisis, of tragedy, are also sounds of comfort and protection. They announce a watchful presence for those who need looking after. His father's siren finally silenced by a wetback on a routine traffic stop, a wetback who happened to be packing a .45.

The child screams again. Whitney removes his shoes and closes the sliding glass door. In his bedroom, he strips the comforter and folds it on the chair. He lies across the flat sheets, watching the length of himself stretched out in the closet mirror, his ankles crossed. He breathes deep; he closes his eyes. He thinks about the woman outside, the mother with her milk-heavy breasts. He can still hear her child crying, although it seems to be tiring, exchanging drawn-out gasps for a more guttural murmur. The sounds of surrender. Soon the husband will return to their hot, little room. The mother will melt ice cubes on the child's forehead until the child falls asleep. The shirtless man will make love to the girl and they will watch themselves in the shadows of their own closet mirror or in the rounded reflection of their dim television screen. Quietly, so as not to wake their colic child, their bare legs wrapped up in twisted ribbons of white sheet.

Bare legs and bare, milk-laden breasts. The milk from those breasts, white cream on dark, refugee skin. The smell of those people. He remembers traveling with his mother to support groups and to English lessons and to small, tight gatherings of immigrants, defectors and the like; how their fragrance followed him everywhere. How their smell filled him with desire even as a child, before he could name the thing—something mixed up with the magia of their mother country. He carried the smell home with him. Now as an older man, as a lifelong bachelor and arguably the most respected man in Arcadia, he sometimes follows their scent into the steaming night.

He would go tonight, if he weren't needed tomorrow. He thinks of going anyway but reminds himself he must be fresh for the morning advance. When the feds arrive and start pushing everyone around—his men will look to him for order.

Before he opted for greater safety and higher pay in small-town Arcadia, he'd served with the City of Miami Police Department. In Miami he learned how to be a cop. As good a cop as his father was. Better, even. He established his adult life. He also found his true religion.

And it is a religion for him, so what if he's nearly an old man. On his off-nights sometimes he drives to Miami like enacting some ancient pilgrimage, to the bars and clubs along South Beach, where he pays his tithes in the form of a cover charge to stand sipping bourbon with the other lechers in the back. The now-retired cops he remembers from his days spent there, and other men with humbler origins who are now too old to flirt and too old to dance to the strange music, but who come anyway to watch the girls, the priestesses of this cult who writhe dark and lean in their tight and translucent fabrics. In the visceral pulse of throbbing bodies packed into undulating rooms, something delicious and decadent grips his spirit and surfaces aberrant desires he rarely lets himself entertain.

It would affect his work, otherwise. If he indulged himself too often.

Because women in Miami wear nothing at all. They wear sheer skirts high on their hips. They wear high heels that cause their legs to curve and stretch like cords. They move together beneath patterns of lights on a dance floor that shakes from the driving bass. Watching from the corner are leather-clad men who stand out of reach but not out of sight. These women are temptations, like the sirens of old: a trap. Because they each have boyfriends—and each boyfriend is larger than the last. And the boyfriends watch their women grind upon the dance floor, worshiped, driving other men wild with lust. Canons shower the dance floor with a thickly cool, white fog so dense Whitney cannot see his own hands or his forty-dollar shoes. When the fog begins to lift he scans the dance floor to see women rising from their knees, steadying themselves against the thick thighs of their men, wiping their mouths as their boyfriends slip back to their places against the wall and adjust their flies in unison, nodding to one another in time with the relentless, knee-buckling sound. Whitney's head swims with lights and music, like a primal serum poured directly into his brain. When the lights finally come on, four or five o'clock in the morning, he staggers blinking into the daylight toward his car parked along the beach, carrying his shoes, the cuffs of his linen pants weighted with water and sand.

He swings his legs off the bed. He pads into the bathroom where his uniform is draped over the shower rod. His undershirt is bunched along the counter. He wrings the undershirt over the sink and then holds the cloth to his nose, inhaling the smell of rainwater but also grass and summer and also somehow the redolence of sandy, waterlogged breath. His uniform is damp to the touch. His head pulses. He can hear the pulse from those South Beach clubs, two hundred miles away.

Dropping to the floor, he does a hundred and twenty pushups. When he finishes, his face is red and he is breathless but he no longer feels the same temptations. He thinks about the morning and the way everything will go down. He's ready to make those phone calls now; he feels like a sheriff again.

He returns to the bedroom. He no longer hears the child crying. He perches on the edge of the bed, watching his looming image in the closet mirror. Flexing his hands and watching the veins twitch along his arms.

An old bull, he tells himself. Toro Viejo.

EDIE HEARS the car pull into the driveway. She hears the approach and the slow, heavy grind of tires on gravel. Its headlights cut the darkness of the pond and swing across the yard where she stands between the shed and the house. Then the headlights are gone. There are lights on inside the house: Mae getting ready to leave for work. The boys, Edie knows, are settling in to watch a little television before bed.

Above the tree line she has spotted Gemini. She still remembers the names of all the points — all but number six, which even when she knew most every star in every constellation she could never remember. Still, the circuitry of this nighttime nexus mimics her own scattered but imaginatively-connected thoughts. Notions of right or wrong; guilt or innocence; forgiveness or damnation. Each a matter of interpretation, so she hopes. Or so she might pray if she could convince herself it might make a difference. In the backyard she has dug a shallow pit four-foot wide.

She hears the car door slam. Vester has returned. She opens a bag of garden rocks and empties the bag into the shallow pit. On her hands and knees, she smoothes the rocks and then pulls into the pit the compost she collected, the twigs and leaves and grass trimmings. The gasoline can at her side is red and rusted on its bottom; she opens the yellow valve on the back and uncaps the nozzle. Balancing on the balls of her feet, she douses the compost and the rock pit with kerosene, the smell of it speeding her back to San Francisco, briefly, before she lights a match and drops it. The flames rise quickly, consuming even the outer edges of the hole. She watches the flames, marveling at the heat. She expects to see her past rise out of them. She expects a voice to speak to her like Moses and the burning bush.

That's a good way to lose your eyebrows, Vester says. He has come around the house carrying her green hiker's pack. Step back a little.

She retreats from the fire. The twigs and leaves begin to catch. He kneels beside her and opens the backpack.

Everything went fine, he says. I didn't see anyone. No one saw me.

Did you replace the top soil like I told you to? Did you flatten the turf grass?

All of it like you said. Once I was finished, the grave looked like it hadn't been touched.

He slides swaths of fabric from the backpack. He unfurls each cloth and a series of bones roll into the fire. There are more than she expected. She watches with a certain detachment. She is waiting for her stomach to roll. It doesn't—until he removes something heavy and round from the pack and then pulls back the folds of cloth to reveal the dead girl's skull. Edie turns from the flames and vomits into the underbrush.

No shame in that, he says.

She doesn't watch him drop the skull into the fire. She waits until he's closed the backpack and tossed it to the side, out of sight.

He says, Back in the war, plenty of good men lost their lunches at the strangest times. Not necessarily when you expected them to. Prison was the same, actually.

Don't let them go too long, she manages.

Not too long. But they need to burn a while. They need to be recognizable as bones, but that's all.

They stand there for a long time not saying anything. Watching the white bones turn yellow and then black. She adds more leaves and branches and when she tosses more kerosene on the fire the flames burst and then die down again.

This proposition, he finally says. The pastor offered. What's in it for you?

The chance to disappear, she says. Once and for all.

He pokes at the fire with a long branch, turning over the fire's contents so they burn evenly black. He says almost to himself, I know what it's like to look back over the things you've done and wonder what sort of person you must be to have done those things. When you see yourself for who you truly are. And you find out maybe you're a coward. Or maybe you're a mean-spirited person. Or maybe you end up being nothing bad at all. But you're in a whole new ballgame now. Way out of my league.

The side door opens. Mae comes outside, backlit by the kitchen.

I'm leaving, she says, but noticing the fire steps down into the yard. What's this?

Edie drops a handful of compost into the flames. Vester positions himself between the fire and his wife and uses the branch to push the compost over that which it would conceal.

Marshmallows, Edie says. S'mores. We thought it would be fun for the boys.

Mae crosses the yard in that heavy-footed way of hers until the front of her is lit by the light of the fire. Do we have all the right stuff?

I just ran to the store, Vester says. You'll be home at your usual time?

Maybe early, Mae says. Our census is low.

Edie watches the woman watching the flames and wonders how she would react if she knew. She pities her for an instant, her sad, long life. That even now, with her husband having returned to make amends, there are still things her loved ones keep from her—betraying her trust, her faith in them.

You two are a regular sideshow act, the woman says. Never a dull moment.

Vester glances sidelong at Edie and she catches the look, both of them wondering how long Mae will stand out here, how long before the compost burns away to reveal the charred, smoking skeleton parts of a girl nine-years dead.

We'll save some for you, Edie tells her. You can heat them up when you get home.

I like my marshmallows with the black outside and a gooey middle.

We'll do that, he says.

And then Mae shuffles back across the yard to where her car is parked. The relief is palpable between the two of them crouching by the fire—they both exhale as one. Edie watches the woman recede until she is swallowed by the shadows. A car door opens and shuts, the engine turns over, and when the headlights come on Edie knows she will not see the woman again. Better to end like this—she has never been one for goodbyes.

When Mae is gone, Edie says, I'm going to check on the boys.

But Vester gestures with the stick he holds. I'm coming with you tonight.

It's not for you, she says.

He reaches through the darkness and wraps his hand around her wrist. His grip surprises her. His fingers are thick and rough and she can feel his tremors and his grip tightening to steady them.

You need a professional, he says. Otherwise, a little girl like you could really get hurt.

I'm not so little.

And I'm no professional, but what the hell.

He removes his hand. She remembers to breathe.

If they catch you, she says, you'll go to jail.

Prison don't bother me.

But you're working now. You have a family again.

He laughs but ends up choking on the sound. Smoke, he says, waving at what little smoke rises from the flames. He wipes his mouth, his eyes watering. He says, Maybe you haven't noticed. But things between me and Mae ain't going so well. She's different now. She's been making sure I know she don't need me around.

She still loves you.

All the more reason for me to get. The last thing she needs is in a year, maybe less, to be looking after me while I'm on my deathbed.

He reaches into his shirt pocket, looking for cigarettes. He pulls back: his hand is shaking too much for him to work his fingers around the pack. He sits back on his haunches, clutching his arm, waiting for the tremors to subside. Edie goes to him and reaches into his shirt pocket; she removes the crumpled pack of cigarettes and slides one cigarette out from the others. She places it on his lips; she finds his lighter and puts the flame to the end of his cigarette where it trembles in his mouth.

He says, This sickness I got inside — there's no fighting it.

Then come with me, she says. We'll find you help. We'll sit in that hospital until they agree to see you, until they give you the medicine you need.

He shakes his head. If I don't have Mae, then I don't have anyone. She's the only good thing about this shit-ass life I've led. Her, and the boys. I won't cause them more expense.

John Whitney listens to the sirens pass. The sirens might be headed anywhere. A fire, or some twisted wreckage. A stroke victim, or a domestic disturbance. The sirens might be headed for someone he knows. One day they will be. One day, they will be headed for him.

There is one type of man he considers most base: the man who preys on innocents. Men like this he has no pity for. Rapists, pedophiles — they deserve no mercy. But terrorists too have only victims.

The man who shot his father in the face; his father leaning inside the car window, Son do you know how fast you were driving?

Upon noticing the driver was Hispanic, ¿Hijo, usted sabe rápidemente usted iba?

Whitney's boyhood fantasy: A struggle ensues. His father fights bravely until finally being overcome by ten or twelve strong men.

The certainty of adulthood: The gunshot was brief and senseless and instantly deadly. It scattered his father's brains across Interstate 95 northbound. The driver later apprehended on an unrelated charge; the driver plea-bargaining his way into thirty years without parole for the murder of Officer John "Jack" Whitney, Sr. Leaving behind a wife, age thirty-four, and a child age twelve. A boy with two bloodlines: one cowardly, one brave.

The ringing phone pulls Whitney from his past. When he answers, it is Cyrus Capron sounding panic-stricken and very much awake.

The new development out on Roan, the deputy says. This fucker is big.

SEVEN

In the end it was Edie who came for me. Edie with her sugary breath; Edie with her touch light as breath as I waited for her, like I always did, with eyes closed. Awake, not breathing, waiting to feel the palm of her hand against my head or her nose against mine—only then would I know that she was there and that I was not dreaming. When my mother came for me the bed tilted beneath the weight of her and that was how I always knew it was time to get up. But with Edie it was as if part of my dream began whispering for me to open my eyes.

The nest of warm covers held me fast asleep—Edie wrapped her arms beneath me and gathered me into her. She set me upright. The floorboards were cold and I felt their chill through my bare feet. My toes couldn't reach the floor and I would not open my eyes—not yet. I was listening for something that was speaking to me moments before I smelled Edie's cherry-berry breath: the Maharajah. It had been weeks since he last came.

The Maharajah told me things. The twisted feeling in my stomach was a sign that he had visited me sometime in the night.

Evan, wake up now, Edie said. It's time for you to be awake.

The room was dark, the curtains drawn. Edie slid socks over my feet and wrestled my feet into shoes. I was still wearing pajamas, the plaid ones she gave me for Christmas and that I always wore as soon as they came out of the wash. Across the bedroom, my dad helped Troy into his boots. Troy asked where we were going. His voice was heavy with sleep.

We're taking a ride in the car, Dad said. We're going to surprise your mom.

My father spoke and my stomach twisted again. There was a smell in the room I almost recognized — the smell of earthy things, moss or raspberries left too long on the vine. But weren't we finished with surprises? Weren't my brother and I done accompanying our father on dark missions late into the night? I wanted to sleep again to hear what the Maharajah came to say.

We were herded into the entryway, my brother and me. Edie said, Hold out your arms. She pulled my winter coat over them and buttoned the coat around me. She tugged a toboggan hat over my head and I saw myself in the hallway mirror, dressed oddly with my pajama bottoms tucked into my shoes and my mittens hanging from my wrists like spent teabags. It was never cold enough to use the mittens, but Edie said people did use them, other places.

When the front door opened I felt the air outside and saw that it was still dark. Why were we awake? Edie went out and then my dad and then my brother.

The Maharajah said, Hurry up and don't get left behind.

It was him after all. The Maharajah spoke words only I understood — that only I heard. Although he never spoke to me in waking — so perhaps I was still asleep. Perhaps we were moving through a dream and it was not waking after all.

For the fun of it, so Dad said (again my stomach in knots), the four of us crowded the front bench of the station wagon. The back seat was covered by blankets that seemed to conceal what I didn't know; a funny smell, the smell of yard work on days my brother and I were told to stay inside. The smell of chemical juice my mom sprayed across the flowerbeds and along the edges of the pond.

I leaned against my brother. He shook me off. Now that he'd

reached a certain age, he didn't like to be touched. He didn't seem to care; he didn't seem to be afraid of where they were taking us. His profile was lighted and then dark, alternately as the car passed through pools of streetlights. He smelled different too. His clothes smelled stale when he came in from outside, his body trailing fumes, the smell of someone who had just been outside and come in. Watching my brother grow older was like watching all the things that would one day happen to me. It was not altogether bad, although I hoped for more.

Edie said, or half-sung, the nursery rhyme about the kookaburra.

Her voice was soft. She waited for my brother to start up too. When he didn't, our dad chimed in, repeating the first line as Edie sang the next. They finished the first verse but Troy made no sound. He thought the song was for babies. If my mom were there, she'd have made him sing. It was one of her favorite songs. I wished he would sing because the song was stupid with only two people singing. I knew the next verse, and so did my brother, but his not singing was part of the changes too.

The Maharajah said that one day I would be ready for changes. The Maharajah had plenty of hair under his arms and on the backs of his hands and hair that spiraled on his enormous belly. His moustache was wide and curled over his lips. He wore narrow shoes and pants that ballooned; his vest glittered. He kept everything he owned piled beneath his hat.

He came from the desert far away. He first came to me the night our father left my brother and me in the bar. We sat on the floor, moving cigarette butts like toy cars through the saw dust.

Are we going to Sunday school?

Troy's voice shattered the endless song. I was glad no one started up again—the song was sad even if people often sang it when they were happy. We were coming up to the church. I saw the big sign and the fountain lit different colors. I wouldn't have minded going to church, to see my friends. But we'd never gone to church in our pajamas before and we'd never gone to church in the night.

The parking lot was empty. Dad killed the engine and we sat looking out at the dark.

There's no one here, Troy said. I want to go home.

But Edie reached across me and ran her fingers through my brother's hair. I need you to stay in this car until someone comes to get you out. Understood?

We bobbed our heads. She kissed us both. Our dad was already out of the car when she opened her door and then she was out of the car too. Then the driver's side door opened again. Dad reached in and laid a blanket over us. The blanket he brought from home smelled like my mom and I missed her right then. I thought we were going to surprise her. I thought she would be there. Dad tucked the blanket around us and then leaned his hands on the dashboard, filling the open door, his eyes flickering back and forth between my brother and me.

Are you going away again? Troy asked. It was less a question and more an accusation.

Dad wiped his mouth and stared at his shoes. I love you boys. No need to mince words. I love you boys, and I love your mother. And no matter what your mother or anybody else says about it, those two things are true. No matter how you end up remembering me, you remember that.

He did this thing like clearing out the space between his ear and jaw, a swallowing, muscular click. He did this and said, Your mother will be here soon.

When he closed the door, it felt final and alone, like being shut inside a freezer.

There was a woman in the bar that night. She kept saying,

Little darlings. If nobody comes to claim them, I'll take them home with me. Such darling boys. Such little darlings.

The back hatch opened. Cold air filled the car. Dad and then Edie slid large bags out of the trunk. Then the trunk shut again and everything was quiet and not so cold.

I reached for Troy's hand but he shook me off. He pushed the blanket away and slid behind the steering wheel. He might have driven us out of there, but instead folded his arms and closed his eyes. Soon his breathing was just like when he was asleep.

I locked the car doors. I didn't see Dad or Edie—just dark land everywhere, the dark church.

Don't cry, my brother said. You big baby.

That night as he drove us to where our mother worked in the hospital, the sheriff said, You boys better learn to look after one another now. Don't seem like anybody else is going to do it for you.

I'm trying to catch a few winks here, my brother said. Stop your bawling.

I closed my eyes. I didn't know whether I was awake or asleep. That's why I was crying. Awake or asleep—real or unreal.

Adults knew the difference between things that were real and things that were unreal. Our last Sunday school class was about this very thing—real or not real. Our teacher made a long list on the whiteboard. In one column we wrote down the things that were not real, like dragons and ghosts, werewolves, vampires and elves. In a second column we listed things that were real—Jesus, angels, and the Devil. There were other real things. Bad Men Who May Hurt You were real, but not common. Santa Claus was not real, although it was important to pretend because people like my mom, and Edie, still believed in him.

In the car with my brother, I began thinking of other things we might have listed on the board. The Holy Ghost: real. Batman: not real. The nightmares I had sometimes were not real, which was maybe why I never remembered them. And the Maharajah…he might be real or he might not be. The things he said were always true. But thinking of things as being real or not real helped me feel like I could manage. That's what Mom always said: get so we can manage.

Take a good look at your father, all soakin' wet out in that pond. Take a good look at him and don't forget. Don't you ever forget.

When we finished with the lists, the teacher told us again how Jesus was real and that believing Jesus was real was how we got to Heaven. If we didn't believe Jesus was real: no Heaven. No matter what people said, even if people made fun of you, or if they said they were going to hurt you, say that Jesus was real. If bad people try to get you to say that Jesus isn't real, don't say it, or if you do, you won't go to Heaven.

Two men burst through the door then. They wore striped suits and funny hats. They carried guns but the guns were obviously fake—just toys. One gun had a big wheel beneath the barrel and the man held it with two hands. The other man carried a water pistol. I didn't know the names of the men but they both went to our church.

Up against the wall, they said.

All of us got up out of our chairs to stand in the front of the classroom. Our teacher stood with us. The men were trying to be serious but some of the other kids knew them and soon all of us were trying to keep from laughing. We laughed until the man with the moustache said, We want you to deny Jesus as savior and king.

Our teacher stepped forward. He said none of us would ever deny Jesus and we said, That's right, never. When our teacher spoke, his Adam's apple rose and fell like the hammer throw at Cypress Gardens.

The men said again, If you don't deny Jesus, we will shoot you and you will die.

They came down the row, waving their guns, asking each one of us if we thought Jesus was Lord or if we thought that Jesus saved. All of us said, Yes, that's what we believe. Some of the kids were still sort of laughing and treating it like a big joke, but most of us were acting serious because our teacher was acting serious, and he usually only acted serious at altar call or if one of us misbehaved.

When they finished coming down the line, the men stood in front of us again and said they would kill us if we didn't deny that Jesus was Lord. Maybe it was the way they said it, but after that, nobody laughed. Nobody moved. The man with the moustache said he would count down from three, to give us all one more chance to live. He said we could still deny Jesus and this was our last chance. Then he counted down from three and nobody moved and nobody said anything. When he said zero the men pretended to mow us down with the guns they carried. We all pretended to die, either pitching forward like the bullets had ripped through us or staggering backward to collapse beneath the whiteboard, beneath the columns of real or unreal. We moaned and clutched our guts just like they do in the movies.

Everyone but Troy, who after all of us had died, still stood. He didn't flinch as the bullets flew, as the rest of us flailed about him. The men shot at him but still he wouldn't go down. He was bulletproof.

Know why I didn't die? he asked me on our way home that morning. Because it wasn't real.

IN THE CAR outside the church I fell asleep. There was nothing else to do. And then I am awake, except that I must still be dreaming because the sky is red and everything around us has the wavering quality of heat rising from blacktop. The sound of an old tree splintering — the sound comes from far off. Our front wheels lift and drop and when my brother and I climb back onto the bench we see fiery rain smoldering on the windshield and leaving charred half-circles on the glass. Before the next explosion there is a rush of air and then a moment of perfect stillness before a concussion rocks our car again and the ground shakes. The windshield is warm when I put my hand to it.

Once, driving through north Florida, Mom stopped our car on the side of the highway so that we could watch a farmer set fire to his crops. The orange flames dithered along the planted rows and the flames spread for acres. But that burning land was nothing compared to this: Black smoke boulders in the red sky; tongues of flame leap from the rooftops of the houses and the flames seem to dance, to raise their arms like our congregation worships during Pentecost — a dance of fire. Shingles take to the air like flat birds — the air suddenly filled with crows and ash and heat blacking out the stars. The sound of these crows rides on furious. We choke on the smell of gasoline; the way my brother's hands smell after he cuts the grass.

Troy wraps his arms around me. I want to ask if we are safe, if we are far enough away. But I feel him shaking — not shivering — but something deep inside of him on the move. With each new blast we jump out of our skins and I am the one who needs to be brave, to be the older brother.

I want to tell him it will be all right. But the last time I spoke, our father left us for good.

Dad, I said then. What does patriot mean? If someone is a patriot. What's it mean?

After that, the sheriff found my brother and me on the floor in the bar. Why my voice drives people away, I don't know. I didn't want my dad to leave and I've been quiet ever since. Like he always told me to. I've been quiet too since Edie arrived because I like her and I want desperately for her to stay. But now that Dad has come back she seems to be going—she hasn't said so, but I know. I'm old enough to know when people are getting ripe to leave.

Sirens are coming closer. Maybe our mother. If I speak now, who will I drive away? There's no one left. Maybe, if I concentrate, the sound of my voice will take us, my brother and me, away— someplace else, someplace far from this fire and from this church, so far you can't even drive there or call us on the telephone. It would be perfect, just the two of us, without all this other sad stuff.

Our car is suddenly surrounded by flashing lights. I count two fire engines and four squad cars. I unlock the car door and outside the red rain has stopped falling. There are blasts going off somewhere deep in the subdivision's belly. A fireman reaches inside the car with his vinyl arms and pulls first me and then my brother out of the front seat.

Strange faces are shouting at us and then bowing close to our own faces to see who we are. They lead us away from the car and toward an ambulance—the parking lot is darkness and spinning lights and a rush of people shouting. There is no one I recognize. My brother takes my hand and someone drapes us in a scratchy blanket and it is only then I realize how cold it is outside. We are seated on the back of the ambulance and told to wait.

It was Dad. Troy wipes his nose with the back of his hand. And Edie. It was them started this.

Already I can feel the back of my tongue loosening. I wonder what my voice will sound like when I finally speak. I wonder how it feels to generate sound. I wonder will I change too, without the Maharajah telling me what to do.

Because he's already gone. Everyone I feared to lose—the Maharajah, our father, and Edie—are gone and now it's time for me to speak.

Troy, I say. My brother looks at me and seems suddenly afraid to touch me, he's so surprised. You were right about Sunday school. It isn't real. I don't want to ever go back, okay?

He nods his head, yes.

EIGHT

The sky burns with a hundred suns above two hundred acres set ablaze. Windfall Estates consumed by fire and smoke poured out against the sky. John Whitney has never seen a sky so red and he has never seen smoke swirl the atmosphere like limestone swirls the quarry in marble. The world turned upside down: His men stare not up through long-fingered clouds but down through gaping earth — the flames not climbing but lashing out.

Against this apocalypse, fire trucks unwind great lengths of hose. Emergency crews set their commands at the foot of the long boulevard where the palm fronds lining it now hang black and withered like shreds from so many torn umbrellas. The empty guardhouse, the rigid gate: The entrance to the subdivision is heat and smoke and men shouting against the roar of the conflagration and against the screaming call of the sirens. When the fire trucks unleash their snaggle-toothed streams, the charges bow against the wind and fall impotently across the flames.

The wind just ain't on our side, Cyrus Capron says.

Whitney has seen before the effects of wildfire, along state road 70 ten years ago when fires scorched acres of forest preserve. How the animals were driven before the wind, leaving the appearance of a great churning in the ground, the insides now turned outside black and smoldering. Still the burn lines display themselves on every pine. But the fire that has consumed Windfall Estates is no happy accident of nature. The houses cast sheet metal and roofing and bits of insulation into the sky, raining threads of carpeting and iron shavings and the melted shards of crown molding. The houses exhale like burners on hot air balloons, contained but terrifying. The houses burn as if choreographed; the houses burn in perfect symmetry. Nature's chaos adheres more to pattern than proportion but these fires display aesthetic balance: timing, meter and rhythm. These fires are nothing if not manmade.

Some of his men retreat from the blaze. They hustle out of the darkness singed and shaken. The heat is unrelenting. If the wind doesn't change soon they'll need to pull back.

Where's the Chief? Whitney shouts above the noise. They huddle with two other officers who were first on the scene. One of them, Kissler, gestures vaguely toward the fire.

Any idea what started this? Capron asks.

Lightning, says the other officer, Seal, and everyone but the sheriff laughs.

We found a car in the church parking lot, Kissler says. Two boys. Ages six and eight.

Maybe those boys saw something. Bring them here.

There is the subdivision, Whitney knows, and there is, facing the road, the church of Christ by the Sea. Between these lies dark land; between these lies the solar farm dark and still. He tries to recall the last report. He remembers Capron coming out here in the fall and imposing new security measures.

He takes his deputy by the arm. You were out here last October.

Sure enough, Capron says.

You had them put up a new fence?

A new fence, and they ended up hiring a night watchman.

Last I heard it was Vester, Seal says.

It is Vester, Capron agrees. Splitting time between the solar farm and here.

Hiring Vester as security, that's hard to believe.

Relax Sheriff. Kissler taps a cigarette out of his pack. We ain't going anywhere tonight.

He offers the pack to each man and each man waits for a light. But when Kissler turns to hold the match to the end of the sheriff's cigarette, Whitney is gone.

NOT FEAR BUT sense of duty drives John Whitney from the fire. His reaction nothing more than a trained emergency response.

He finds his flashlight in the squad car. He releases the shotgun clipped to the dash, a sawed-off Remington 870. The 12-gauge is loaded with two slugs; he drops a magazine tube into his jacket pocket before setting off down the road, double-time.

His breath comes easier now, removed from the blaze and the overwhelming stench of burning gas. The artistry—if he can call it that—of the crime is evident in the residue it leaves behind in his nose and eyes. That is why the officers made the crack about the lightning. The fire was no accident. The fire was manmade. Not hoodlums playing carelessly with firecrackers, not some construction worker's errant cigarette, but arson: whoever set the fire turned on the gas in every home and lit the main gas line aflame.

The sheriff turns from the road, stumbling through the wild growth of the drainage ditch, up a short embankment to the fence line. The fence hems the solar farm. His back is to the road and to his right the sky burns crimson. He shoulders the shotgun; he pitches his flashlight over the fence and then follows the flashlight, hauling himself up and past and down again with some effort. Old bones. He recovers the flashlight and wipes dust from its face but does not turn it on.

A dirt road circles the solar farm like a horseshoe. He finds himself in the back of the lot. He hurries across the path. He moves along the back row of solar panels, the frames silent and still. The glass reflects stars in the sky that look not like stars but rose petals cast upon dark water. Turned red by the wavering heat of the sky. He comes to a wide aisle that leads toward the infield where the solar tower rises ominous and hard. No sooner does he round the corner than he sees two figures standing at the base—shadows talking animatedly with one another. He ducks behind a dish unit. He crouches there, letting his eyes adjust to the strange visions around him, rows upon rows of dim mirrors and metal frames. Above all, listening. But he cannot make out the conversation of the shadows. He waits until his breath is steady, until every part of him again is quieted, before he moves into the aisle.

He sees them more clearly now. Edie, he is sure, is the slighter shadow; the taller can only be Vester. It is just as he suspected. He advances one unit at a time, pausing before ducking out into the aisle, advancing, and ducking in again. Finally he is hidden not ten yards from them, close enough to smell them, almost. They fall quiet. They too are listening. Maybe they heard something, or saw the shadow of him moving through the dish arrays. He waits, breathing through his nose, thinking that what they heard was the sound of dogged retribution, the old bull, coming for them.

He is shielded by the frame of one unit and the mirrors that it supports. The mirrors cast only darkness toward the central tower, the burning sky. He wonders should he call for backup, now that he is sure of his mark. But it is too late for that. They will hear the squawk of his radio and his position will be compromised. He'll go it alone, then. He imagines, briefly, his face on the nightly news, the commendations that will surely come his way when he apprehends not only Vester Carson, ridding Arcadia once and for all of his drunken menace, but also Edie Aberdeen, federal criminal. He thinks that after this night, the office of mayor will not hold him—he will aim for something grander, the Florida Corrections Commission perhaps, something with statewide sway.

And it will be personal as well, he thinks, because he will relish the takedown—not so much the girl, whom he has come to care for over time, having pulled her out of the storm and saved her from drowning, having taken pride in the way she assimilated herself into the community, before now, a fatherly sort of pride he imagines, something like his father would feel for him, were he alive. But Vester: that will be personal. It was Whitney who had introduced him to Mae and it was Whitney who had hauled him twice now outside county lines. It will not happen a third time— Vester's inglorious run ends tonight.

He finds a rhythm and matches his breathing to it, counting. He will rise from behind the dish array and throw down. He expects no resistance. He begins to move—and in his mind continues to move into the aisle even as he fails to notice the shadows change behind him, the one shadow charging and swinging a long, flat cut of lumber, the one blow falling across his shoulder, a breathtaking blow—and a second strike across his back before he drops, crying out, into unconsciousness.

HE WAKES in a room. The room is dark. The walls are rusted, unpainted steel. He is crumpled on the floor, hands bound behind his back by his own handcuffs. He hears a rustling across the room, something human, and knows that he is not alone.

Evening, John. Although I suppose it's morning now.

A voice from the darkness. The room begins to take shape, the rounded, suffocating room and in the center, balancing the Remington 870, is Vester Carson.

Of all the mistakes you've made in your life, the sheriff says, this is by far the worst.

Vester makes a sound that might be a laugh but it collapses into a wheezing cough. When he catches his breath he says, Welcome to the barbeque.

The sheriff asks, Where's the girl?

Yo no hablo tu pinche idoma, gringo.

A donde esta Edie Aberdeen.

No hay ninguna Edie Aberdeen aqui. I'm only half the equation.

Whitney sees more clearly now Vester not pacing but drifting to the right and to the left across his line of vision. He works his hands against their ties without success.

Half the equation, he mutters. I'll get her sure enough.

You won't. Vester pauses and when he is finally still the sheriff sees how his hands shake, the barrel of the shotgun wavering. She's dead.

Edie?

Fires can be dangerous. Accidents happen.

He's lying of course — of this, the sheriff is certain. When Vester notices the tremors in his own hands he resumes his pacing, but the movement does not hide the inward shuddering or the tic in his face and neck. It's been a long time since the sheriff has seen Vester Carson — he heard that he was sick.

Women are hard to control, Vester says, although the sheriff has said nothing. That's why I admire you, John. Devoted to your job. Too devoted to be bothered with things like family.

What are you going to do? the sheriff asks. Blast a hole in me? Every policeman in three counties is right up the street.

Through the dawn light seeping through fissures in the steel walls he sees Vester smile. But the smile droops as if one side of his face is stricken by palsy. His captor holds a radio — the sheriff's radio. He turns the dial and waits for someone to answer.

Capron's voice, Over.

Deputy, this is Vester Carson. Night watchman. I'm down here at the solar farm and I just come upon the sheriff. I'm using his radio.

I can hear that, Vester.

The sheriff, he's badly injured. And the girl—Edie—she's dead. You better get people down here right away.

They do not listen to the deputy's response: Vester snaps off the radio.

Brave, Whitney says. You're a real fucking hero.

Two steps across the room and Vester swings the butt of the shotgun, knocking Whitney flat across the floor.

What do you know about bravery? he says. What do you know about heroes? Arcadia's finest, picking no-good drunks like me off barroom floors.

The sheriff's mouth is full of blood. He spits it out, tasting iron and phlegm. His voice is lost somewhere deep inside his gut, in his testicles.

You abandoned those boys, he says finally. And you're no kind of husband to that woman.

I was a soldier. You don't know a thing about it.

The sheriff lies flat on his back. Vester looms over him, no longer balancing but waving the 12-gauge in his hand.

I know you left Mae to raise those two boys on her own, he says. I know you lack the courage to be any kind of real criminal. Or any kind of patriot. A patriot doesn't run. Not from his obligation—not from his family.

When Vester comes again the sheriff is ready. His legs are outstretched and when Vester moves to strike, the sheriff kicks, scissor-like, and drops his assailant to the ground. Then he is up— on his knees—and driving the full weight of his shoulder into the other man's face.

They struggle. Vester regains the upper hand. Both men turn over in the shadows of the room, in the dust from the dirt floor kicking up, both of them cursing and out of breath but both men unwilling or unable to concede to the other. Bound, the sheriff loses the advantage. Vester is on top of him, astride him, swinging wildly with his fists. But only half the blows land, and of these, most glance harmlessly away.

And then Vester is off of him and moving across the room, still carrying the shotgun. He finds the door and when the door opens the sound of sirens and the blinding light of the outside world flood the room. Vester is gone through the door and out across the dirt infield before the sheriff can find his feet.

Officers Kissler and Seal greet him at the door. Capron follows and, finding the sheriff bound, fumbles with the handcuffs and finally frees them from his wrists.

He get you any? the deputy asks.

Only a little. Whitney tries to gain his bearing, half-blinded, his ears ringing.

He went up the tower, Capron says. I pulled the men back. He's armed. And there ain't nowhere for him to go anyway.

Whitney sees now they stand near the tin drum. Across the infield, the bottom cage of the solar tower is thrown open. Through the ironwork he sees the shadow of Vester Carson ascend the inner stairs.

Did you find the girl? he asks.

Capron swallows and shakes his head and has to look away. For a moment, the sheriff pities him. If he were a certain type of man he might blame the deputy for all of this—he was the one who wanted to stop for the girl that night in the rainstorm, who insisted upon taking her in as one of his own.

Kissler says, We found...remains.

She's dead, Sheriff, Seal says. Fire got to her.

Whitney laughs. She ain't dead.

She's burned up pretty good, Sheriff. Trust us, she's dead.

Hand me a piece.

Seal slides the standard Glock from his holster and hands it over. Whitney checks the handgun and, finding it loaded, says, If that girl's dead then I'm the king of Prussia. Keep looking.

What are you going to do? Capron asks.

I'm going after him.

I think we should be patient, John. Let us talk him down.

I'm going after him, he says again. Keep the rest of our guys back.

As a rookie in the City of Miami Police Department, his superiors laughed at him and named him Toro because he had a tendency to run headlong after those perps that fled into darkened yards or across busy streets or down rain-swept roads with hairpin turns. Drug addicts or gun smugglers or men who fled for no reason other than that they'd been taught all their lives to run from cops — no matter what. They made the justice harder for themselves when it finally came. Most cops never chased perps — they had families to think of. But not Toro — Toro always gave chase.

But this, ascending the staircase of the solar tower in the still-red light of dawn, the smoke lying heavy across the land, is a dogged pursuit, a plodding and inevitable tracking. John Whitney climbs each iron stair and above him waits Vester Carson; Vester having returned to Arcadia once more only to find, in the end, nowhere to run. To find himself wingless when wings are the only things that can save him now.

The sheriff is out of breath when he reaches the top. He finds the hatch closed. He swallows against a searing pain in his shoulder and waits for it to pass. Once he has his breath again, he throws his weight against the hatch and the hatch flies open. He reaches up and pulls first his head and then his shoulders through just as a single shotgun blast rips the door from its hinges. He feels the heat of the shell and the air pushing past; he turns to see Vester Carson propped against the far rail, grinning. The wind is deafening at this great height: it disorients him, the chaotic white noise it creates. He pushes up and with one last effort pulls his legs through. Then he is standing face to face with his predator now his prey.

I missed on purpose, Vester says. Don't come no further.

It's simple math, he thinks. Two shells were in the shotgun when he himself pulled it from the squad car, before Vester knocked him out cold and ran off with it. Only one remains. He glances over the rail and the dizzying vista takes his breath away. He gauges the height at a hundred feet easy.

Vester gestures with the weapon he holds. You can go ahead and slide that pop-gun my way.

The sheriff moves very slowly to ease the pistol from his holster and, bending down, slides it across the floor. Vester stops the slide of the weapon with his foot and then kicks it over the platform's edge. They don't hear it land. Then Whitney is on his feet again, moving toward the rail, letting Vester think he plans on keeping his distance, that he's only come up here to talk.

He says, You've been admiring your handiwork, I take it.

From this vantage point, the carnage is striking. The flames die down and in their wake leave mansions reduced to their foundations, pock-marking the bleak, primordial landscape simmering. The devastation is total. Not one house remains.

Where would you estimate the cost of that? Vester asks. Millions?

He laughs, but again the laugh is stifled by a noisy shifting in his throat or in his lungs. The man is hideous in the daylight, his face limp, his eyes watery, some raised rash across his neck and arms. The whole sad mass of him trembling.

My men wanted to leave you up here, Whitney says. They wanted to let you go ahead and do what you came up here to do.

See that? Vester points the barrel of the shotgun over the rail, indicating the ravished land. Christ by the Sea sits untouched, the burn line from the development running up against and stopping at the newly-built wall behind the church.

The sheriff says, If I didn't know better, I'd say this was all premeditated.

I ain't much for meditating, Vester admits. But you Sheriff, you're a churchgoing man.

You know that I am.

It's fitting we find ourselves up here. In the Upper Room, so to speak. Where the apostles were blessed with the gift of tongues. After Jesus died. And rose from the grave. And ascended.

I reckon.

Not just tongues, Vester says. But the gifts of prophecy and healing. Other crazy things too. But you know what the Apostle Paul called the gift of tongues?

What did he call them, Vester?

He called them the weakest of the spiritual gifts. The glamour gift. The glitz. Take one look at my body and tell me, after all the hollering, what I could have used more. Babble? Or healing?

It is not a showdown Vester wants, nor justice. Whitney decides the man has come up here to die. The sheriff's own presence is incidental. The man has done what he set out to do. He has burned the new development to the ground. He has vouched for the girl Edie's death. Only one thing remains. One shell.

You'll keep looking after my family, Vester says.

It's not too late, Vester.

But why, he wonders, shouldn't he just let him do it? After all Vester has put his family through, after all the trouble he's caused. The sheriff has seen it first-hand, the way Mae suffers. The way the youngest boy won't talk. But he also knows what it's like to lose a father and that's no kind of way to grow up.

Tell my boys, Vester says, that all those songs they sing, heavenly mansions and so forth, streets paved in gold, it's nothing but a way to keep us in step.

Tell them yourself, Vester.

Soldiers fight because they're told. They don't care one way or another.

Whitney knows he must act now. He judges the distance between them, Vester leaning against the rail not balancing the shotgun but resting it on the rail, trembling.

Your boys need a brave man to look up to, the sheriff says.

Vester's eyes freeze the sheriff's heart. Plenty of those.

He swings the shotgun and turns the barrel on himself. He raises the sleek barrel to his lips. He pulls the trigger. The sound of the blast shatters the bleak mid-winter dawn. Whitney lunges for the man and feels warm liquid on his face. Too late—he moved too late. But his momentum carries him forward. Meeting no resistance in the suddenly lifeless body of Vester Carson, Whitney carries both himself and the man he now has wrapped up in his arms across the platform. To the rail and then over it, or almost: They push against the rail as he struggles to free himself from the body, to grab hold of something else, to catch his balance, but there is too much momentum and not enough time to stop. They teeter, they lean, and then both men go over the rail. They are over the rail and past it; they are past the rail and down sailing quick and true through smoke-filled air. Falling, their images grow larger in the field of solar panels below. Their reflections ever larger in the mirrored glass as they fall toward earth; their bodies, now one body, tangled, burst the blue-paned glass of a single mirror in a field of mirrors that, although now dark, will one day shine again.

NINE

One morning late in spring, the timeshares and condominiums and vacation homes empty out at once. Cars and minivans stuffed with suitcases and favorite pillows and presents for the grandchildren up north make their way down Oak Street to state road 70, away from Arcadia, fleeing the onset of the unbearable summer.

Evan Carson watches traffic pass along the strip. He rides a dirt-bike back and forth on the sidewalk, popping wheelies, braking suddenly to swing the back end of the bike forward, him standing upright still gripping the handlebars, acting as the pin while the body of the bicycle swings beneath him. The bike is the blue of Freeze Ice; a gold racing stripe cuts the frame. Cars pass on Oak Street and sometimes the passengers wave at him or honk their horns.

But he pretends not to notice. He pedals hard and then pivots, leaning over his handlebars. The boy and bicycle pause mid-motion, preening, a flamboyant pose. Women old enough to be his grandmother blow kisses at him through their open car windows but he does not look at them. He does not smile for them because a smile would reveal his true intentions—as long as he does not see them he is only a boy on a recently-gifted, slightly-used dirt-bike, nothing more.

His brother would call him a show-off. His mother too.

Although he pretends not to, although his nonchalance is practiced, he notices each car passing and registers each passenger. He pretends not to, but he is watching—and none of the cars carry Edie. Each day he waits for her, knowing none of the cars could possibly hold her, but hoping for it anyway.

The pastor, and Cyrus Capron, and his mother all said that she was dead—that she'd gone home to be with Jesus. The memorial service they held for her afterward; the third that day, after Sheriff Whitney; after his father. Each in the same room at the church, in the Great Hall. Almost as bad as rolling one coffin out and rolling in the next—hardly a break between.

Pastor Dancer stood beside the closed coffin and read a homily for the girl. The sermon ran long. There were television cameras and newsmen from far-away places like Texas and Oklahoma and one beat writer from San Francisco. The coffin was closed. There would be no viewing of the body. Instead, a photograph of Edie balanced on the coffin lid, her face flickering in the light of a candle set beside the frame. Beside them, a vase with a single white rose. Nothing out of the ordinary but that as the pastor spoke, Evan caught a betrayal in his words.

A matter of phrasing. A matter of tense. When the pastor spoke of Edie he spoke as if she were still alive—Edie is this or she is that—not what she had done but that which she continues to do.

Did you hear that? Evan asked his brother. They made their way through the procession line, winding from the front of the hall past the photograph, vase and candle.

Troy ignored him, acting like the question was absurd. People do it all the time. They talk about dead people like they're still alive. It's just habit.

The brothers moved toward the casket. Ahead of them, older women from the church bowed their heads and whispered prayers. Behind them, cameramen filmed the mourners. The camera lights made everything seem staged.

Evan knew the casket was closed because the body was badly burned. Everyone agreed Edie would not have wanted a thousand people to view her lying lifeless in a black box—she who was so full of life would have wanted to be remembered that way. The coffin was closed and the pastor spoke in the present tense as if she were still alive and Evan thought maybe it added up to something or maybe it didn't.

The third coffin that day—the third procession. With his father and the sheriff, their caskets had been open and the men lay there like waxy reproductions of themselves. Seeing his father had scared Evan, his father looking rosy-cheeked and filled-out, the way he looked before he got sick, not the gentler, scarred version that brought Christmas trees home and fell with the sheriff from the solar tower. With both men, passing both caskets, there had been a smell—not an unpleasant smell, but overly clean, a smell that was one part sour chemical and one part roses. But passing Edie's coffin, the photograph of her taken in the Carson kitchen, her holding up both arms smeared to the elbows with icing, he smelled nothing. No chemicals. No fragrance. Almonds and vanilla: That's what she had smelled like the first day she came to live with them. She had held her wrist to his nose.

She's not in there, he told his brother. They were bowing their heads, pretending to pray.

Shut up, Troy hissed.

She's not in there and I'll show you, Evan said and reached for the coffin lid.

The handle was flourished with grape leaves and copper berries. Evan gripped the handle with both hands and pushed with all his weight. When the lid lifted, the photograph and the candle and the white rose slid the length of the mahogany plane and clattered to the floor—the lid was open six or seven inches, almost a foot then before his mother and someone from the church and the funeral director swarmed over him, slamming closed the lid and dragging him from the hall. Carrying his squirming and struggling body away as he shouted to the congregation, There's no one inside.

I liked you better when you couldn't talk, Troy said.

But Evan added it up like any simple math equation: closed casket, no smell, nothing inside the casket when he opened the lid. And maybe it all added up to something, or maybe it didn't.

He rides his dirt-bike between two alleyways, the length of a city block almost, from morning through into afternoon. Until all the cars have passed. He doesn't know a better way to make himself seen — to be more visible. No one could miss a six-year-old — almost seven — doing tricks on his dirt-bike along Oak Street. Anyone coming or going. And if Edie is in one of the cars she will stop — she will want to see all of his new tricks.

Three months after her funeral and Evan has made up his mind: there was no body in the coffin because Edie isn't dead. She is only hiding somewhere until it's safe to come out again, a grown-up game of Hide 'n Seek. He knows this is true because he knows she wouldn't leave them both — him and Troy — unless there was a good reason. He knows she will come back to them as soon as she can. She misses them, he's sure.

When the traffic slows along the boulevard and the sun sits low in the sky, he turns from the sidewalk, down an alley to a long stretch of blacktop. He pedals through the parking lot and finds the dumpsters behind the Chinese Fortune, the piles of cardboard boxes and fishy-smelling pallets. Shrugging the backpack from his shoulder, he crouches outside the kitchen door and unzips the pack. He has not even removed a single tin of cat food before several stray cats drift like steam from behind the boxes and crates. The sound of the zipper is enough, like a dinner bell calling them.

Chow time, he says.

He barely has time or room to unpeel the lids before the cats swarm. They rub themselves against him, stretching into his knees and burrowing their heads in the creases and folds of his clothes. The tins he sets in a circle around him, seven tins the cats share. Some eat with their entire faces submerged; others scoop at the food with one paw extended and drag some of the wetness and the goop to eat off the ground. He doesn't have names for any of them; he doesn't think it should be his decision alone.

When the food is gone the cats remain, waiting to see if he'll offer anything more. The tins arrayed are empty shells. With so many empty tins each day he wonders could he make something useful, a gift for his mother maybe. The tins reminding him of the ashtrays she keeps everywhere around the house, the ashtrays marked with colorful, faraway places. At school, his teacher has been helping him find these places on the globe in the back of their classroom. Most are in other countries where they don't speak English. Places he can't go until he's older. Places his mother has never been.

When they study different countries, his teacher places cartoon pictures on the whiteboard, typical scenes from typical days in other countries. Men and women both, boys and girls—but Evan can only imagine Edie; eating croissants in a Parisian café; kicking a soccer ball with children in Brazil; slurping rice noodles along a busy Tokyo street. Edie standing in for all the iconography and clichéd representations. The world not sharp enough on its own; needing the lens of Edie Richards—Edie Aberdeen they call her now—to see it clearly.

Evan collects the empty tins and dumps them in the trash. The cats disperse to their daylight hiding places. The sun is very low in the sky and he knows he should be getting home; his mother will worry otherwise.

He thinks of what he's learned — the world is vast. He is only just starting to get his mind around it. Sometimes he stands in the back of the classroom and spins the globe, allowing the tilted earth to turn beneath his one finger extended, tracing a wavering line across oceans and continents, his fingernail traversing thousands upon thousands of miles in a few brief wobbling rotations. Spinning ever-eastward. Entire continents beneath his finger, the touch of mountain ranges and rivers that vanish in an eastward spin to reappear on the other side, rotating always in his direction, always coming back to him. Hoping the next rotation will return Edie to him, the sight of her balancing on the rounded edge of the world.

He climbs onto his bike. He pushes off toward home.

Credits and Permissions

Acknowledgments

To Joe Taylor and all the Old Masters at Livingston Press; Laurel Yourke and the University of Wisconsin-Madison Writers' Institute; S.L. Wisenberg and the Northwestern University MCW Program; Brock Clarke; Heather Dewar; Steve Hendershot, Jodee Lewis, and The Spares; David Kennedy; and Andrew Yankech: I am forever grateful.

Certain resources proved invaluable in the creation of this book, including write-ups by Scriblerus at Everything2.com; Redheadjokes.com; and Brian O'Connor's exhaustive website, *Animal Crackers.*

My deepest thanks to everyone who kept asking about this novel even when I would have rather forgotten all about it, including my friends in Chicago; Owen Duffy; Cara and Isaac; the in-laws and out-laws; and my parents, Lyle and Ro.

Finally, to my wife and first-reader, Amelia: Thank you. You will always be the better (and classier) half of our *duprass.*

An award-winning short-story writer and editor, L. C. Fiore has also appeared on NPR and has published in various baseball venues. He and his wife live in Durham, North Carolina.